AN EXTRAORDINARY FEW

THE EXTRAORDINARY SERIES

PAM EATON

Pam Eaton

COOPER AVE PRESS

Editor - Jana Miller

Cover Design - Molly Phipps with We Got You Covered Book Design

ISBN-13: 978-0-9996787-0-1

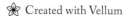 Created with Vellum

To my parents.
Thank you for filling our home with books.

CONTENTS

ONE

This probably isn't the best idea I've ever had. Definitely not in the top ten. Actually, I feel like I'm in the opening of a horror movie. Any minute, a man in some ridiculous mask is going to come out of the woods to my left. And I'll be the no-name girl who gets murdered because I thought it was such a great idea to come run the unlit track at night. Next, the school's security guard will come running, try to save me, and fall victim as well. If this were a movie, my name in the credits would read "Rebecca Hunter: teenage girl runner who dies in scene one."

It doesn't help that the track is on the edge of campus, bordering the nature preserve. It *also* doesn't help that every freaking twig snap, leaf crunch, and owl hoot is amplified thanks to the track being surrounded by trees. It's the perfect amphitheater for terrifying noises.

Did that bush just move?

It totally did.

Don't people say that fear has a scent?

I'm definitely going to attract every predator within a mile.

And yet, my feet still thud against the gravel track. The woods surrounding me are more of a flimsy barrier than a place for a murderer to hide. The light from my dorm pierces through the branches. And what serial killer cares about prep school kids? Still, my eyes scan the darkness. Running at midnight isn't a great idea, but ever since my knee surgery, my gait is super awkward. I need it to be what it used to be. I need to get my speed back. Maybe even reclaim my scholarship.

I round the bend. Only a hundred meters left and I'm done. The distant sound of tires crushing gravel makes my head swing to the right. Crap. If the night guard finds me, it'll be detention for a week. I pick up the pace, my knee twinging, and cross my imaginary finish line.

A car door slams.

I stumble. Should I drop to the grass, make a break for the woods, or succumb to my fate? No, I can't have detention, because the idea of being in Miss Aniballi's class any more than necessary makes me want to rip my hair out. And hers too, if I'm being honest.

The distant sound of several male voices makes my decision for me. There's only one security guard at night. I make for the trees. Barely five feet in and my knee buckles. "Mother –"

Gravel crunches under heavy feet.

I drag myself over to the closest tree. Hundreds of curses flow through my mind as I try to slowly lower myself to the ground. Pretty sure if my knee had a mouth, it'd be cursing too, along with my doctor. Bark cuts into my fingers, but I refuse to be murdered at my high school's track.

"Think she saw us?" a man with a deep rasp asks.

She? *Me?*

Cold fingers of fear scrape down my back.

I look around the trees and see two men standing on the track. It's too dark to make out anything other than their basic shapes.

"Who knows. They aren't watching her, though, so she hasn't changed," the other man says. This guy must be in charge. Something in the tenor of his voice practically sings dominance. Fear like I've never known before seizes me, crushing my lungs. How do they know about the change? About me? "She's worthless to us right now. Why don't you fan out and see if you can spot anything."

My mouth drops in horror as I watch two men quickly turn into six. Who the hell are these guys? One of the guys steps away, and like some bad sci-fi movie, four men break off from the one guy. They all start walking in different directions on the track. Suddenly, they all turn as one. Man, that's freaky. "It's too dark. And I doubt you want me using flashlights. But if you want, we can search and grab her," the one in the center of the five guy says.

"Those aren't our orders. Yet."

Yet? I have to tell someone about this. But what am I going to say, "Some creepy guys were hanging out at the track talking about me"? That'll get me in huge trouble. And I'm not sure my principal would believe me. Not to mention their rules are pretty iron clad, especially the no-tolerance ones.

I shift, causing pain to blast through my knee. I rock to my side. Tears stream down my face and I shove a fist in my mouth to silence my agonized moans.

The fading crunch of gravel loosens the tightness in my chest.

Car doors slam, and relieved tears course down my cheeks.

The sound of the engine firing and pulling away clears the clogging fear from my mind. Time to leave.

My hand still grips the bark of the tree. I pry it loose and rub at my chest. My heart is pounding so hard I'm afraid it'll burst through my shirt.

Who was that?

What was that?

I have to get out of here. What if they come back? My fingers dig into dirt and decaying leaves. I hop up on one leg and test how much strength I can put on my other one. Not too bad. But after a few inches, I need a break.

I flop onto my back. Heavy breaths leave my lips. I'll just rest a minute. Yeah, that's a good idea.

A sob rips out of me. I'm going to die here. They're going to come back.

I can't even run away.

I'm going to be the girl they point at in the school's yearbook and say, "This is why you don't go out after curfew."

Tears continue to stream down my face. I test my knee again. It hurts, but I can make it. I take a deep breath...

A wave of pain erupts behind my eyes, eclipsing the agony of my knee. It shoots down my neck. My chest kills like it's being shredded by a ravenous beast. Flames of pure agony lick up my legs and into my arms, burning and biting at every pore. My muscles stretch and flex like an over-used rubber band. I bite down on my lip to silence the scream that wants to break through. Blood pools in my mouth from my cut lip.

My body arches off the ground, tearing a piercing scream from my mouth, scattering the once-sleeping birds above.

***

THE FAMILIAR SMELLS of Band-Aids and bleach are the first things to register.

I slowly open my eyes. The infirmary.

"I'm sorry, Mr. Hunter, we have a no-tolerance policy. It's not negotiable. She's suspended for two weeks," my principal, Mrs. Knell says.

I follow the sound of her voice. Grandpa Joe and Mrs. Knell stand near the door.

I close my eyes again, wishing for the all-encompassing blackness to return.

Suspension?

Forget any chance of getting my scholarship back now.

"Fine," Grandpa says.

Heels click away and the soft footsteps of my grandpa come closer. The smells of Old Spice and coffee flood my nose. Scents of home.

"You can open your eyes now," he says.

"Busted," I say, my voice hoarse.

I open my eyes and stare into a pair of familiar blue ones. They look tired. One of his soft, weathered hands brushes the hair off my forehead. "You scared us," he says.

Things click, and it finally registers where I am. I latch on to his arm, causing him to stumble forward. "Grandpa, *it* happened."

His eyes scan the room. "Not here," he orders me.

"But —"

"Not. Here. Calm yourself," he tells me.

I nod my head.

"You heard, so you know that you have to leave school. How are you feeling?"

I go to bend my knee, bracing for the pain.

Nothing happens.

Not even a whisper.

My eyes go wide.

I flex my fingers.

Point my toes.

"Perfect," I whisper. Even I can hear the awe in my voice.

"What do you mean perfect?" His voice jars me.

"My knee. It feels like nothing ever happened to it." My voice gets louder.

He shushes me with his hands. "All right. We'll talk more in the car. For now, we need to get to your room and grab your stuff. Probably most of it." The last part he mutters more to himself than to me.

I sit up and swing my legs off the bed, getting ready to stand, when I'm drawn back to what occurred to me moments ago.

"I just received my—"

Grandpa covers my mouth.

Powers, I finish in my mind.

Wait. A huge knot forms in my stomach. If I just received my powers, it can only mean one thing.

My mom's dead.

TWO

"Tell me everything," Grandpa says as he puts the car in drive.

"I was out running—don't look at me like that. You know why." He makes a noise low in his throat. "I know, but I didn't want to stop trying," I tell him.

He lets out a heavy sigh. "You might have to give it up now," he says in a gentle tone.

"Why?" I ask.

"Becca," he responds, but the tone of his voice says, *Really?*

"What?" My voice rises with my temper.

He shakes his head, eyes never leaving the road. "Finish," he commands.

So I tell him about running, the men, the moment the pain seized me.

"You're sure they didn't see you?" he asks.

I lean my head back against the seat. "That's what I'm hoping. They didn't hang around or search for me."

His hand starts tapping on the steering wheel, the pace slowly increasing. I watch, fascinated, as this former D.C. hotshot lawyer shows his nerves.

The tapping abruptly stops.

"I got a call from Grandma before we left."

Bomb dropped.

My stomach starts to knot. "Yeah?"

"Yes." His tone sounds weighted.

I already knew she was dead. That's the only way I would have received my powers, and that's the only thing she ever told my grandparents about it. Some people inherit a house or money. I got saddled with a power I know nothing about. Part of me wants to see what this power is, but a large part is afraid. Maybe it's the unknown that frightens me the most. Ever since my grandparents sat me down after my tenth birthday and told me about it, it's almost felt like our family's dirty secret. I thought I'd have years before I had to worry about this.

What's going to happen to me? My dad's parents have done their best to shield the outside world from who my mother was, but I've already felt like an outsider my whole life not having my parents. An outcast, even among my own family. Really, this unknown is downright cruel.

"And?" I ask, almost afraid to confirm the suspicion bouncing around in my mind.

He clears his throat once, twice, three times. "She overdosed."

I rub a fist across my chest, desperately trying to get rid of the hollow feeling that's beginning to spread.

"Okay," I say.

"Do you—"

I slice my arm through the air, cutting him off.

I lay my head against the window, closing my eyes and trying to close off any feelings of sadness for a woman who once again chose drugs over me.

"GRANDMA?" I call as we walk in the front door.

I'm immediately encompassed by the smell of cinnamon and sugar, more scents of home. The familiar smell alone eases some of the tension in my shoulders. At least I can take comfort in being here in my safe haven. Sitting at the kitchen table, Grandma gives me a forced smile and raises one finger to her lips before talking into the phone. "Yes, Friday at noon should be okay."

Her face drops. Her eyes quickly fill with sorrow and glisten with unshed tears. "Exactly, the grave right next to our son, Jonathan."

Sometimes I forget that I even had a father. I never got the chance to know him. How sad is that? It's pretty freaking pathetic, if you ask me.

She hangs up the phone and motions to me with open arms. We squeeze each other tightly. "Was that about my mom's funeral?"

She gently strokes my hair, pushing stray locks behind my ears, and nods her head. "We're just going to have a graveside service. I figured that would be okay with you. I don't think anyone will be there besides us."

I shrug my shoulders, pretending to be indifferent. "Fine by me."

I shift my gaze to over her shoulder, avoiding her eyes. "Do you think it's bad that I probably won't cry? It's not like she was a part of my life."

I look back toward her face, catching her cringe and her eyes flashing with disappointment. "You know, she wasn't the best mother and was pretty absent in your life. But I know she loved you, and I know that your father loved her dearly. If you feel like crying, then cry, but if you don't, that's fine too."

I stay silent, eating the words that will only disappoint her more.

But my silence causes her to press her lips tightly together. She stares at me for a moment, then releases her pinched mouth. "We'll have the service in two days."

"Okay" is the only response I can give her.

THREE

"What's left is but a shell. For the soul is where our true hearts and minds reside. But today we pay respect to the body that housed this glorious soul."

This minister is absolutely full of it. Would it be completely inappropriate to laugh? My mom was a lot of things, but I highly doubt she had a glorious soul. And she left behind a lot more than a shell.

It should be raining. Right? Doesn't it usually rain during funerals? It's not supposed to be this warm fall day. I'm pretty sure I hear birds singing. And this grass is ridiculously green. Then again, why would it rain? It's not like the earth would mourn the loss of my mom.

The minister's ridiculous words bring me back. "As we remember to celebrate her life..."

Does this guy not realize he's at the funeral of a drug addict and possible prostitute? Are we celebrating the fact that she abandoned her daughter as a baby? Or how about the fact that she died from an overdose?

I snort. I can't help it. Grandpa Joe gives me his *behave* look, tight mouth and pissed-off eyes. Luckily the minister keeps going, but as I look to Grandma Mae for her reaction, she's stuck in her own head like usual.

Her eyes are focused on her son's grave, my long-gone dad. She discreetly wipes tears from her eyes as she slowly gravitates toward him. His eternal resting place is nothing special, a smooth stone with his name and the dates of his life. He could have done remarkable things or been a monster, but I'd never know that from standing above him. All of his deeds, memories and sacrifices died with him. I don't want that to be me as well. I'm only seventeen. I want to leave some sort of imprint on this world.

This has to be the cruelest place for Grandma Mae to be. Her son is here, and I can see she yearns to be with him by the way she strokes the tombstone and clears away the debris with one hand while the other strangles the daises in her grasp. The grief is evident on her face, her eyes reflecting the hollowness of the grave below her. Her only child lies dead beneath her feet. I don't understand her heartache. How could I? I never had a chance to love my parents like she loved her son.

"Let us pray."

Prayer. I prayed for years that my mom would get herself clean. Trying to picture her in my mind now, all I see is a pathetic woman, covered in dirt, clothes torn, begging in a gutter. Am I an awful person to feel this way? If I could have been at the hospital before she died, I would have screamed and shaken her. Even now I can feel the rage inside of me. I squeeze my eyes shut and bite down on my cheek to keep from cursing. How could she just leave me? I want to know why she's gone, why she never saw me, why she didn't love me. Why was I never enough?

Stop.

She didn't care about me. Wondering about these questions isn't going to solve anything.

"We ask thee, oh Father, to please bless Rebecca and her grand-parents."

Something pricks the hairs on the back of my neck and the cool autumn breeze makes me shiver. I turn and scan the rows of graves. Someone moves from the base of a tree and walks away. I can't see them, but I felt their eyes zeroed in on me. Or I'm overreacting. Hopefully the latter. But everything has changed now, and I don't feel safe anymore. Not since the night she died. My mind wanders back to the woods, causing my body to start trembling. "Get it together, Becca," I whisper to myself.

"AND NOW WE return this shell to earth and will mourn the beautiful light that has been extinguished."

I brace myself right before they lower her and slip on my steel mask of indifference. I've had a lot of years to perfect this face, to make it seem like I'm not affected by my mother. I take a white rose and place it on top of the casket. In a low, angry whisper I say, "Thanks for nothing, Mom, just like old times."

It's hard, but regardless of what I feel, she was my mother and brought me into a world with these amazing grandparents. I should at least be grateful to her for that.

As my hand grazes the top of the casket, an unexpected surge of electricity rushes over me, pushing me down to my knees.

Not again.

Liquid lightning shoots straight through my veins and I grasp desperately for the grass. The feeling is exhilarating, exciting and frightening all at the same time. My feet slip underneath me as I try to stand and back away from the casket.

"Are you okay?" Grandpa asks, helping me steady my feet as he pulls me aside.

I gaze hard into his eyes, trying to figure out what the heck just happened. His body may appear calm, but I see the panic in his eyes. "I...I don't know what happened. It was like what I felt the other day."

He shoots a cautious look at the perplexed minister and assures him, "She's okay, just overcome with grief."

The minister nods his head like this is a normal occurrence, and the funeral home workers begin to lower my mother into the ground. I look toward my grandma, but she's tenderly touching the headstone of her son's grave again, lost in her own world of sorrow. Wiping tears from her rosy cheeks, she bends down and her fingers unclamp the daises so she can lay them next to his grave. For a moment she stands there in silence and then turns back to my grandpa. Her bottom lip quivers. "I just miss him so much, Joe."

He nods his head in agreement. We all stand and continue to watch as my mom disappears into the ground.

"May God bless her soul."

And please bless mine as well, because I have no idea what power I just inherited from my *dearly* departed mother.

FOUR

I train my eyes on the colorful leaves outside the car window. "That was a lovely service," Grandma says.

Grandpa pats her hand. "Sure was."

"Don't you agree, Becca?" Grandma asks.

"It was more than she deserved," I answer.

She sucks in a harsh breath and before Grandpa can scold me I say, "Sorry, Grandma, I'm just not myself today."

She turns and faces me. Her eyes soften as they sweep my face. "Grief takes on so many forms, and funerals don't make it any easier. But don't hold on to that anger for too long. It'll eat you up inside, turning into poison," Grandma tells me.

"I wish she didn't leave us in the dark about this power," I say.

"I know, sweets," Grandpa says.

I would love to know what's happening to me. I would love not to worry about being hauled off to Area 51. Why didn't my mom leave me a letter, a note, or anything in the form of an explanation of what to do right now or what power I have? But of course, that would be too much to ask. She was always too busy finding her next fix or *working* for her next dollar. I was always extra baggage she needed to unload. Never mind a note saying: "Hey, daughter I never see. Just a heads up: the power you're going to inherit from me is (fill in the blank here)." What if I can turn things into gold? But then again, what if I can perform the *killing curse* without a magical wand? Do the wrong thing and poof, I'm now on some secret top-ten most-wanted list.

"We'll figure this out as a family. I promise," Grandpa tells me.

He'll keep to his promise. I don't doubt that. What's making my palms sweat is who else might know about me. It doesn't help that I keep thinking about how people with any special abilities get treated in movies. I shouldn't have watched X-Men last week. Now I'm going to have nightmares about underground government facilities.

"Wait, what if I start shooting laser beams out of my eyes?" I sound hysterical even to my own ears, but come on.

"Don't be ridiculous. Besides, that would have already happened," Grandpa says in a nonchalant tone.

How can he sound so calm about this when I'm having a panic attack in the back seat?

We pull down the lane to our home. My shoulders start to droop. Being angry is exhausting. "I'm going for a run," I tell them after we pull into the driveway.

I TAKE off down our maple-lined street at a slow jog. Testing my knee. I shake my head in disbelief. I can't believe how great it feels. Wait, does this mean I have super healing abilities?

I turn into the woods.

I have to test this.

My feet brush away the fallen leaves, looking for a small branch.

There.

I pick it up and bring it down across my knee, breaking it in two. My eyes fix on the sharp end.

Deep breath.

The tip digs into my arm—

"Holy— ow!"

Blood pools and I press my hand over the gash on my arm.

"Stupid friggin' branch." I probably have splinters on top of the cut. A squirrel most likely pissed on this, and now I'm going to get rabies or something. Going to need a tetanus shot too.

This was a bad idea. Another to add to the list recently.

I pull my hand off my arm. Guess I can check off *no* on the miraculous healing bit. Now I need to run home and get a Band-Aid. Along with a bath of disinfectant.

I take off, continuing to cut through the woods.

Ahead, a fallen tree blocks my path. I pick up the speed, planning my jump.

I pump my legs harder.

My feet leave the ground. Everything blurs.

Blink.

I land with a thud, kicking up leaves and dirt. I didn't put *that* much effort into my jump.

Blink.

Where's the tree? I slowly turn.

The fallen tree is fifty feet behind me.

Whoa. I stumble into the closest tree, sagging against it. "How..." I whisper.

I scramble to my feet and head toward the log, scanning the ground.

No footprints.

No disturbed leaves aside from where I landed.

What the...? I grip the back of my neck. Did I fly? No, that sounds too crazy. *Because having some sort of power isn't crazy enough.* Maybe I can jump long distances?

I rock back on my heels and leap forward. But I only go a few feet. Was it the sprinting?

The snapping of a twig causes me to freeze. "Hello?"

Nothing but silence greets me. And that's just super creepy.

My feet slowly shuffle backwards. Time to head home, but slowly. Can't let anyone see.

FIVE

The porch swing sways from the pressure of my foot on the rail. Hushed voices drift through the screen door. Too quiet for me to even eavesdrop. Wouldn't matter; my mind is too busy processing my run.

Car doors slam, making my gaze snap to the street. I'm met by a very pleasant surprise.

My eyes involuntary survey the perfect specimen coming toward me. Standing at about 6'2" is one of the most gorgeous guys I have ever encountered. His brown hair curls just slightly above his ears, and he has vibrant green eyes. He's wearing a white button-down shirt fitted across his broad shoulders and chest. He has to be in his early twenties.

He strolls toward me, and I finally catch he's not alone. Striding next to him is a beautiful, tall blonde. With her long legs, platinum hair, killer blue eyes, and toned body, life tells me again that it's unfair.

He walks toward my spot on the porch, full of purpose and confidence. I stay seated and pray he doesn't notice me gawking at him. With an almost knowing smile, he approaches. "Rebecca Hunter?"

Never has the sound of my name seemed so alluring until now. Definitely need to record him saying my name. "Umm yes, that's me." I wince at the sound of my voice cracking.

"Gregory Johnson. Nice to meet you."

He's polite enough to overlook my cracking voice as he extends his hand, and I stand to shake it. As our hands touch, warmth surges all over my body. It's not like the electricity I felt at my mother's funeral or when I realized she had passed away. No, it's more intense, exhilarating, and makes my heart flutter. He smiles and I swear the green in his eyes becomes more vibrant.

"All right" is my witty reply.

He finally drops my hand. I can't believe I was still holding it. My mind is racing with the stupidity of my actions right now. Really, all I can get out of my mouth is "all right"? This amazing-looking guy is standing in front of me and all I can say is "all right"? Mental face palm.

"Ania Kowalski," the blonde says, her voice basically purring with a thick Slavic accent.

Gregory pulls something off his belt and then shows me his badge. "We're with the FBI."

"You don't look like feds." More like models.

They've got to know something about me or my mother—the timing is just too convenient. About seven years ago, two men who looked straight out of *Men in Black* came knocking on our door looking for her. My grandma ushered me into the kitchen, but I could hear my grandpa telling them he didn't know where she was and didn't care either. I don't know why they thought she would be at their home. She never came to visit. Their stay was short, and I was glad. They brought uneasiness with them into our home, and both my grandparents refused to talk about it.

"We're sorry for your loss," he tells me, bringing my attention back.

"Did you know her?" I ask.

"No," he says.

"Didn't think so."

His eyes hold mine with a thoughtful expression on his face. "Why?" he asks.

I wrap my arms around myself. "You wouldn't be saying sorry if you did."

He takes a step forward, but stops as the front door slams shut. Crap.

"Becca!" my grandpa shouts from behind me. Guess he heard that. "Sorry, she's still angry." He looks at me with a frown on his face and my eyes dart to the ground.

"Can we come in?" Ania asks.

"Yes," Grandpa says and starts ushering us all in.

We all start to sit on the couches as Grandma walks into the living room, wringing her hands. Unexpected company always puts her on edge. Or maybe she's remembering the last time people showed up from the FBI.

"We know about the gift you've inherited," Gregory says.

Wow, he doesn't waste any time. And of course they know.

"What?" Grandma asks, her voice a harsh whisper.

"Am I being dragged off for testing?" I ask, and my grandpa lets out an irritated sigh next to me. I'll just ignore that.

"No. Quite the opposite, actually. We're here to recruit you."

Grandpa leans forward. "Recruit for what?" he asks. Oh, that tone. That's his *I think you're full of it* voice.

"Totally X-Men," I mutter, shifting the attention off Grandpa.

"Sorry?" Gregory asks.

"Nothing," I quickly reply.

"We have an internship program for people like Becca. People with—" she hesitates a moment "—gifts," Ania says.

"Yes." Gregory's eyes lock on mine. "And Becca, I'm guessing you already experienced something odd. Probably pertaining to your gift?"

What's with the word *gift*? Is the house bugged? I know I've needed to keep this quiet, but why are they seriously evasive?

"No, she—" I must have made a noise, because everyone focuses on me. "Becca?" Grandpa asks.

I clear my throat. "During my run," I admit.

Grandpa drags a hand across his face. "Later" is his curt reply.

"How do we know you're who you say you are?" I ask.

"Your grandpa has contacts he can call to verify us," he says, and my grandpa makes a choking noise next to me. Odd.

I look between the two men. Gregory's face seems to say *like we don't know all about you*, while grandpa seems shell-shocked.

Huh, never seen anyone put Grandpa in his place. Never mind someone young enough to be his own grandchild.

Gregory holds out a card. "Here. As soon as you confirm we're legit, call the number and set up a time to come down so we can tell you more."

Grandpa snatches the card and Gregory and Ania stand up.

Ania clears her throat, making me tear my eyes away from Grandpa and his erratic behavior. "You're going to need help with this. Don't wait too long." Her voice is almost pleading, like she understands.

"You're not alone," Gregory tells me, his voice strong and reassuring.

They head for the door and I follow them out, alone. "We'll see you soon," Gregory says, seeming totally confident that they will.

I stand on the porch as they walk away. The view of him from behind is almost as enjoyable as the front.

He stumbles on the path.

Guess even the pretty ones have some flaws.

He shakes his head, and I'm fairly certain he just put some swagger in his walk.

I stay on the porch, watching as they pull away.

Definitely stalling, though.

"Becca!"

My head and shoulders slump.

Can't stall anymore.

SIX

I settle back into the couch, waiting for something. A lecture, a discussion—I don't know what, but something.

A knock at the door makes us all jump. What is with today?

Grandpa motions for us to stay seated and proceeds cautiously toward the window behind the couch. He pulls the curtain back a fraction of an inch and looks through it, then his tense shoulders relax. "Just the mailman; no need to worry. Becca, why don't you go out and get the mail from him?"

I step onto to the porch and eye the man in front of me. I'm becoming paranoid. He's just an average guy standing at the door waiting in his postal worker uniform. There's nothing extraordinary about him. His eyes though—they tell a whole different story. They're piercing grey and filled with rage. I've always heard the joke about crazy postal workers, but this seems a little too intense. Since when do mailmen knock, anyway? He shoves the mail, including a small box, into my hands and an uneasy feeling washes over me as his gaze doesn't break with mine. "Thank you," I tell him.

He lingers for a moment—a moment too long—and then heads back toward the road, rounding the hedge and out of view. I have no idea where his truck is. I look up and down the street, but nothing. Something else catches my attention; a gold sedan parked across the street. Goosebumps race up my arms and the hair on my neck stands, alerting me of danger. I don't like that car.

My heart races. I return back inside and make sure to deadbolt the door. I don't know what good it will do, but it gives me some sort of comfort. "How long has that car been out there?"

"Don't be paranoid, dear," my grandma says.

Really? Did we not just have two government agents show up at our house asking to recruit me? How can I not be paranoid? Granted, my grandparents always accuse me of being paranoid. But it's kind of hard not to be when you're worried that someone is going to come collect a debt from your mother or that someone will find out you'll have powers someday. It's the reason I room alone at school. I don't trust a lot of people.

Grandpa rubs a hand over his tired face. "I want to make a few phone calls. This seems a little *too* timely. I want to make sure it's legitimate."

He turns on his heel and walks into his office as I sit here staring at my grandmother.

I look back down at the small box I still have clutched in my hands. It's addressed to the family of Linda Hunter. "What's that?" Grandma asks.

I hand the box over to her. "It's got my mom's name on it."

She looks down at the address and then back up at me. "You should open it, sweetie. You are her family."

I take the package back carefully. Because apparently I think it could bite me or something. *Just a box.* I pull the tape off and pull open the flaps. A large woman's wallet lays at the bottom with a note. I grab the letter. "What's it say?" Grandma asks.

I scan it over. "It's from the hospital. It's her things that she was brought in with." I put down the letter and grab the wallet.

As I start to unzip it, a large gold coin drops in my lap. The phrase *To Thine Own Self Be True* are inscribed on it. I let my fingers run over the words. "Do you know what this is?" I ask, handing it to my grandma.

She looks at both sides. "Huh." Her face scrunches up.

"What?" I ask leaning forward.

She looks at it for a moment longer. "This is a medallion from Alcoholics Anonymous for a year of sobriety."

I slump back against the couch. "Sobriety? But she just over-dosed." The words just flow out of my mouth.

She levels me with a pity-filled look. "You don't stop being an addict. That's why they say they're in recovery. Sometimes people slip. Even after years of working toward being clean."

I look back down at my lap; at the wallet still lying there. A piece of newspaper sticks out. I tug it out and unfold it. It's a picture. Of me. From a basketball game last year. What's she doing with this? I shove it all back in the box. I can't deal with this now.

I look back up at my grandma and with a fake smile ask, "What now?"

Her expression matches mine, but her eyes give her away and I wonder if mine do too. This has been a rough day for her too. She's probably still thinking about my dad. I don't know the last time she's been to his grave before today. This visit just made it worse.

"Hmm, how about we get dinner ready?" she asks, thankfully dropping anything to do with my mom's wallet.

I nod and walk into the kitchen with her. Sitting on the table are potatoes she's already washed. I start peeling them. After thirty minutes of painful silence, Grandpa finally makes an appearance. Our eyes focus on him. "Well, Joe, what did you find out?"

He pulls out the chair next to mine and drops into it. His hair looks as if he's been pulling on it. His eyes show his age, and his normally strong shoulders slump forward with an unseen weight. "Everything they told us is true. One of my friends at the Capitol confirmed they're from the FBI."

Grandpa used to be an important lawyer for the federal govern-ment. After Dad died, they took me in and Grandpa took an early retirement. I don't know if he regrets it. He does a great job keeping that secret. As I've gotten older, I've had a feeling that he only retired because my grandma couldn't raise me. I look a lot like my father. I have the same shade of dishwater blonde hair, the single dimple in my left cheek, and the same stubborn set of my jaw when I'm angry. I truly believe the sight of me causes her pain. The older I get, though, the better she does, but not well enough for me not to notice the occasional sad looks.

Even though he's retired, Grandpa goes back to Washington D.C. every now and then as a consultant. He still stays in contact with some of his high-power friends, but that's about it. None of his friends know about Mom's and my secret. They still must wonder why I live with him. I asked him once what he told people. He told me that he didn't lie, just told them that their daughter-in-law was an unfit mother.

"What do you think, Becca?" he asks, breaking the running monologue in my head.

I tried to think about it earlier while peeling potatoes for dinner, but now fear keeps creeping up on me. "Would it be a smart idea? Should we trust them?" I grimace at the frightened sound of my voice.

"Well, it couldn't hurt to look into it. Maybe they could help you understand your powers or you could be an asset to them. I think they would be able to help you more than I could ever dream to.

"Your grandmother and I just don't know how to help you." He pauses and drops his gaze from my eyes and continues. "Also, it might be a good idea if you actually withdraw from school for a while. We really have no idea what this means or what...or what could happen. We're out of our element here."

I inhale sharply from the blow those words just landed. I can't leave school. I still have so much to look forward to. I'm supposed to go to homecoming at the end of the month. What about the senior trip to New York? What about my friends? I have plans, and none of them involve staying here, holed up in my grandparents' house.

"Leave school? But...I'm in my senior year. What about graduating? What about college? You can't expect me to give up my entire life and go join the FBI." And I know I'm whining like a five-year-old, but I don't know what else to do.

Regret fills his eyes, and my grandma won't even attempt to look directly at me. "We understand, Becca, but there's a lot more at risk here. Let's just play it by ear and see how things go. You already have enough credits to graduate, and college will always be there. You never know, it could turn into something good. Just take some time to think about it. You don't have to make any decisions yet."

A part of me—a large part, to be honest, wants to throw a toddler-like tantrum. Really embrace it. But I know Grandpa, and it'll just make things worse. They're already super stressed. I can't imagine making it worse.

But that doesn't stop me from stomping up the stairs to my room.

No door slamming at least, but I fall into bed without even bothering to get out of my clothes.

I fall into a deep slumber.

Almost instantly, the dream begins.

Wind whips past my face. Its embrace is warm and inviting. Miles below me are specks of green and brown.

I'm flying.

The sky is a spotted canvas of crystal blue, and it feels effortless up here in the clouds. Wisps of white and grey clouds part before me in a fluid motion. A hint of moisture clings to my skin as I gracefully dive up and down, spiraling through the air.

Suddenly, my beautiful flight is stopped as I feel a slight tug at my ankle. I kick, releasing whatever is there. Lightning flashes in the distance and the sky turns black as a storm quickly approaches. The blood in my body turns to ice and my eyes widen at the impossible speed of the storm heading for me. Lightning strikes all around me. I falter in the air with violent gusts of wind rocking me. I gulp for air, but it's so heavy and dense. Something pulls hard at my ankle again. My eyes shoot down, but there's nothing there. I can't kick off this invisible force! It feels like multiple hands are dragging me down. Stop! Please let me go! *I can't scream. I can't move.* Oh please, someone help me! Please! *I keep fighting, but the harder I fight, the harder they pull me down.*

Down into the dark.

"Becca, wake up. It's just a dream. Come on, you can wake up now," Grandpa's voice penetrates the all-consuming void.

I gasp. "Grandpa?" Unshed tears fill my eyes.

He pulls me into his arms. "It's okay, Becca, it was just a dream. You're safe here. It was just a dream."

I find his loving eyes with the small amount of moonlight shining through the blinds. They take the weight of the dream away. My body slowly relaxes. He strokes my hair until I fall back into a dreamless sleep.

SEVEN

Through the front window I notice the gold sedan parked across the street again. Our neighbors, the Miles, don't own a sedan. The windows are way too tinted to even see if anyone is inside of it. As soon as I see their van pull into the driveway, the car leaves. I need to get a picture of that car. First the dark shadow at the cemetery, and now that strange car parked outside. My nightmare from the other night still haunts me. I might be overreacting, but the sight of that car doesn't sit well with me. My fingers rub the coin from my mom's wallet. I don't know why I'm carrying this thing in my pocket, but I've got more questions than answers now.

"What are you looking at?" Grandpa asks from beside me. My free hand grabs at chest, completely startled.

"Sorry," he says.

"Uh, did the Miles get a new car?" I ask.

He looks out the window, but the car is probably already a mile away. "I don't believe so," he says.

"Huh."

He puts a gentle hand on my shoulder. "I just got off the phone."

His hand moves to my arm, slowly turning me. I look into his resolute eyes. "I spoke with the secretary for Mr. Smith. He's the director of the division you'll be interviewing with," he says.

"Mr. Smith? That's seriously his name? Grandpa, that kind of a name sounds like a lame cover. And what's the name of division?" Grandma makes a very un-lady-like snort at my comment, and Grandpa raises an eyebrow at his wife and turns back toward me.

He waves away my comment. "No one said its name. The government and its agencies like to keep everything secret and done in person. Anyway, they want you to come in immediately for an interview and physical. You'd better get an overnight bag packed. We're leaving in an hour."

Grandpa and I make the long trip down to a suburb near D.C. for my Tuesday morning interview. He wants to stay at a friend's house instead of a hotel.

My stomach is tight with apprehension about tomorrow. "Isn't is kind of weird that we didn't ask more questions about this?"

"Well, it is the FBI, and I don't think they're allowed to disclose what this all requires without first meeting with you. I'm sure when you go through the interview and they lay out the parameters of what they're offering, you'll still have the option of whether to stay or not."

I exhale heavily. "Grandpa, this is like Conspiracy Theory 101. I highly doubt there are going to be any 'options' for me."

"Don't worry. Everything will work out. And I trust the friend I verified everything with."

Such a typical reassurance, but he has a lot more knowledge of these things than I do. I don't think he would ever intentionally steer me wrong. He's always been the one person I can count on to be in my corner as my biggest advocate.

When I first presented the idea of going away for high school, Grandma protested. She hated when I was in the spotlight, which I was a lot because of sports. She was always afraid people would start digging into our past and ask questions about my parents. They never really did, but I kind of wish they had, because then maybe I would have more answers about my dad. Grandpa was the one to have the final say about me going to Rosemary Academy. He knew it would be the best thing for me, so I have to believe now that going and doing this is something that he believes is good for me as well.

As we approach the home, all the windows are dark and only the front light is on. No one's there, just as Grandpa said he expected.

We exit the car and grab our bags. He pulls an envelope from his coat pocket, opens it, and produces a key for the door. "The guest rooms are on the second floor. Xander said we should find them all ready for us."

Xander is another lawyer from some foreign embassy. That's all Grandpa told me, and I didn't bother prying. If he wanted me to know more, he would have told me. I follow him up the stairs and he ushers me into the room I assume is mine. I take the hint that he's weary from the drive. Four hours in a car would do that to anyone. "I'm just going to go to bed. I'll see you in the morning. Night, sweets," he says and then kisses me on the forehead.

I lie in the dark for a while with my mind going a mile a minute. The wind blows outside, causing tree branches to lightly scrape the side of the house. I creep out of bed. The window offers an unobstructed view of the stars above and the lawn below. I hear a faint sound, barely a whisper. It could be the trees. *Please let it be the freaking trees.*

Down below, shadows move. All I can hear now is the sound of my heart beating wildly in my chest. I duck down by the sill and pray that the darkness conceals me. I do my best to still my heart and breath. Slowly, getting to my knees, I look out the window to the street near the house. Everything below my nose is hidden by the windowsill, but I swear I can feel eyes watching me. As my own eyes adjust, I can make out two shapes standing below on the sidewalk. One leaves and heads farther down the street. I wish I could see their faces or hear what they said to one another. A sedan is parked on the street, but it's too dark to determine the make or color. Maybe the FBI is watching us, but I don't know why they would bother.

If I take a picture with my phone, they're going to discover me.

It's probably just the neighbors. That's what I'll keep telling myself.

I crawl back to my bed, too afraid to get back up because what if they see me? Whether friend or foe, I don't want whoever it is to be aware that I have seen them. I lie back in bed. My hands grip the blanket. The door is locked, my window is locked, but that doesn't drive away my fear. I don't know how long I've been lying here when exhaustion finally wins. A dreamless sleep occupies my night, and for that I am grateful.

THE SUN PEEKS into my room. I move slowly to the window, making sure I am somewhat obscured by the curtains. I finally chance a look out the window, but the shadows from last night are gone, along with the car. Could I have dreamed that? I scoot down the wall, plopping onto the floor. I rub my palm against my forehead. I can't keep driving myself crazy with these shadows and possible cars. Today is a big day and I need to get ready.

Multiple jets spray a warm mist all over my body when I step into the shower, causing my muscles to relax. It would be so nice if time could just stop in this moment, but I finish quickly and hop back out.

A few minutes later, a knock at the door makes me jump. "Becca, are you almost ready? I've got breakfast downstairs waiting. I may not be Grandma, but I can still make a mean pancake."

I take a deep breath and try to calm my racing heart. It's just Grandpa. I'm still on edge. I'm going to have a freaking heart attack if I don't get myself under control. "Just doing the final touches. I'll be down in a second."

His footsteps fade as he walks away. I turn back toward the mirror and stare at my wet dirty-blonde hair falling close to the middle of my back. I quickly throw it into a fishtail braid. Should I even bother with makeup? My hazel eyes do look a little bland. I wonder if Gregory will be there. He probably will.

Decision made.

I whip out my mascara and apply it, liberally. It makes my eyes pop.

I brush my hands down the green blouse Grandma made me pack, along with the black pants. At least she let me pack flats instead of heels. I'm tall enough as it is at 5'9", and heels make me feel like I tower over everyone.

The smell of breakfast cooking lures me down the stairs quickly. I can't hide my excitement for his legendary pancakes. I follow the smell into the kitchen. "Good thing you're cooking, otherwise I never would have found you in this monster of a place."

He laughs and hands me a plate of pancakes.

I devour them.

After taking his last few bites, Grandpa brushes the crumbs from his mouth. "You about ready to take off? We should get an early start."

What I really want to tell him is no, I want to go home, but I know that answer will not suffice. "Yeah, let's get going. I have a feeling this is going to be a long day."

He offers a small smile. "Probably. That's why I set up some consultation appointments to fill my time while you're in the interview. No offense, my dear, but I have no desire to sit in the waiting room all day."

My lips curve into a strained smile. "That's okay, Grandpa. I don't blame you."

The drive to FBI headquarters is short, but I notice a gold sedan behind us. And cue mini panic attack. *It's just another car*, I tell myself. But there's something that I need to ask him.

"Grandpa, did you hear anything outside last night?"

He mulls over my question longer than necessary. "Hmm, not that I recall. Why?"

Should I even bother him with what I think I saw? I go for it. "I just thought I heard people outside last night. Maybe I was dreaming it."

He brushes off my comment with a humming noise, looking at the road and not acknowledging my statement.

We continue making turns down streets I've never been on. We pull up in front of a large 70's style concrete building with lots of squares. I turn around to look for the gold sedan, but it's disappeared.

The building looms over us, casting a shadow that swallows us whole. A burly-looking guard approaches the car as soon as we enter the garage. He leans over the driver's side window and his shirt strains against his broad shoulders. "Name and purpose, please."

"Rebecca Hunter. I have an interview with a Mr. Smith."

He checks the clipboard in his hand. His face shows no emotion at the mention of Mr. Smith. "Yes, here you are. Proceed to the third level of the parking garage. At the north end of the garage you'll find a set of double doors. Continue in and inform the attendant at the desk who you are. Your companion will only be able to drop you off, not accompany you inside the building. Have a good day now."

Continuing into the garage, Grandpa places his large hand over mine. "Don't worry, Becca. It'll be all right. It's better that I just drop you off anyway so I can make it to my appointments."

I know he doesn't want to sit and wait for me, but I really wish he could. I pull my shoulders back and tilt my chin up a notch. "Thanks. I don't know why I'm so nervous, but I'm sure it'll pass."

He stops at the double doors. I give him a lingering hug and slowly exit the car, wonder how long I can actually prolong this. As I walk inside, I'm immediately greeted by a middle-aged woman sitting behind a desk. I'm expecting a stern look, but she takes me off guard with a smile when she looks up at me. "How can I help you, dear?"

I kind of thought that since we were at the FBI everyone would be like a drill sergeant. "My name is Rebecca Hunter. I have an appointment with a Mr. Smith. The guard downstairs told me to come here."

She checks a paper on her desk. "Right you are. Have a seat and I'll call your escort."

I sit on the edge of a padded chair. They really need to invest in magazines to pass the time, or something to do with my hands to help stop the shaking. The lobby itself is pleasant enough, with paintings and soft music playing in the background.

Suddenly, the elevator doors behind the desk open. That was a lot quicker than I expected. I figured it would be like waiting for the doctor, which always takes forever.

When the doors fully open, I am met by a very unexpected but pleasant surprise.

EIGHT

I give my sweaty hands one more good wipe on my pants and stand. "Coming to get me?" I ask.

Gregory strides toward me, his body moving with purpose. His shirt is pulled so tight across his shoulders, one wrong move and he's going to be tearing some seams. I wouldn't normally call a guy beautiful, but man, he totally is. His arm stretches out toward me as I stay in the same exact spot. Time freezes, just like in those corny romance movies. "Didn't know I'd be seeing you again so soon," he says as he takes my hand and shakes it.

The familiar electric warmth rushes through my skin at his touch, like a contact high. Is he happy he's seeing me? Just surprised? Indifferent? And now my own questions are sounding pathetic to even me.

"Made a phone call and they set it up. Guess they didn't want to waste any time," I tell him. Now that I think about it, it was all pretty quick. But given what happened in the woods, maybe that's not such a bad thing.

My eyes focus back on Gregory. He seems to be studying me. Probably because I'm still holding his hand! What is wrong with me?

I've become one of those seriously awkward people. Well, at least when I'm around him. I feel my face flame as I drop his hand. "Sorry," I say.

"This way." He motions back to the elevator. And I could kiss him for ignoring my sudden issues with touching people I hardly know. They're going to throw me out of here on account of not passing any psychological tests today.

We step in and the doors close. Sealing us in. Classical music plays softly overhead. I thought all awkwardness would fade, but I guess karma hates me today, because the elevator is covered in mirrors. So now I can't covertly check him out. I can't do anything but stare at myself like some narcissistic jerk. And apparently I'm a super twitchy person; who knew? Obviously Gregory does now, since all my fidgety movements are on display. Like what the hell is going on with my left eye? Am I having a stroke?

"Nervous?" he asks.

"No," I lie. I'm so freaking nervous I can't even come up with any good replies.

I watch in the mirror as his green eyes crinkle and his lips thin. He's totally trying to rein in his laughter. "Be like Elsa, man. Let it go," I tell him, and yes that definitely sounded a lot cheesier coming out of my mouth than in my brain. But really, if I was in an elevator with someone acting like me, I wouldn't be able to contain myself.

He lets out a deep laugh. I think I'm in love.

The elevator dings, bringing us to our destination. And all the humor that was between us is gone. He clears his throat and then steps aside, letting me exit first. Such a gentleman.

"Soooo what's next?" I ask. I'm not really liking the fact that I have no clue what to expect.

"You'll be starting the physical portion first," he tells me, all business now.

We enter a hall devoid of color and originality. Stark white walls, white tiled floors, florescent lights lining the ceiling. The waiting room had paintings at least, but apparently down here white is the only thing allowed.

"Physical?" I ask.

His eyes finally meet mine. "Just standard protocol."

"Of course, *standard protocol*." I make air quotes around the last bit. "Is that code for *poking, prodding, experimenting*?"

He smiles slightly and shakes his head like *I'm* being ridiculous. "Just your normal doctor's physical. With a little running on the treadmill."

My steps falter. Maybe what happened in the woods was a fluke. "Everything okay?" he asks, lightly touching my arm.

"Yeah. Totally. Perfect." I nod my head, trying to convince him as well as myself.

"Okay." He draws out the word.

I give him a bright, forced smile. And then I point at it. "See? Wouldn't be smiling if I wasn't okay."

He stares at me, his features drawn. But he comes to some conclusion, because we keep walking down the bleak hallway.

As we approach a set of double doors, he swipes a badge from inside his pants pocket and we walk inside. "This is a little more extensive physical than average. I'm going to show you to a locker room where you'll find clothes to change into."

Awesome. I hadn't even thought about needing a change of clothes. I figured it would be just like getting a physical for school, and you don't need a change of clothes for that. "How do you know what size I need?"

A smile lights up his gorgeous face. "Well, Miss Hunter, this is the government. What don't we know?"

I guess he's right, but it's still freaking creepy. He opens another door and leaves me to walk into the locker room. "I'll be waiting right here for you after you change."

I nod and proceed in. Around the corner, on a bench is a pair of shorts, shirt, socks, and a pair of shoes. Even the shoes are the right size. Bizarre.

I step out of the locker room and find Gregory leaning against the wall. He has to be model. Who knew leaning could look so attractive? Have to get him do it more often.

"Ready?" he asks.

"Guess so. Any tips?" I ask.

"Don't fall on your face," he tells me.

My mouth falls open and I have to scramble to catch up with him. "Did you just make a joke?"

"Why does that shock you? I'm not a cyborg." No, just a gorgeous man. He needs a flaw. That stumble the other day doesn't even count.

He stops in front of a metal door. "I'll come and get you after you're done. And don't worry, Dr. Wilkes is a good guy. No top-secret government experiments will happen today."

"Today?" I ask, my voice rising to an unattractive octave.

He opens the door and we walk into a large room. It looks like an operating room had a baby with an interrogation room. One whole wall is the kind of large mirror that you always see in cop shows. A treadmill takes up another corner, along with an exam table and some machines whose purpose is beyond me.

Standing in the center of the room in a white lab coat is an older man with a clipboard. His face is round, as is the rest of his body. His hair matches the color of the walls, white as snow.

"Hello, Rebecca." Dr. Wilkes extends his hand to me, and it's like touching an ice cube. I quickly drop it.

He gives a deep laugh. It's like watching Santa. "Sorry about that, forget sometimes."

Umm, okay?

"Don't worry, Gregory. I'll let you know when I'm done," Dr. Wilkes says and then he waves a hand behind him. A lady steps out from behind him. Where did she come from? "This is my assistant, Carrie. She'll be taking notes today too."

At least it won't be just the two of us alone. In the creepy lab. In the bowels of the FBI.

Gregory gives me a wink and leaves me alone with Mr. Freeze.

"Why don't you hop up on the table and we'll get started," he says, interrupting my inner monologue.

Fifteen minutes later and now I know exactly how a lab rat feels. I've never been poked and prodded so much in my life. Of course, there was the standard blood pressure, listening to my lungs, taking my temperature, and weighing me. But did he really have to take *that* much blood? And was it really necessary to pinch my sides to see how much body fat I have? It took everything in me not to stare at the mirror to see if I could see past it. I've watched enough movies to know that there's a good chance someone's back there, but I'll never be able to tell. And I'd rather not be remembered as the girl who put her face up to the glass.

"Let's get you on that treadmill now," he tells me as his eyes stay focused on his clipboard.

Freezing for a minute, I'm not sure what to do. Walking and jogging aren't the issue, but what if he wants me to sprint? I haven't dared since the woods.

I take a deep breath and walk over to it. I keep chanting to myself, *They're here to help me*, over and over in my mind.

"All right, I'm just going to attach some electrodes to you so we can monitor you heart rate."

"Okay, doc," I tell him and it causes him to smile. He should smile more often; it would help with the creepy-basement-government-facility vibe I get from this room.

I step onto the treadmill and try to swallow the lump in my throat. I start off at a walking pace and slowly he speeds me up to a slight jog. Okay, this is not too bad. I can definitely handle this. Nothing weird seems to be happening.

He leans over and ups the speed. Spoke too soon.

Every minute he increases my speed one mph, and before I know it, I'm in an all-out sprint. I can scarcely feel the ground anymore with my feet. It's like I'm barely skimming the treadmill. I'm literally running on air. And I kind of wonder if my legs look like they're going a mile a minute. I try so hard to keep composure in my face and

I sneak a peek at the doctor, but he's just writing on his clipboard like he doesn't even notice anything strange. Like there isn't a girl who looks like one of those cartoons. Because my legs are definitely pumping in the air.

He decreases the speed gradually. My hands rest on my hips as I drag in deep breaths. I tilt my head back and my eyes snag on the mirror. Crap. My gaze sharpens on the glass. I clench my hands, hoping to stop their shaking. Maybe no one is behind the mirror and I'm just over reacting. Maybe it's just a mirror after all and not one of those two-way ones. Maybe no one can see me drenched in sweat and in desperate need of a lung transplant right now.

I know they *know* about me, but feeling the need to hide about it is a hard thing to stop.

The doctor snaps me back into reality. "Okay, Rebecca, we're going to have you do an obstacle course now. Just follow me to the next room and we can begin."

I groan and shuffle after the doctor to the other room. The room is larger than I expected, and the size alone makes me feel tired. There are ropes courses, climbing walls, and large boulders. Who would have thought that this building would hold these types of rooms?

The scope of everything in this room is overwhelming. I really hope they don't expect me to do all of this, because that would be crazy. "I know this room seems a little intimidating, but don't worry. We just want to see how fast you can scale this wall," he assures me.

He points to the wall and my calves start to ache. Of course they want me scale that wall. You know, just an average day at the FBI. Not only do I have to scale it; they're going to time me on top of that. Someone better be prepared to pick me up off the floor when I'm done.

I look at the rest of it, though. "Thank goodness. For a minute there I thought you were going to have me do the entire room. I'm not Wonder Woman."

The doctor laughs and takes me to the starting place. "On the count of three. One...two...three!"

I sprint as fast as I can for the wall, grabbing the rope dangling from it. Up I go at an amazing speed, but a feeling washes over my body. It's the same sensation as when I was sprinting, but my body feels charged, like lightning. It's almost as if I fly over the wall and land on the other side. I would totally be an amazing pole vaulter now.

The doctor just stands there, taking notes, blank face. Did he not just witness the amazingness of my wall climb? "All right, I am going to show you back to the locker room so you can freshen up and change. Mr. Johnson will be waiting for you once you're done," he tells me.

I guess the first hurdle of the day is done. *What's next?*

NINE

Fully dressed and hair fixed, I leave the locker room to find Gregory. I stop short—he's not alone. Ania stands next to him. Unfortunately, they make a striking pair, but she has to be older than him. "Rebecca," she says in her thick accent.

"Germany?" I ask.

Her face pulls into a sneer. Come on! Even that's pretty.

"Poland," she tells me, totally offended.

"Sorry." What did I do?

She waves away my comment.

"It'd be like if we assumed you were Canadian," Gregory tells me.

"Ah," I say, nodding my head. I still don't get it. I'll just make sure never to make that mistake again.

They turn in unison to walk down the hall, their movements in sync. They must work together a lot. We move down another dull hallway, and after a few turns we end up at a large wooden door. It stands out starkly against the continuous white.

Gregory opens the door and we enter a small conference room. A long table occupies most of the space, and at the very end is a man who looks close in age to my grandfather. There's nothing extraordinary about him. He still has most of his hair, but it's grey. He's average height and build, but his eyes change his whole demeanor. The way he looks at you, there's no doubt about who is in control in this room. "Rebecca Hunter, meet Mr. Smith," Gregory informs me.

Ah yes, the man with the unoriginal name. He stands from his chair; his body is rigid as if at attention. He extends his hand for me to shake and I hesitantly accept. "It is very nice to meet you, Rebecca. Please, have a seat."

Our hands touch, and that same electrical feeling I felt with Gregory engulfs me. So much for hoping we were unique. I release his hand and then shake out my own. "Don't worry. You'll get used to it," Mr. Smith says in a companionable way.

We all lower ourselves into seats around the table. "I'm sure you have a lot of questions for us. And we'll get to them, but I'd like to ask mine first. Okay?"

"All right." I rub my palms up and down my pant legs.

"How's school?" he asks.

School? Seriously. They bring me all the way down here to ask about that? "It's fine. It's school." I'm not really sure what type of answers he's looking for.

"Do you enjoy it? Participate in sports? Friends?" he continues.

"Does anyone really enjoy school?" I ask and look to Ania and Gregory for their agreement, but they've both got straight faces. All right, no help from them.

"Uh, it's fine. Kind of necessary since I want to go college. I've got some friends." Who currently aren't talking to me because I dropped off the face of the earth. But it seems necessary right now. "I play sports. I actually had a basketball scholarship in the works until I tore my ACL last season." All my hopes were ripped away when that happened.

"Have you always taken pleasure in playing sports?" Mr. Smith interrupts my thoughts.

"Yes. Ever since I can remember, my grandfather has had me actively playing some sport."

What I don't tell him, since he didn't ask, is that sports have been my outlet for anger, especially around my birthdays and holidays when my mom never called. I would either go out back and shoot hoops or run. I think that was the other reason my grandpa put me in sports. I probably would have been a terror otherwise.

"How's your relationship with your parents?" he asks.

"I'm sorry?" I ask, because I'm not sure I heard him right.

"Just wondering about your feelings concerning your parents," he tells me. But this doesn't make sense. He should know they're dead. And whoa, a little personal, guy.

"Both of my parents died," I tell him. And I know my voice is patronizing, but come on. This is the whole reason they dragged me down here. Well, maybe not dragged, but heavily suggested.

"Yes, our condolences on that," he says, and I'm confused. Is this a test? Is he trying to get me to answer a certain way? "How about before your mom died?" he asks.

I shift in my seat. These are *super* personal questions. "Well, I didn't really have a relationship with my mom. My dad's parents raised me. And that's a great relationship."

"So you never had any contact with your mother?" he asks while leaning toward me.

My palms begin to sweat and I try to dry them on my pants, but it's like I have a faucet for hands. Why does he keep asking me about my mom? I shrug. "Not really. Drugs and alcohol were more important to her than me. She wasn't the best at keeping in touch. You guys have to know about her."

Mr. Smith looks over at Gregory, who nods as if in agreement. What does that look mean? Goosebumps break out across my arms and a cold fist squeezes my heart. Ania rises from her chair with an air of authority. She walks to the door and locks it, making me flinch. Fear begins to bubble up in the pit of my stomach. My throat tightens and it feels like all the air in the room has been sucked out. I grip the table. There is no escape out of the room. I try to stand, but Mr. Smith puts a hand on my shoulder as if to comfort me. Where the heck did he come from? All I want to do is scream and run. Gregory shakes his head in warning, and then a firm pressure plops me back into my seat. Mr. Smith turns his eyes on me.

"And she never told you about us?" he asks.

What on earth do they want? I tilt my head to the side, puzzled. "What...what are you trying to ask me?"

He leans toward me and his eyes become intense, only for a second, before they're back to questioning. I don't know what answer he is looking for. "It's very important that you tell us everything," he says.

I start fidgeting in my seat. I keep shifting my glance between the three of them. Ania is still at the door standing guard and Mr. Smith reigns over me. "All you have to do is ask my grandpa. I can't remember the last time I saw her. There's never been any discussion about any of this. She left me in the dark. *You* guys came to me and told me to come here and learn more about what's going on." Now I'm getting pissed. They may be trying to appear calm, but this still has the feeling of an interrogation.

Mr. Smith shakes his head and frowns at me. "Well, we do know about your mother. You seem to choose your words wisely like she did. I knew Linda personally."

My stomach drops and it feels like someone pushed all the air out of my lungs. He knew my mom. And it makes me grab for that stupid coin I put in my pocket.

I shift my gaze between the three of them again. I don't know what I'm waiting for. They all seem so calm, but I must look like a rabid animal trying to find a way out. How could he know my mother? I didn't even know her. What kind of life did she live that they would know her? But after finding that sobriety chip and newspaper article, what else don't I know?

Gregory's stare stays steady on me, but he's not giving anything away. I'm on the verge of either crying or screaming. Probably screaming. My eyes shoot toward the door, still locked. "We know that your mother was special, and we know that since she has passed away, you have become special yourself," Mr. Smith tells me slowly like I'm a little kid.

Is having a super power not special enough? I feel more like a freak than someone special, and my mother was far from anything good. What makes me mad, though, is that these complete strangers know more about her than I do. My eyes harden as I take in Mr. Smith. My muscles tighten in rage and my breath becomes harsh from trying to control my rising temper. "Why don't you tell me what was so special about my mother," I spit out.

I can't believe I just lashed out at them, and Mr. Smith blinks, surprised at my sudden burst of anger. But how hard does he think he can push until I break, even if he's being somewhat gentle?

He straightens his posture and addresses me with a demeaning air. "There are only a few people in the world who know what we are about to reveal. Keep in mind that everything I say can easily be wiped from your memory if need be."

Mr. Smith says it calmly, like this is an everyday occurrence. Wiped from my memory—what the heck kind of place is this? I swallow hard and nod. He leans forward across the table and grabs my hand. I try to recoil, but his grip stops me. "Calm down. Nothing is going to happen to you. You have inherited powers upon your mother's death. There are ninety-nine other people left who are similar to you. Three of them are in this room right now. All our powers were passed from one of our parents to us.

"Welcome to the extraordinary few."

TEN

Someone's fingers snap in front of my face. What just happened?
"How's it going?" Gregory's face comes into focus above mine. And what a gorgeous face. He smiles, making me smile too.

"Rebecca?" I turn to the voice and see Mr. Smith. Crap, not a dream. I push myself up, struggling to get my legs under me.

"It's okay, calm down," Ania tells me.

I turn my face toward her. "Calm down?! It's one thing to be told there are others like you, it's a whole other thing to be locked in a room with three other people that have super powers. And who the hell knows what those are? How do you expect me to calm down? How about next time you ease a person into it rather than just blurting it out." The last comment is a demand, not really a suggestion.

"Sit down," Mr. Smith says as a command, and everyone sits, because this guy missed his calling as a general.

My mind reels for a minute with the information he just gave me. There are others out there like me. I know they said it before, but it's finally sinking in. I look at the three of them in a completely different light. Gregory was right. I'm not alone in this anymore.

"Go ahead, Ania. Let's show her what you can do," Mr. Smith says without taking his eyes off me.

She stands and smooths down her shirt. She places her hands under the table. And without any change in her face, the table rises into the air. She's not even breaking a sweat. "Strength," she says as she lowers the table.

My hands, which were in my lap until this moment, press against the underside of the table. Yeah, nothing happens.

"Did you just try and lift the table?" Gregory asks me in a low, humor-filled voice.

I shrug my shoulders. I couldn't *not* try.

"Does this help?" Mr. Smith asks.

I nod, because what do you say to watching that just happen? Great to know I'm not the only *special* person in the room.

"Now, let's try this again," Mr. Smith says so calmly, like the fact that I just watched someone lift a wooden conference table like a piece of paper wasn't even a little crazy.

Mr. Smith continues. "Even though there are a hundred of us in the world right now, there used to be thousands upon thousands. As our numbers grew, so did the fear among ordinary men. Many friends turned foe. Our ancestors helped bring some great men to power, but that came with an even higher price to pay.

"There was a great purge of us during the time of Moses. The Egyptians were our people's greatest nemesis. They thirsted for power, and are to blame for so many of us dying. The people claimed that we were the gods on earth, and in turn this made the pharaoh furious. While the pharaoh persecuted the Jews, he took that opportunity to execute many of us, too.

"He was so afraid of the people looking to us to lead, afraid we'd help the Jews and cause his demise. After that great eradication of our people, we went into hiding, only married outsiders to blend in, and never let our powers be known to the outside world. But this wasn't the first time we're mentioned in history.

"Well over two thousand years ago is when the first account of our people is mentioned in Mesopotamia. We've found vague references in writings from the ancient Sumerian city of Ur. Even though we can trace our ancestors back that far, we still have no idea of our exact origins. And even with this great history and legacy, there are only a hundred left."

I slump down in my chair. Well, at least he didn't mention aliens, but I guess anything is possible at this point. Egypt? Ancient Sumerian cities? What's next, is he going to tell me that Atlantis really exists? I actually wouldn't mind that, but now's not the time.

The lines on his forehead become even more pronounced as his face contorts into a frown and his tone becomes gravely serious. "Of the hundred left, not all are good people. Those who seek power and domination align with evil. The most important thing right now is that there are others who will find out that your mother died. And they will find out who you are and what you're capable of. Some of them will want to take you and use you for their own advantage. That or kill you. What we have to offer is security, a chance for you to embrace your powers—your destiny—and do great things."

Well, with that kind of sales pitch, who would say no? Basically I either join up with these guys or die. *Sounds like an amazing future there, Grandpa.*

"This is where you're supposed to be, Becca. Can't you feel it?" Ania asks.

Can I? Can my power be more than a dirty little secret? Can I embrace it and learn to wield it? Whatever *it* is.

The gold sedan flashes in my mind. The shadows outside my window, the feeling of being watched at the graveyard—it all comes flooding back to me. I was being watched; he was right. There's so much more going on than just learning about this power.

Gregory sits up straight, breaking me out of my thoughts. I hold up my hand, stopping him before he can even utter a word. This is a lot of information to take in, but there's been a question gnawing at my brain since before he even talked about the one hundred. I steel myself. "How do you know about my mother, and what do you know about my father?"

Mr. Smith hesitates for a moment. "Your mother was approached in the same manner as you were, with the lure of internship. Her mother, your grandmother, also had powers. Your mother came here at the age of twenty-two, after her mother passed away. She was trained here and participated in our covert operation, which is called Project Lightning. She met your father here. Even though he didn't have powers, he was a brilliant strategist. He was her mentor. They began a relationship, eventually got married, and brought you into this world.

"When he died, your mother decided she no longer wanted anything to do with Project Lightning. She was an amazing woman who did great things in a short amount of time, but the loss of your father destroyed her. She turned to drugs and alcohol to help suppress her powers and her memories."

The honesty and bluntness of his response causes me to sag even more in my seat. I'm not surprised that she fell in love with my dad, though. He was a handsome man, and Grandpa said that he loved to laugh. I bet working alongside him only made the attraction between them grow. I glance over at Gregory, and then quickly look back at Mr. Smith. "Why would I want to be a part of the FBI?"

He breathes in deeply. I can't tell if he's annoyed with me, but I hardly know the man; he can't expect me to just say yes on a whim. "I already know that you feel a change in your body. We all experienced it when our parent with powers died. You felt the charge when you shook our hands. This isn't going to go away, and any of our kind can know you by touch alone. We can help you learn how to control and utilize these powers. The world can be scary for any regular individual, but when you're an extraordinary person amongst ordinary men, it is downright terrifying.

"We were given these powers to accomplish things even the most influential people in the world can't. We have a chance to save this world from itself. Let us train you. Let us show you your worth. Work with us. Serve and protect this country in a way only a few can.

"We can help keep you safe and teach you how to protect yourself, too."

That last comment makes me snap to attention. "So, are you trying to tell me that I'm not safe right now?"

"Make no mistake; people will come for you."

"Yes, but how do I know *you* won't harm me?" For all I know, that could have been Gregory outside my window last night.

Mr. Smith exhales slowly. "If we wanted you dead, it would have already happened. But others will come. I know we're asking a lot of you, but in return we're offering a lot as well. I understand the gravity of the decision you have to make, so maybe you need some motivation."

Ania walks back to the door and unlocks it. I've forgotten about that. But any thought I have is washed away when in walks Grandpa Joe. And his face is completely awash with guilt.

Pure shock washes over me like a sudden downfall of rain. I feel my mouth open in a silent gasp, but as his face registers, my mouth sets into a harsh line and I jerk my face away from him.

I look back up and catch him shake Mr. Smith's hand. There's a familiarity there. My fists curl at the sudden need to hit something for all the lies and secrets he's kept.

He sits down in the chair next to mine and takes my hand. I instantly tense, wanting to rip it away, but he tightens his hold. Crazy strong Grandpa.

I take a deep breath. He's always told me he wants the best for me. I pray that that hasn't changed.

He finally looks me straight in the eye. "I know you're angry and confused. I kept this from you because I wanted to keep you safe. I wanted you to have a life full of opportunities and chances to excel. Grandma and I knew that one day your mom would die, but we had no clue when that would be. I always hoped that she would explain everything to you, but her sudden death came as such a shock to all of us."

"And why not tell me before we got here?" I ask.

"The words never came, and I just thought maybe you'd—"

"You'd let complete strangers tell me?" I interrupt him. And granted, Gregory's hot, but I don't know the guy.

He squeezes my hand. "I didn't even know who they were when they showed up at the house. That's why I made a phone call to D.C. I *never* thought someone would be showing up at the house right after your mother's funeral."

They knew I would have powers—we all knew, but he never told me about any of this. I stare into the eyes that have always been the source of so much comfort and confidence, and in them I see truth and love. I drag my hands over my face. "I don't know what to do, Grandpa."

His eyes stay focused on mine. I couldn't care less what anyone else wants to say. "I can't make this decision for you. I can tell you that you're in good hands and you'll have the chance to do amazing things. Mr. Smith was a good friend to your dad, and I've had the chance to work beside him on legal matters. I don't believe they'll lead you astray, but the decision must be yours."

All those times he told me that he was going to do consultant work, I wonder if he was coming here. "I don't even know what my power is."

Mr. Smith clears his throat. "I think it would be best if I tell you what we assume your powers should be." Great, he knows more about me than I do.

"What do you mean *assume*?" I ask.

"Traditionally, whatever powers you have were passed to you from your parent. The powers don't change, but the person wielding them may be better than the one before. Your mother had the abilities of levitation and speed, almost like flying, but we're not talking superman. It was almost like she was gliding across the ground at incredible speeds. There's something different about you, though, that doesn't make sense. We can already see that you have your mother's powers, but there seems to be more to you than that."

I thought he just said that the powers don't change. "More to me?"

The room becomes very silent and the air is thick with uncertainty. "When we were doing your physical evaluation, the doctor and Gregory noticed something. You, for lack of a better term, flickered."

Guess that was a two-way mirror. Wait, did he just say what I think he said? "You're kidding, right? I flickered, like a bad light bulb? What does that even mean? I didn't sense that."

Mr. Smith drags a hand over his face. Guess he doesn't like the fact that I'm not going according to their plan. "We really don't know what this means either, but hopefully with time, we can figure it out. Of course, this is only going to happen if you take us up on our offer."

I think about school and not being able to finish. Not only that, but what about my friends? I wonder if I would even be allowed to talk to them anymore. What about dating; was that even permitted? I have all these thoughts jumbling in my head, yet something keeps telling me to give it a chance. But what about later in life—husband, kids, and the whole shebang? "I have a question for you, Mr. Smith. Say I join with you, train and help. What happens if I ever want to quit? What future can I even have?"

He looks at me with a smug smile on his face. He must know that I'm leaning toward yes, that my walls are crumbling and all he needs to do is smash some of the stones and I'll come running.

"We're not taking away your future. We're trying to give you one. We need you to have one. We need you to get married one day, have an heir so your power will pass on. I wouldn't worry about it just yet; you're still young. As far as quitting, there are opportunities for jobs within the FBI and not out in the field. If you decide that you want nothing to do with us ever again, we would have to wipe your mind. It's imperative that our secrets are kept. You would no longer have any memory of this place, what you've done or who you've met, but you would still have your powers."

"Is that what you did to my mom?"

I'm met with silence.

"No. We lost track of her," Mr. Smith pauses, and something like pity appears on his face. "Until she was at the hospital."

Where she died. But what about the A. A. meetings? The year sobriety coin? Does anyone know about that? I'm guessing they don't; otherwise maybe she wouldn't have ended up overdosing.

What do I have to lose, besides my life? I've always felt out of place and now I'm virtually an orphan. My parents were able to find some happiness here, so maybe I will too. Maybe someone here can shed light onto my mom—a woman who, it seems, was not what I thought. Honestly, it's not like I can really say no, because if that wasn't them in the gold sedan, who knows what might happen? "By any chance have you guys been following us around in a gold sedan?"

Everyone's head snaps toward mine at that comment. Apparently this is news to them. Mr. Smith's eyes grow wide. "You've been followed?"

Well...hell. I swallow down the lump in my throat. "Yeah, I saw them outside my grandparents', and then last night there were two men outside the house we were staying in. I assumed it was the FBI."

Mr. Smith narrows his eyes at Grandpa. "Joe, did you know about this?"

Grandpa hangs his head. Tapping snags my attention. Gregory's fingers keep drumming the table and he looks like he has murder in his eyes. "I just assumed it was nerves, and Becca never told me about the men outside," Grandpa says.

"That wasn't us, and it concerns me that you're being followed already. That's what I was trying to tell you about possible danger. We can protect you and teach you to protect yourself, but you'd have to agree to stay here," Mr. Smith says.

I feel my free will slowly slipping away from me. I'm not going to lie to myself. This is intense and a lot to digest, but if my Grandpa believes I should do this, then I'm willing to give it a try. What are my alternatives? Maybe I can do the good that my mother never did. No. Not maybe. I will do what Mr. Smith said. I will find my worth, even if she ended up losing hers. I won't be like her.

I take a deep breath and release it slowly. "What choice do I have? I'm willing to try."

Grandpa nods his head in agreement and the decision is made. "So where do we go from here?" I ask.

Mr. Smith smiles at me. "And so it begins."

ELEVEN

Two weeks. Is that even enough time to get my life in order? My packed suitcases mock me from my bed. Time's up.

Grandpa called school last week and informed them of my mom dying. We lied. Said the grief was too much and I'd finish up my classes online. I tried to use that same spin with my friends, but some of them were surprised since I didn't exactly speak kindly of my mom. I laid it on thick, though, claiming to feel ridden with guilt for never healing the breach between us. I almost believed myself—also scared myself with how good of a liar I've become. But that's the new norm with all the secrets I'll be keeping.

But here I sit. Headed to training today and learning to perfect my powers. Life is too freaking crazy. At least one good thing has happened these past two weeks: no gold car. Maybe it was just a fluke. At least that's what I keep telling myself.

I walk down the stairs and out the back door, toward the swing hanging from the old willow tree. Grandpa hung this for me when I was seven after I begged him for weeks to do it. The tree itself is old and strong. Its limbs are as familiar to me as my own. I lean back, closing my eyes, and push off, soaring toward the sky. Is this what it'll feel like when I use my powers?

A cool breeze tangles my hair, soothing my nerves, comforting me. It makes me feel alive. A hand touches the small of my back and pushes me from behind and my body tenses. "It's okay. It's just me, Gregory. I was a little early picking you up and saw you out here swinging."

Everything relaxes. A huge smile appears across my face before I can stop myself, but at least he can't see it. Every time his hand rests on my back, even if only for a few seconds, it's pure bliss, mixed with that same shock that seems to have diminished the more contact we have.

After a few pushes, I hop off and face him. He's dressed simply in jeans and a t-shirt, but he wears them so well. If I met him on the street I would think he's a regular guy, except for the fact that he has a super power and works for a secret government agency. Normal things. "Thanks for that. I just really wanted to come out here and enjoy this." My hand may point to the tree, but a part of me means: enjoying the freedom.

He smiles at me and it reaches his eyes. "No problem. You know, life isn't over just because of where you're going. Think of this as a new chapter, a chance to meet new people and experience things others can only imagine."

He makes everything sound so easy. "I'll go get Grandpa and let him know it's time to head out."

As I walk in the back door, I spot Grandma sitting solemnly on the couch. "What's wrong?" I ask.

Tears begin to well up in her eyes. I wonder if she felt the same way when my dad went away. "I'm just really sad to see you go. It's been so nice having you home. I don't know when I'll get to see you next."

I stiffen my spine. I need to be strong, more for her than myself. I don't know when I'll be able to come again either. "Don't worry," I try and reassure her, "I'll be coming home to see you soon. Do you know where Grandpa is? Gregory's here to escort us."

Grandpa walks in from the kitchen, his hands stuffed in his pockets. "I'm not going to come with you two. I need to stay with Grandma. But I'll come down in a few days."

A large part of me is pissed. And scared. I can't do this on my own. But a small part, a secret part, is excited about the prospect of being alone with Gregory.

They both stand and I give each of them a long hug. Grandpa leans in and gives me a kiss on the forehead. He pushes my hair away from my face and whispers into my ear, "I love you. Don't ever forget that."

I smile at the man who's been my rock. I'm going to miss him so much. Gregory peeks his head in the front door. "Are we ready to go? Joe, where's your bag? Aren't you coming with us?"

"No, I'll join you guys in a few days. I need to stay here with Mae for now."

His voice seems a little off. I can tell he's lying. I doubt I'll see him in a few days.

"All right, well, we should hit the road before it gets too late," Gregory says.

I hug my grandparents one last time. I have to keep chanting *Don't cry* to myself. It'll only make things worse. "Okay. I promise to call you guys as soon as we get there, and Grandpa, I'll see you soon. I love you both."

Gregory stands by the door, my suitcase in his hand, waiting for me. We walk out the door and to the car. "Ready for a road trip?" I ask, getting in.

He smiles, a little crookedly, and we take off down the road.

This is the first time we've been alone together for longer than five minutes. I study his body. I can't help it. His profile is to me and I trace the line of his strong jaw with my eyes. I follow it down the column of his throat to solid, wide shoulders. His forearms are bare and his muscles flex. I didn't think forearms could be attractive, but maybe I need to rethink this. His hands grip the steering wheel, causing those muscles to flex even more. He shifts in his seat. "Becca?" his voice croaks out.

Did he catch me staring? My mind scrambles for a distraction. "Uh, so umm, tell me about yourself."

Great opening there, really smooth.

"Me?" he asks, and there's a hint of relief in his tone.

"Yeah, what's your story?" I ask.

His body relaxes. No more taut forearms for me. He laughs and then raises an eyebrow at the question. "My story, huh?"

I don't think that's too hard of a question, but maybe I'm wrong. "Well, it's just so quiet in the car and we have a long ride, so I figured that you could tell me a little about yourself. You know a lot about me, and I'm assuming we're going to be working together."

He sits there for a minute, not saying anything. *Please say something because I cannot handle this ride in complete silence.* "Actually, I'll probably be your mentor during training and for a little while afterwards."

Excellent.

His smile stays on his face and I can feel the burning in my cheeks. "So, where're you from?"

"I spent some of my childhood in a little farming town in Iowa. Kind of a dull area, but everyone there was always nice."

"Only for part of your childhood?"

He hesitates. "When I was nine, I was told my parents both were killed during a tornado."

He says it so matter-of-factly that it throws me a little bit. And I'm kind of surprised he's telling me this. Then again, he already knows my backstory. But maybe this is like the way people in Project Lightning introduce themselves? Man, that would be depressing. "That's horrible. Wait, told?"

"Yeah, and that's what the newspapers said too. However, when I got older I learned they didn't die in a tornado. I don't really know how they died. I've never been told what actually happened, but I know it was something else."

He jerks slightly. I wonder if maybe he didn't mean to tell me that much.

And I thought the history with *my* parents sucked. "You don't remember how they died?"

He takes a deep breath, probably resigned to the fact that he might as well tell me more. "No. I have no memory of their deaths, just the life I had with them. After they passed away, I was also raised by my grandparents. They gave me a good life, taught me to speak fluent Polish and Russian. With their help, I was able to attend MIT and earned a degree in aerospace engineering. Then I ended up with a job at the FBI."

I wait for more, but nothing comes. That's it, that's all he has to tell me about himself? He seems so evasive and acts like there is still so much more. Stupid guys, don't they realize we hate when they pull this Mr. Mysterious act thinking it's hot?

A strangled cough pulls me from my thoughts. I wait for him to say anything, but he just keeps watching the road. "Sorry, got something stuck in my throat."

Okay.

Everything he tells me is so vague. Like, why is he working in this division and what powers does he have? I look him over. There's no way he could have graduated from MIT. He hardly looks older than me. "MIT? How old are you?"

A sly smile spreads across his face. "I'm nineteen."

My mouth must be hanging open like a fish, because he starts laughing. What, am I with baby Einstein here? He must be some genius to have already graduated from MIT. I can't believe he's only two years older than me. I haven't even graduated high school! I know nothing about him, and what I do know makes him out to be even more secretive. "Did not see that coming. Got any more crazy details to tell me?"

He barks a laugh at me. "In time you'll learn more about me, along with the others."

I'm not going to lie; I want to know much more about him now. And what I have learned has made me more attracted to him. Wait, did he just say others? What does that mean? Better yet, *who* does that mean? "Will Ania be with us during training?"

I cringe at my question, but wait for the answer.

"Yes, she's got a lot of knowledge that you'll find useful."

I was hoping she would be off on some mission. I didn't really talk to her before I left our last meeting. Her beauty really intimidates me. How can I possibly compare to that? Maybe if I knew more about her she wouldn't seem so perfect. "If you won't tell me more about yourself, what's Ania's deal?"

He perks up in his seat, eager enough to talk about her. *Rub it in, why don't you?* "Well, Ania is an interesting and sad case. She was born and raised in Poland with her parents until she was fifteen. She's special like you. She received her powers at fifteen. Her mom was also part of Project Lightning. But she was actually tried and executed for treason in Russia. I'm not allowed to divulge all the details, but she'll probably tell you when she's ready. After her mom was executed, Ania's father brought her to America and the FBI. "

Do none of our parents die from old age? I wonder if everyone's story is going to be tragic. "That sounds really rough. Is anyone's power like hers?"

"No, every one of the surviving hundred possesses a different power. Sort of like snowflakes, no two are the same, but some are similar. With Ania's strength she has amazing fighting skills. That's because she has the strength of a hundred men. She's been training at the FBI since she was a teenager. Her knowledge on weapons is more extensive than almost anyone on the planet."

All right, that's a little scary. "Sounds a little—well actually, *very* — intimidating. I would hate to get on her bad side."

"She's a firecracker, but she's been a good friend, with a lot of advice and experience to offer."

I have the sudden urge to shake my fist at the sky.

I wonder if they're more than just friends. She looks older than him, and even more so now that I know he's only nineteen.

"What's your power?" I ask him.

He rubs the back of his. "I'm not at liberty to tell." His voice is hesitant.

"Why?" I ask.

"Orders." I wait for more of a response, but that's the only one he gives me.

We drive for a long time in silence. Nothing to do but watch the trees pass by and try to imagine what the future has in store. Will I be alone? I should have asked more questions. I never ask enough questions.

Gregory finally breaks the silence in the car. "We should be there in about forty-five minutes, so let me give you a run-down on how tonight will go. Once we get there, I'll show you to where you'll be staying. It'll kind of be like living in a dorm room again, but it's not too bad. After that, you'll attend an orientation where they'll go over ground rules and you'll be able to meet others like yourself."

"How many others are there?"

"I think around twelve or so. Mr. Smith usually does orientation once a year around this time, if there are new recruits."

"Rough year?" I ask, completely shocked.

The atmosphere changes. And his whole body seems to slump. "You have no idea," he says in a voice filled with regret and a sadness I don't understand.

This must have been a seriously bad year for them.

"This sounds a lot like freshman orientation," I say, desperately grasping at the fun banter we had not long before.

He attempts a smirk at that comment. "Yeah, it's sort of like that, but a lot more intense, and thankfully shorter. You'll see what I mean when we get there. Won't be too long now." I try to swallow the lump in my throat.

"Did you come in with a lot of people too?" I ask.

"No. It was just me, actually," he says.

"Did that suck?" I ask.

He laughs. "Yeah. Nothing like being the center of attention." He sobers quickly. "Just so you know, we won't be telling anyone about your power."

"Why?" I ask.

"Since you're showing signs of being different, we want to keep it quiet. We don't know how some of the others will react. I'm sure it'll be fine, but better to be cautious."

Well, this should be interesting.

TWELVE

The hall leading to my room reminds me of the hospital-like feeling I got during my interview. Very plain and sterile. If it weren't for the number three next to my door, I'd never find the room.

Gregory opens the door so we can drop my bags off. I shouldn't be surprised really; look at the rest of the place. But would it kill them to use another color besides white? Like blue, that's still subtle. "Lots and lots of white," I say.

"Uniformity," he tells me.

"Does my personal space have to stay this way? Because this will drive me crazy."

He grabs the door and closes it. "I'm sure you can add your own touches to it, but you won't be staying here for your entire training."

He starts walking, but I stay in the same spot. Leaving? I run to catch up with him. "Where else am I going?"

His face doesn't give away anything. "You'll see eventually. Let's get to the meeting. You might find out where else you'll be training."

We walk down another long, dull hallway until we come to a room that reminds me of a high school classroom. Desks in rows, a whiteboard at the front, and Mr. Smith standing at a podium like a stern math teacher. I didn't know my dad, but I can't figure out how he could have been friends with this guy. Sure, he was *okay* when I met him, but he just has that military feel about him.

Sitting around the room are twelve other people ranging from teens to maybe early twenties. Beside everyone looking under thirty, there are no other similarities. It's a mix of genders and ethnicities.

"You're late. Have a seat so we can get going," Mr. Smith says to me.

A little embarrassed, I grab the seat next to another girl who looks close to my age. I give a polite smile and she returns it with a grimace. *All right, then.*

We turn our attention to Mr. Smith at his podium. "First and foremost, I would like to welcome you here and thank you for accepting the opportunity to be a part of Project Lightning. All thirteen of you have met with me individually already throughout the last few months. After I have finished my presentation, you'll have a chance to talk and get to know each other. Some of you will be working together, so try to build a good rapport with one another. But we won't be discussing powers right now. We'll leave that for another time. Some of you might not even have a grasp on what your power is."

That sucks. I really wanted to know what power everyone has. And there's thirteen of us—like that's not a bad omen or anything.

"All of you come from a long line of gifted people. All of you have a different power, which means different strengths and different weaknesses, but that's what makes Project Lightning great. Here you'll learn more about your history and the history of our people. I believe it's vital to understand where you've come from. We have been persecuted and our ancestors have been murdered. We won't let that happen again.

"You'll learn to master your powers and overcome your weaknesses, as well as have opportunities to perform a great service to our country. In order to accomplish these tasks, there are ground rules that have to be followed."

Of course.

"The first and most important rule is that you won't be able to contact the outside world for a while. Secrecy is essential, and we cannot risk exposure. So for now, communication with anyone outside of training is forbidden. This is the reason all of your phones are have been taken. Don't worry. I don't want to keep them; you'll get them back"

A hand shoots up from across the room. The owner of it's a guy who looks to be in his early twenties. He has dark brown hair and alluring eyes, along with olive tone skin. He's pretty hot, but no Gregory. "What is this, the fortress of solitude?" the guy asks.

Mr. Smith levels him with an exasperated look. "Anthony, it's vital right now to keep silent. In time you'll be able to communicate with friends and family, but not yet. I would also recommend that you learn to control these outbursts." Anthony leans back in his chair and throws his arm around the seat. I swear I see Mr. Smith holding back an eye roll.

"Moving on." His eyes stay locked on Anthony. "As you may notice, many of you are close in age. There can be no improper fraternization with each other, so there will be curfews in place and we will be closely monitoring you. You'll need to be focusing on training and educating yourself. That will require you to devote all your attention to your training. Make friends and allies, but keep it at that."

I wonder if my parents broke this rule. They were mentor and student who fell in love, so either they broke the rules or are the reason behind it.

"Most of you will be training here, but a few of you will be taken later to an off-campus site. While you are here or anywhere else, I want to you to remember that I'm not a maid, and the mentors aren't either. Clean up your rooms and after yourself.

"That's it for tonight. Tomorrow I'll meet with each of you individually and go over specific goals and training strategies. For now, get to know one another and I'll see you tomorrow."

He leaves his podium and exits the room. Gregory said that I probably won't stay here long. Maybe some of these guys will be coming with me.

We all sit in our chairs staring at each other, not really knowing what to say. There are different walks of life in the room. I've already taken notice of Anthony and the girl next to me. A guy in his mid-twenties with thick glasses is hiding in the back corner with ragged clothes and messy hair. Poor guy looks like he's someone who was teased in school.

Right next to the podium sits a beautiful redhead whose hair runs down her shoulders in a shower of curls. She has piercing blue eyes and a curvy frame. Another guy catches my eye. He's close to my age, but built like a freaking ox. He totally flexes his arms when Miss Redhead turns his way. Guy must have worked out for hours to get that body.

So many different types of people, but they're all here for the same reason.

What *do* you say when you realize you're in a room filled with people who have powers? This isn't a typical get-to-know-you situation. What are we supposed to say? Should we all apologize to each other because we've all lost a parent recently? A minute of the most awful silence passes and finally Anthony stands up. "I feel like I'm at an AA meeting."

We all give a nervous, forced laugh. I'm not surprised that he's the first to stand. "Well, you heard Mr. Smith call me Anthony, but I go by Tony. I'm eighteen, from Boston, was planning on going to college, but that's out of the question for now. Let's see what else I can tell you. I enjoy long walks on the beach and lots of inappropriate fraternization."

We all laugh for real this time and his eyes lock with mine. My cheeks flame and I avert my eyes. It's a nice release to have someone crack a joke, though. Around the room people take turns standing, introducing themselves, and saying a little about who they are. The redhead's name is Arianna. When she talks it isn't hard to tell she's from the South. All the guys in the room hang on her every word. The nerdy-looking guy in the corner is Dexter, possibly a cruel joke by his parents. All he tells us is his name. The big ox is Mike. He goes on for several minutes about his successful high school sports career and how upset he is to not shine in the college or pro arena. Pretty sure if there was a mirror in here he'd be flexing.

Finally, the girl sitting next to me stands up. She's average; nothing about her stands out except for her eyes. They're as dark as night and hard—there's no softness there. "My name is Sariah. I'm eighteen, was a freshman in college with plans to become a doctor. It took a lot of arm twisting and convincing to get me here. We're all here because one of our parents died not too long ago, and it was my mom's dying wish for me to be here."

Well, that shuts us all up.

Sariah sits down. Guess it's my turn. I stand and address everyone. "Well, I guess I'm last. My name is Rebecca, but I prefer being called Becca. I'm seventeen and scared out of my mind to be here. I don't know what I've gotten myself into, but like the rest of you I'm here now. I guess the last thing I have to add is, here's hoping that we all make it out of this alive and live to have improper fraternizations in the future."

Tony shoots me a smile and adds a "Hear, hear!"

We all exit the classroom to find Gregory leaning against the wall. I smile at him. Tony may be good looking, but I can't help getting excited when I see Gregory.

"So you're hoping to live through training to have 'improper fraternizations'?"

I can feel my face turning as red as a stop sign. I had no idea he was listening to us. And seriously, when's the last time I blushed this much? "Well you know, I thought I would leave everyone with a dose of humor instead of seriousness."

The smile on his face slowly leaves as his demeanor changes. "That was a good choice. The next few days are going to be pretty rough, and you'll need humor to get you through it."

"How come everyone else's mentors aren't escorting them back to their rooms?" He's the only one.

"You're sort of a special case." I raise a brow at that. "Since we don't really know what all your powers are. I thought it would be better to be safe than sorry."

We walk side by side down the hall and I occasionally catch a hint of cloves, sweat, and something that has to be Gregory's natural scent. Whatever it is, it's delicious.

"I've got a question," I say.

"Shoot."

"So we're supposed to be working with everyone? But we can't talk about what we do?"

His eyes stay fixed ahead, and then he nods his head like he's come to some sort of decision. "Not yet. There are so few of us left and we invite everyone here, but there's a chance that some won't stay. Or that some are plants."

"Plants?" I ask.

"Some of the one hundred who no longer work with us have their own faction. Only about sixty of the hundred have anything to do Project Lightning. But of that other forty, their decedents have come to us before saying that they want nothing to do with that group. Most of the time it's true. But there have been a few cases where it wasn't," he says.

Whoa.

"So the next little bit, if that's the case, they'll be weeded out," he says.

"What happens to them?" I ask.

"They get their memory wiped," he says.

"But what if they leave before that?" I ask.

"That's a rarity," he tells me.

"Not with my mom," I counter.

His gaze leaves mine. "She was a rarity," he says.

Apparently.

He approaches my door and I realize I'm going to get lost in the place. He's got to know that. But somewhere in the back of my girlish head I'm fantasizing, hoping that he's walking me back to my room as an excuse to be with me. "You're not going to be camping outside my door all night, now are you?"

He laughs, making me feel so naive. "Well, I know you would probably enjoy that, but I need my sleep as well."

I swear he must know what I'm thinking. That or I'm just completely obvious.

"All right, I'll see you in the morning after breakfast. Get some sleep; you'll need it for tomorrow. Training is really exhausting at first."

Sleep. Sure, because that'll come easily.

THIRTEEN

The dream is familiar. I'm flying through the air again. That same feeling of exhilaration washes over me as I weave in and out of the clouds. Suddenly the clouds start to darken and the wind is blowing fierce and cold. Cutting my thrilling flight short.

I hear a voice, but it's too distant to make out.

A feeling, like a heavy shove, pushes me toward earth. I thrash my arms and legs, attempting to fight it. But fighting it just seems to make the pull harder and increasingly faster toward the ground.

I make a choice.

I stop fighting and release myself to this unseen force. Everything goes dark and my body feels suspended in the air. A whisper in the wind pierces me, as if passing through my soul. "Becca, we don't have much time. Don't trust anyone. Don't tell your secrets, and keep your guard up. Listen to your instincts and never doubt yourself."

Sirens roar in the darkness. Am I still in the dream? My eyes snap open and I'm back in the small dorm room. A voice booms over a loudspeaker. "This is a wakeup call! All trainees are to wake up and proceed to breakfast!"

Not a dream.

Well, that's one way to wake up. Guess there's no need for an alarm clock?

I sit up quickly in bed. Maybe today is the day we'll figure out what the heck my power is.

I didn't unpack last night, so I fish my toothbrush and paste out of my suitcase. Looking in the mirror, I don't see my reflection, just flashes of the dream. It was strange, even surreal. I'm not sure it even happened. It was just a dream, and nothing really comes of dreams, but there was something eerily familiar about that voice. With all the weird things occurring right now, it couldn't hurt to heed the warning.

After countless wrong turns and endless white halls, I follow the smell of food. The cafeteria is already full of people sitting and eating. I wonder if they're some of the one hundred, or if they just happen to work for Project Lightning.

Grabbing my breakfast, I feel like I'm in high school again trying to find a place to sit.

"Becca, come join us over here," Tony says from behind me.

Four sets of eyes assess me, besides Tony. "Sorry guys, you're going to have to remind me of your names again. I wasn't paying the best attention last night," I say with a sheepish shrug.

Thankfully, Tony jumps in with introductions. "Well, I'm Tony, but how could you forget that? This is Mike, Paul, Jessica, and Steve."

The chair next to me pulls out. "And I'm Gregory."

Tony narrows his eyes. "I don't remember you from last night."

Everyone looks at Gregory, and I suddenly feel protective of my mentor. "It's okay, I can vouch for Gregory. He's with me."

Tony keeps looking between the two of us. Searching.

That's followed up with blank stares, and I look at Gregory for help. "Yes, I'm her mentor. Each of you will meet with yours if you haven't already. Probably after your first workout."

"What's the deal with the workout?" Tony asks.

"We need to see where you're at physically. Some of you have been athletes. Some have a little martial arts training. It's really just to get a baseline on you guys."

We dig into our food, and that's when I notice Dexter out of the corner of my eye. He's just standing there, holding a tray and looking a little lost. No one seems to notice.

"Hey Dexter, come sit with us," I yell out to him.

His shoulders relax, and a bright smile spreads across his face as he walks toward us.

He takes a seat at our table, and everyone introduces themselves again. He looks at me. "Thanks for that. For a minute there I had a horrible flashback to eighth grade."

I laugh at the exact same thing I thought when I walked in here. "Me too, Dex. Me too."

He smiles at the nickname I've already bestowed on him.

As soon as our plates are empty, we're herded into a large training room. Today is the first day of our group workout. Everyone stands around the mat assessing one another. Dexter and I stand next to each other, and Tony takes his place to my left. His eyes survey the room, really only focusing on the girls. Typical guy, with too many hormones roving around. Mike stands next to him, and I can hear them talking in hushed voices. "They really need to drop the rule of no 'fraternizations.' There are some real hotties in the room," Mike says.

Gross.

Tony strokes his stubble. "Well, if no one finds out, then no harm, no foul."

He gives a chin lift to Sariah across the mat. Her eyes haven't really looked anywhere else but at Tony. I wish someone would tell her to wipe the drool from her lips. "She's not half bad, eh?" Mike asks.

Tony smiles at her. "No, she's not, but I prefer someone else."

He turns from Sariah and his eyes meet mine. I've been caught eavesdropping. "You ready for today's session, Becca?" he asks, laughter heavy in his voice.

Suddenly the wall is super interesting, but only because I'm completely mortified. Yup, he was totally aware I was listening. I nod, too embarrassed to answer. Because I don't really need him to know how humiliated I am.

The training room door crashes open, and through it steps Ania. Quite the entrance. A bunch of others follow her in and line the walls. These must be the other mentors.

At once, every guy in the room turns and stares at her. It's like dogs looking at a bone. I'm pretty sure some of their mouths are salivating. She's got to use her looks to throw off opponents.

What's it like to have every guy in the room want you? I know I'm not ugly, but my body is more muscular than lean, nowhere near the modelesse of Ania. Girls always tell me that if I did more with my hair and wore makeup I would be a knock-out, but that's too much hassle. The only thing I care about right now is that I'm in better shape than most of the other trainees.

Thank goodness for grandpa and all of his grueling drills on the basketball court or at the batting cages. Most girls got to go to Brownies or tea parties, and poor Grandma Mae tried so hard to put me in dresses with bows in my hair. Her efforts failed. More often than not I came home with my tights torn, hair a mess, and grass stains all over. Which would cause her to put her hands on her hips, give a disapproving sigh, and say, "Oh Rebecca, what am I going to do with you? You need to start acting like a little lady." Fat chance of that.

Ania positions herself before all of us on the mats. "Today we're going to work on some self-defense tactics. Later, as you progress in your training, you'll have the opportunity to learn different types of martial arts and combat styles. These will be useful, as you never know where you'll be or what you'll need to survive. Now, can I have a volunteer?"

Mike steps forward immediately. His eyes scan her slowly from head to toe like he's undressing her with his eyes. Total creeper. He rubs his hands together and a huge, smug smile sits on his face. He may be big, but that's going to be his downfall. "I'll gladly take you on."

The sound of his voice makes my skin crawl. He's one of those guys you wouldn't want to be alone with. I don't know if I'm the only one who knows her power is unbelievable strength. I smile to myself. It'll be such a pleasure to watch this. "Well, come up here and we'll see how long you keep that smile on your face, *tępak*," Ania says.

"Well this should be interesting," Dexter says from beside me. And I couldn't agree more.

The hairs on my neck stand up as the warmth of a body presses against mine. "I bet she wipes the floor with him," Tony whispers.

I snort at his comment. I have no doubt that she'll easily subdue him. When I glance back up, Sariah's shooting daggers at me. I highly doubt we're going to become friends. Oh well. If she wanted to giggle with Tony, all she had to do was walk over here and stand next to him.

Mike looks poised on the mat. "Okay, I want you to come at me and don't hold back," Ania instructs. "There's nothing more irritating than a man who can't take control."

She's baiting him. He seems like the type of guy who refuses to lose and would never be outdone by a woman. He stalks around her, surveying her body. I want nothing more than to go retch in a corner. What a sleaze. I wonder if she thinks he's gross as well.

He rushes to grab her from behind. But without any effort she turns, lifts him in the air, and slams him onto his stomach, twisting his arm into an unnatural position behind his back. It all happened smoothly and quickly, like she was dancing. All her movements were well planned. His lips are pinched and his eyes are slits, and that's the best thing I've seen all week. His pride is completely wounded.

Silence fills the room. No one seems to know what to make of what just happened. A small part of my brain would love to laugh, but I know better. I start to clap slowly. That was amazing, after all. All eyes swing to me. Tony joins in and the rest of the room soon follows. The clapping and shouting becomes a roar and Mike's face reddens even more. He crawls back to his spot alongside Tony and shoots me a dirty stare. I give him an innocent shrug. I'm not really making a lot of friends, but he deserved it.

Ania stands triumphantly on the mat, but not without a smile on her face. "Never underestimate an opponent because of their size. Dexter, come up here and we'll show everyone some easy moves to break holds."

Dexter freezes for a moment and then gives me a horrified look. I pat his shoulder. Poor guy. But he soon joins Ania on the mat. She shows us different ways to get away from an attacker. After a couple rounds Dexter's face is covered in sweat, while Ania stands there without a hair out of place.

She pats the poor guy on the shoulder. "All right, let's break up into partners and work on these simple tasks together. We'll start on how to break free from an opponent by sweeping them off their feet."

Sariah saunters over toward Tony, while Ania walks toward me. "I'm going to have you go off with Gregory to work today," Ania says.

She points to the door behind me and there he stands, leaned up against the door frame. How long has he been standing there? He always seems to appear out of thin air. As I approach, he smiles and I understand how Sariah must feel when Tony looks at her, because my stomach starts to do flips. "Are you always lurking by some door?"

"I love this part of the training. Ania is always able to draw out the one creep who just wants a chance to put his hands on her. Their facial reaction makes my day every time."

I look back at Mike, and he's partnered with Ania. He looks like a scared little kid, but that's not who Gregory is paying attention to. "I don't think Tony really likes me," Gregory tells me.

My gaze shifts to Tony. A scowl mars his handsome face, his eyes looking at Gregory. "I think he feels like his turf is being threatened," he says.

I laugh at the notion. "What, with me?" I ask.

He smiles and grabs my hand to pull me out of the room. Tony watches us leave, still looking annoyed. "You and I have some training to do ourselves."

FOURTEEN

The training arena reminds me of the rec center at school. Various weight machines, treadmills, elliptical machines, and a rock wall. The major differences are the boxing ring, sparring area, and a door marked *Caution: Shooting Range.* I stop to marvel at the sword-fighting area. Why they have swords I'll never understand, because last time I checked, this was not medieval times.

Gregory walks over to the boxing ring. As I approach, he flashes his brilliant smile and produces a pair of boxing gloves. "Lucky for us, you're already in pretty good shape. However, you need to learn to defend yourself and fight. Today we'll work on boxing to teach you how to block and move. Any questions?"

"Yeah, why am I boxing alone with you?"

He smirks. "You better feel lucky you get to spar with just me. Be grateful that it's not Ania you're working with. We're alone because until we have a better handle on your powers, we don't want to expose you to the others."

More secrets and more seclusion. Just add another reason for the others not to like me.

I put my gloves on and follow him into the ring. I hop from foot to foot. I've never boxed, but this is what they always do in the movies.

He starts me with basic techniques of blocking shots, jabbing, dipping, and reacting quickly. My muscles scream in protest, especially since I've been benched for a while. But man, does it feel good to release all of these pent-up emotions. He's quick to anticipate my moves and we continue for close to an hour in the ring.

My hands grip my knees. I'm going to die. Gregory grabs my sweat-drenched arm and leads me to a bench. He hands me a bottle of water. "That was a really good workout. I know you're tired, but after working at this for a while, you'll be able to handle much more. It's vital that we stay in top shape. Rest a minute, and then I'll take you to the classroom."

In the classroom are Ania and Mr. Smith, but no one else. It isn't really a classroom, but more like an office. The desk at the front is hidden under various stacks of papers. The walls are covered with different type of maps, as well as a picture of Mr. Smith shaking someone's hand. I'm guessing the guy in the picture is important, but I have no clue who he is. There's only one picture on his desk. He's a lot younger in it, dressed in army fatigues with two other men. There's no picture of a wife or children. How depressing.

Mr. Smith gestures for Gregory and me to sit down. "Welcome to your history lesson, Rebecca. We're going to talk about a lot of important things in here. I need you to stay silent about what you learn, even with the others in the program. Do you understand?"

"Honestly, no," I tell him.

"May I?" Gregory asks Mr. Smith.

"Go ahead," is his reply.

Gregory looks at me. "Remember what we talked about last night?" I nod. "You're getting a little crash course. The rest of the recruits will be eased into it more than you."

"It'll make more sense soon," Mr. Smith says.

Maybe, but in the meantime, this feels ridiculous.

"As I said the other night, our heritage stretches back thousands of years. Our ancestors have been a part of most major historical events and have often caused the loss or win of a war. They've been immortalized in myths and stories. A prime example would be the Greek gods."

Really, Greek gods, is he serious? "Are you really trying to tell me that I am related to Zeus and Ania's related to Aries? Am I actually at the FBI?"

Gregory and Ania try to smother their laughs, and Mr. Smith desperately tries to keep a serious face. Ania really could be descended from Aries; she is freakishly strong, after all. "No, you're not related to the Zeus of legends, but those stories were based on real people. There is truth in all folklore and history. You basically floated across the ground when you ran fast, kind of like Hermes. Imagine yourself back in ancient Greece. How else would people explain us? They called us gods because of the things we were able to do.

"Our ancestors have been vital to this world and especially to this country. The Revolutionary War wouldn't have happened without them. Of course, the FBI wasn't established yet, but Project Lightning has been involved with this nation's government since its inception. That's when it had its founding. Our task is sometimes a thankless one. We won't be written about in any history books but our own. Now, not all hundred live in the U.S. and not all work with us, but many have come to work here or are operating overseas.

"Our ancestors have invested a lot and provided a great service to this country, one I hope you will want to continue."

I guess I come from a long line of unsung heroes.

"There's a new threat on the horizon that we're currently monitoring. We're not telling any of the new recruits, but some of our agents have been kidnapped."

What?

"This is one of the reasons there are so many of you right now, and why we didn't waste time in recruiting you so soon after your mother's death. We know some of the agents are being killed after kidnapping. But the others, we have no clue."

This sick feeling spreads throughout my body.

"The guys in the gold sedan?" I ask.

"Maybe. I don't know, but we're not taking any chances," Mr. Smith tells me.

"I'm only telling you this so you can understand why we're going to push you rather hard in training. In a week or two, you'll be going to a different location for further preparation."

"How can I be more valuable than the others?"

"There's a lot we can't tell you right now. It's better for you to be ignorant. Trust us. I know your grandfather would want you to."

A tidal wave of anger hits me. He had to play the grandpa card. But what is the alternative? The dream I had last night flashes in my memory. My head aches and my heart is weighed down. Regardless, I have to go along with this, for now. "Trust is earned, and it's hard for me to trust when so much is kept from me."

His hands grip the desk, but immediately he releases them and takes a deep breath. "We understand, and in time more and more will be revealed to you. Don't forget you're only seventeen and we've been at this a lot longer than you have. Other lives besides your own have to be considered. Trust is a two-way street, and we need to ensure that you aren't planning on running like your mother."

Low. Blow. And seriously, way to be patronizing.

The mention of her is like a punch to the gut. "First of all, I'm nothing like my mother." My voice comes out harsh. "Second, I may be seventeen, but I had to grow up pretty fast with a dead father and absentee mother. I'll accept your offer for now, because you haven't really given me much of a choice."

A slow smile spreads across his face. "Good. Now I'd like you to have lunch with Ania, and afterwards you're going to be with her for the rest of the day."

We leave the room. It's so intimidating walking next to her. Not only is she a killing machine; she's also drop dead gorgeous. "He's not always that—" Ania pauses, probably searching for a kinder word "—intense."

"So it's just me?" Sarcasm drips from my words.

"I think it's the situation with what's been going with the missing agents. Plus we've never had to question someone's power. It's a game changer."

Fantastic.

After grabbing our lunches, we head to a table and I see Tony motion for me to come and sit with him. I smile and gesture toward Ania. He nods his head in understanding. I seem to be the only one who's ever accompanied by non-recruits. "The food here is kind of lousy. When we leave here it will get better."

My eyes widen in surprise. "So you'll be coming too?" I ask.

"Yes, and Gregory will be coming with us as well. There might be another recruit coming, but that decision hasn't been made yet."

The mention of Gregory makes my heart pick up speed a little. "Gregory speaks very highly of you."

Her lips twitch. "He does, does he? And what has he been saying?"

I squirm in my seat. "He just told me a little about you. Where you're from, about your mom, and coming here to the U.S..." I hesitate "...and about the extent of your powers."

She wipes her face of any emotion. Is she mad that he told me about her? "Well, that seems more than just a little," she says in a flat voice.

She's right; that's a lot more than a little. "Really just the *Reader's Digest* version."

She shrugs as if it's inconsequential. "I've known Gregory for a long time. He's a good friend." Her eyes lock with mine. "What do you think about what he told you?"

What do I think and what am I willing to tell her? I opt for *some* truth. "Honestly, I think that you could kick my butt."

She shakes her head, a small grin forming.

I take a deep breath. "But I also think it's sad about your mom. That must have been really hard for you, especially at a young age."

Her mouth quickly transforms into a grim twist when I mention her mom. "I do miss my mom. A lot. I'm very thankful to still have my father. But you lost your mom, so you should understand."

"Not really. Hard to love someone you don't know. But I do love my grandparents, and I can't imagine losing them."

She starts shifting in her seat at the talk of my drug-addict mother. It usually makes people uncomfortable. "I'm sorry for that. How about we change the subject to something a little lighter? We can talk on the way to training."

"Good idea," I say, and we both dig in and finish off the rest of our lunches.

We throw our trash away and head out of the dining hall.

As we walk down the hall I blurt out, "So, how well do you know Gregory?"

She gives me a knowing look. "Cute, isn't he?"

I can *feel* my face turning red. She sees right through me. I wonder if it's that obvious to everyone else. What am I, twelve? There's nothing wrong with admitting that someone is attractive. I laugh nervously. "Yeah, he's definitely not bad to look at."

Ania snorts. "Let me give you a piece of advice. Make friends here—it'll come in handy to be able to confide in the people you'll have missions with. But when it comes to love, I have always found that it's better not to mix work and pleasure."

That might be sound advice, but it's no good, because I still have a crush on him.

We walk through yet another set of double doors and come upon a swimming pool. This place never ceases to amaze me, but why we would swim? "Ania, I don't have a swim suit."

"Oh, we're not swimming. Look up."

The ceiling goes up about three stories and on the second level is a suspended track. "I'm going to have you run. It should help us get a better grasp on what's going on with you. We also have this entire place to ourselves." Her arm sweeps the area and I take in the stillness.

It's eerie to be alone in such a large space. Mr. Smith wasn't kidding when he mentioned that he wanted to keep information on my powers under wraps. All of this secrecy is making it hard to forge any relationships with the others. Too many secrets, too many things to keep hidden, and I've just begun here.

We climb the stairs to the second level, the track stretching out before us. Seriously, how much of this building does Project Lightning take up?

Ania motions me to start stretching alongside her and I fall in line. We work our arms and legs. I'd better stretch well or I'll be paying for it tomorrow. "Before you get to top speed, I'll do a couple of laps with you at a jogging pace. I also want to see at what speed things begin to change."

We start jogging, Ania setting the pace. Little by little she increases our speed. Running the track is the first time I've felt comfortable here. I'm back in my element, running. I've missed this so much. We round a bend and I feel a surge of energy rush through my body, as if I'm a battery being charged. My feet feel light. Ania must sense something too, because she looks over at me. "I'm going to stop so I can observe better. Concentrate on completing your laps and increase the speed at whatever rate feels comfortable."

When I sprinted earlier for the physical, it didn't last too long, but nothing is going to stop me now. "What's going to happen?"

She shrugs, looking as confused, scared, and excited as I feel. "I have no clue. We'll just have to wait and see."

I take off from her and begin increasing my speed, focusing on each step I take. When some people run, you can hear the pounding of their feet, but that's a sign of a bad runner. I've learned to roll my steps and how to run at fast speeds, but I can hardly even feel my feet rolling. The ground is there. I can see it. And I think I can feel it, but I'm not sure.

Time to sprint. My heart starts pounding as I start. The crystal blue pool snags my gaze. Man, I want to take a dip in that water.

A roaring sound fills my ears. Something's forced down my throat. I try to scream, but I can't breathe. My eyes are burning, and everything's blurred. What's going on? There's a pull at my arm. Is this another dream, another nightmare? I struggle to swing my arms and legs, but the pull is too strong. My head hits something hard and unforgiving.

Air finally hits my lungs, causing me to gasp.

Ania leans over me, water dripping from her hair and face. "Becca? Becca, are you okay?"

I roll to my side, coughing up large amounts of water. I look down at my now-drenched clothes. "What...what happened? Why am I soaking wet?"

I study her face, but it's completely blank. "Well, I'm not really sure. One minute you were sprinting, the next you disappeared and I heard you thrashing in the water."

I still don't understand. "Did I jump over the ledge or something?"

"No, you just literally disappeared in front of my eyes. What was going through your mind?"

I disappeared? I sit in silence for a few seconds and try to recall my thoughts. "I was concentrating on running like you told me to, and then I got a glimpse of the pool. The thought just popped into my head that it would be nice to swim when I was done. Next thing I knew I couldn't breathe or scream, and something was pulling me." A waking nightmare.

She runs a hand absently over her jaw and looks back at the door. When she turns back to me, there's a firm resolve in her eyes. "Let's get you dried off. I'm going to need to go and talk with Mr. Smith. He'll want to know this for sure. For now though, keep this to yourself and tell no one, and I mean no one."

"Okay," I tell her, and my gut is telling me not to disobey. She helps me to my feet and we walk out of the pool area.

FIFTEEN

The ceiling above my bed looms over me like a weight on my chest. Doesn't help that being underground translates into no windows. It's like a coffin.

I wonder what Mr. Smith will think of what happened today. I don't even know what to think about it myself. I feel like a science experiment, being poked and prodded, trying to figure out exactly how I work. Except not only am I the experiment; I'm a scientist as well.

Maybe I can try it again. I close my eyes tight and think of my bedroom back home.

I crack my eyelids open. Nothing.

Okay, maybe I need to...I don't know what the heck to do. Shouldn't this be easy? But I'm too afraid to push any more. With my luck, I'd end up sending myself Alaska. Wait, I could totally get myself trapped somewhere if I don't figure out how to control this. And when I do figure this out, I can go anywhere. Granted I won't have any money, but the places I'll be able to see, that'll be amazing.

A knock at the door stirs me out of my thoughts. "Come in."

The door opens slightly and Gregory's face appears around it. "Skipping dinner, are we?"

I glance at the clock. I've lost track of time. I'm not surprised he came looking for me. He's been my shadow ever since I got here. "No, just forgot what time it was."

"Well, dinner is still going on, so why don't you come with me and we'll get you something to eat?"

I don't really feel like eating, but I can't tell him no. I pull on my shoes and we head down the hallway. He stops me with a hand on my arm. "Is something wrong?"

All I want to do is tell him about what happened at the pool, but I was told to keep quiet. I want to tell him everything about today and how I'm feeling, but I know I can't. He may have his secrets from me, but I would tell him everything if he asked. I resolve on lying, but I don't enjoy the idea. "Yeah, I'm fine, just really tired from all the exercise. It's been a while since I've worked out that hard."

He nods, but it's plain to see that he doesn't believe me. He can read me like an open book. He doesn't move, like he's waiting for me to say something else. Ania made it very clear to keep quiet, but I feel so ashamed for lying.

We enter the dining room to find Ania eagerly awaiting us at a table. There are already full plates waiting for us. She smiles but it's a little strained. "I've been waiting for you guys. Hurry up and dig in before the food gets cold. Oh, by the way, Becca, we need to go talk with Mr. Smith after you finish up."

I sit down and feel a knot forming in my stomach. Did she mean to ruin my appetite? How can I eat and have a panic attack at the same time?

Ania and Gregory look at one another, a conversation happening without even speaking a word. She puts a hand on my shoulder. "Don't worry; you aren't in trouble or anything. He just wants to talk to you about today."

I wish I was sitting with my grandparents eating in our home. That dinner table was always full of laughter and talk of things that happened throughout the day, but those days are gone now. I want nothing more than to be able to tell my grandpa what's going on. Not being able to talk with him is killing me. I can picture us sitting on the front porch in the rocking chairs. He would always just sit there and listen to me, not interrupting or judging me. That's where we discussed my fears about private school, my regret of realizing I might have ruined my college scholarship when I got hurt, and how angry I was with my mom.

I so desperately want to be there right now with him. I can see the dark-stained chairs rocking in the wind, the flower box empty from the autumn frosts, and the cool air blowing leaves around the porch floor. Suddenly, Gregory grabs my arm firmly. Startled, I pull my arm back forcibly. "Hey, what's the big deal?"

He leans in smiling, like he's going to tell me something amusing. "You began to flicker," he whispers into my ear.

My stomach drops and my eyes dart around the room. Maybe no one noticed. But then my eyes lock with Dexter. He looks at me, but keeps blinking, completely confused. I've been caught, but I think he's at a loss as much as I am. He saw something. But I'm still trying to figure out the whole flicker thing myself as. "He saw," I say in a harsh whisper.

"I wouldn't worry too much about him. I don't think he even knows what he just witnessed."

Ania quickly gathers our trays. "We should probably go talk with Mr. Smith. Don't you think so, Gregory?" she asks.

"Definitely. He's going to want to know about what just happened."

I take one more gulp of water and the three of us head toward the door. Nope, we're not conspicuous at all. Totally normal. But I can still feel Tony's eyes fixed on me, so I look back at him and smile. He waves and then turns back to his tablemates.

We walk down the long corridor toward Mr. Smith's office. As soon as I enter the room, he motions for me to take a seat across to him. His desk is still cluttered with files and paperwork. The room smells stale and so does he, like he hasn't left his office since yesterday. I fixate on the photo of the soldiers again, stalling. I know one of them has to be him, but who are the others? His lost brothers or best friends?

Mr. Smith runs his fingers through his hair.

"Well, young lady, you're just full of surprises, aren't you?"

Before I can even respond to him, Gregory chimes in. "Before you talk about the pool, you should know that she flickered at dinner just now."

My eyes shoot toward Ania. I thought we weren't supposed to tell anyone. She has the nerve to pat my hand. "Don't worry; Gregory knows about today. We felt it important he knew since he'll be training you too."

Mr. Smith strokes his chin for what seems like an eternity. He moves some papers around on his desk, searching, scanning. He stops when he finds a packet, but quickly puts his hands on top of it before I can read what it says. His eyes meet mine. "Becca, why don't you tell me what happened at the track today? I've heard Ania's account, but I want to hear it from you."

I begin to relay the story about how we started out running together around the track. "The next thing I knew, Ania was pulling me out of the pool soaking wet."

Mr. Smith sits there for a few moments studying me. "What about tonight at dinner?"

"I didn't even know that I had flickered until Gregory told me. I wasn't even running."

His face remains a blank mask. "Was there anything in particular you were thinking about?"

I squirm in my seat under his piercing gaze. "I was thinking about my grandpa and how much I missed him. I was envisioning my home, eating dinner with my grandparents. I also thought a lot about sitting on the front porch in the rocking chairs with him and telling him everything I was thinking and going through. I wanted to talk to him about what was going on. I wanted to be there."

I look down at the floor and feel the flush creeping up my neck. I'm practically a grown woman and shouldn't be experiencing homesickness, but I can't help it. I want to run home, back to a life without these types of responsibilities. I want to go to practice and hang out with my friends.

Gregory rests his hand on my arm, pulling me out of my inner turmoil. "It's okay to miss your grandpa; he's probably the only person outside of here who knows what's going on. We've isolated you a lot from the others. You're not alone, though. Everyone in this room knows how you feel."

Mr. Smith and Ania nod in agreement. I'm one of them, and they understand, but it still hurts. "We are asking a lot of you, just as a lot was asked of us and everyone else here," Mr. Smith says. "However, it's important that we not disclose to too many people what you are capable of. It seems that your powers can be tied heavily to your emotions. You lack control, and that's something I can't let everyone know."

He shifts his gaze to Ania and Gregory. The air in the room seems to become heavier. "We might need to move up the time of relocation. It's getting too risky to have Becca stay here. We also need to make a decision on which other trainee will be coming with you." He completely disregards me; it's like I'm no longer sitting here.

I don't like being left out of this conversation like I don't exist. Yes, I agreed to come here and join them, but they should at least let me know matters that concern me. "What other location?" I ask.

Mr. Smith holds up his hand to quiet me like a small child. "Remember, we talked previously about taking you somewhere else to continue training. That time has come much sooner than anticipated. I cannot tell you yet where you'll be going, but we'll fill you in soon enough. For now, let's have Gregory escort you back to your room and we can discuss more tomorrow."

He dismisses us with the wave of his hand and starts poring over the papers that cover his desk. Gregory and I exit the room and walk down the same boring hallways toward my room. Maybe he can sense my uneasiness, or maybe he knows me better than I thought, but he puts his arm around my shoulder and pulls me in close. My body relaxes at the comfort he gives. "I know this doesn't seem fair, but just trust that we have good intentions and that everything will keep unfolding for you." He stops, letting his arm fall, and places a hand on my cheek. "You can trust me."

I smile at him. He has such an ease about him that always settles my nerves but makes my heart race. I may have met him a short time ago, but I do trust him.

We reach my door and say goodnight to each other. I walk into my room and sprawl out on my bed. I can still smell him on my clothes, and a smile lights up my face. Looking up at the ceiling, I try to imagine where we'll move for training, who might be coming with us, and how long I'll be there. As my thoughts wander, I begin to drift off to sleep.

SIXTEEN

A m I dreaming? I can feel something moving in the darkness of my room. I rub my eyes, but it does no good. Blackness encompasses everything. My heart quickens as I hear movement again. A whoosh of air and a hand is clamped over my mouth. My arms and legs thrash, trying to break free. But then a familiar voice whispers into my ear. My body seems to recognize it better than my mind because I immediately relax. "Becca, calm down. Don't worry. I'm going to move my hand and turn on the light, but you need to stay quiet."

With the flick of the light switch, I blink rapidly, glaring at the lights. As my eyes adjust I see Gregory kneeling before me at my bedside as he turns off a flashlight. I pull my covers up to my chin. It's not like I'm half-dressed, but I feel vulnerable nonetheless. "What on earth are you doing in my bedroom?"

His eyes shift from me to the door and back again. "Your bags are packed and ready to go."

My eyes go wide and I see them sitting by the door. "Excuse me?"

"I threw stuff in your bag. Don't worry about it. But the timetable has been moved up. We have to leave right now."

This has got to be a dream. They would never drag me out of here in the middle of the night. And he totally just handled my underwear. A look of horror must have come over my face, because he puts a hand on my knee. "Trust me. I need you to do that now. And don't worry, I didn't look at your stuff; I just grabbed it and threw it in the bag."

I look into his sincere eyes and for a fleeting moment it seems like he's looking into my soul. A calm washes over me and I search his eyes for any type of deceit. None. "I trust you."

There's no relief in his face, only the pressing need for us to get going. "Good, but we don't have a lot of time. We need to leave. Let's go."

I swing my legs out of bed, and grab my mom's A. A. coin off the nightstand. The clock reads three a.m. What's with the urgency in leaving so early? As I pull my shoes on, Gregory grabs my bags, throws them over his shoulder, and ushers me out the door and down the hallway.

We race down the hall toward the elevator. My hair flies in my face and I push back the tangles. Ugh, I bet my breath reeks right now. With everything going on, it's ridiculous how concerned I am about morning breath.

The elevator doors open and there stands Ania...with Tony and more suitcases. I look at Gregory. "What the...?"

Before I can even finish my sentence, Ania pulls me into the elevator. Tony gasps at my appearance, but then a slow smile spreads across his face. Gregory rolls his eyes at Tony. Well great, this'll make things more interesting.

She pulls me close and whispers into my ear. "I get how confusing things are right now, but we'll explain as soon as we can. I just need you to stay quiet and calm, and continue trusting us."

I nod at Ania, afraid to make even the slightest sound. Tony gives me a wink. He better not know more than me about what's going on.

We reach the basement level and walk swiftly into the parking garage. Gregory waves at the guard in the security shack and we head toward a row of black SUVs. Figures. Anytime you see anything regarding the government, they're always driving around in black SUVs.

Next to the SUVs, though, is a small silver sedan. Gregory pops the trunk and throws my bags in and the others as well. He looks over his shoulder with his charming smile. "Only the big wigs get to travel in style. We get to travel in a normal car. Draws less attention anyway."

Why do we need to draw less attention? Is someone going to follow us?

Ania gets into the passenger seat and I sit behind her next to Tony. Gregory turns the key and as he's about to put the car into reverse, there's a tap at the window. We all jump. "Sweet goodness," I rasp. Tony shoots me an amused glance.

Gregory slightly cracks the window. It's the guard from the security shack. My breath whooshes out of me. "Mr. Smith just called and told me to inform you not to stop; get as much distance in as you can." He backs away from the car and we drive out of the parking garage.

After a few minutes of silence, I can't take it anymore. "Can we talk yet? I'm dying back here. And if we can't talk, then please at least turn the radio on. But if we can talk, what the heck was that all about?"

Gregory looks up at me through the rearview mirror. He tries to smile, but it doesn't reach his eyes. "Just keep the conversation light."

Really, keep it light? I just got dragged out of my room in the middle of the night and some guard told us to get a move on. This whole situation is crazy. Tony has an evil smirk on his face and turns toward me. "Gregory says keep it light. I say we make it entertaining. So Becca, what do you look for in a man?"

Ania starts laughing and my mouth gapes like a fish. She looks back at Tony and says, "Goodness kid, Gregory said keep it light. Ever heard of subtle? Why don't you start with *what's your favorite color?*"

They both laugh, and it gives me time to regain my motor functions. "Well, Tony, I really like the color green, and I like my men to be athletic, charming, smart, and funny."

He looks shocked at receiving an actual response, but recovers quickly. "Well, how do three out of the four sound?"

He has such a smug look on his face. I laugh and shake my head. I wonder which three traits he thinks he has. Out of the corner of my eye, I catch Gregory's glance. "Gregory, you've been really quiet. What about you, what do you look for in a girl?"

I thought he was part of the merriment in the car, but apparently I'm wrong. "How about those who aren't driving get some sleep and let me focus on the road?" His voice is unyielding.

Well, someone is a little pissy. He glances up at the rearview mirror again and his eyes are flat. He's not smiling. Everyone seems to withdraw to their own little corner of the car. I lean my head against the window and drift off to sleep.

"Becca, just remember to keep your secrets and trust no one." I know I'm in a dream just now. The voice is so familiar to me and though I can't place it, it makes me feel so comfortable. I'm sitting on the tree swing in my grandparents' backyard, feeling the warmth of the sun on my skin and the cool breeze dancing through my hair. It's summer, not the cold biting frost of winter that's coming. Bliss is the best word to describe this moment.

Thunder pounds in the distance, and with that, my bliss turns to terror. Shadows grow and creep outward from the tree line. They take the forms of men and beasts, but I can't make them out completely. I keep twisting in the tree swing to see if someone's coming. Beads of sweat dot my brow and my heart pounds like a bass drum. The wind becomes more violent. It lashes at me and makes the shadows dance in the blackness. Snap! I spin around at the sound of a branch breaking and a man is standing there, cloaked in darkness. My skin erupts in goose bumps. I can't see his face. My throat begins to tighten, my wind pipe crushed. All the oxygen is being sucked out of my body. "A raging storm is coming. Question Gregory."

They said Gregory's name. I can't breathe. I try drawing in air, but it won't come. My knees give out. I slump to the ground and the man stands over me now. I can't make out his face. I need to see his face. Lightning strikes; everything blurs. I can feel myself fading, fading into the darkness that completely encloses me. The shadows of the beasts and men flank me until everything is black.

In the darkness I can hear a whisper of sound. I move toward it like the lifeline it is. "Becca! Becca, breathe!" Tony screams.

Gasp! I draw in huge gulps of air. The car. Just the car. Everyone's gaze flits from one to another. I fidget in my seat, unsure why they keep looking at me like I'm a mental patient. Tony slowly reaches across the seat and lays his hand on my arm. He touches me like I'm a scared animal. Maybe I am. I draw up as much bravado as I can muster. "Sorry guys, it was just a bad dream."

I turn and look out the window, trying to make it seem like it isn't a big deal. I can still feel their eyes fixed on me. The silence in the car is deafening. Looking out the window, I realize that we've pulled over. It's late morning—I can't believe that I slept that long. Did I sleep through a pit stop? I must have.

I keep my eyes focused on the window, not wanting them to see my tears and the humiliation on my face. "So, where are we now?" I have to push the words past my tears.

No one responds to my question. We must have gone south; there would have been snow if we had gone north. The trees are pretty much still green, but there are signs of the season changing here as well. Finally, Ania breaks the stifling silence. "We're just about there. We pulled over because it sounded like you were choking."

I can't shake the horrible feeling that the dream left me with. I wipe my face on my sleeve and then turn, catching Gregory's eyes. He looks so unsure. "I'm fine. We can keep going."

He turns back around and puts the car into gear. About two miles from where we stopped, we turn off the main road and onto a dirt one. We drive for about thirty minutes deeper into the forest. Nothing but tall pine trees, rocks, shrubbery, and dirt flanks the car. Finally, the car stops, and directly in front of us is a dilapidated cabin.

The wood looks old and weathered, the paint on the shutters is flaking off, and there's a huge hole in the screen door. Gregory shuts the car off and turns toward us. "Welcome to your new home."

Tony laughs without humor. "What, no Hilton or Ritz?"

Ania shoots a disapproving glance at him. As we move up the front steps of the cabin, I step gingerly, feeling that at any moment the wood is going to crumble. It reminds me of one of those cabins in horror movies. When was the last time someone was here? Walking toward the front door, I feel chills race down my spine and I look into the woods at the shadows forming. This is ridiculous. It was just a dream. I drop my bags on the porch and turn to find Ania. "How long are we going to be here for?"

"I have no idea. That'll be decided by Mr. Smith. I do know that we have a lot of training to do, and I haven't forgotten that I promised you some explanations."

That isn't exactly the answer I'm looking for, but what else is new? Gregory comes up from behind us and unlocks the door. Peering into the darkness, I barely make out the staircase to the right and a furnished living room to the left. Once Gregory finds a light switch, I'm pleasantly surprised.

Even though the outside looks like it's about to fall apart, the inside is clean and crisp. It has new furniture, freshly painted walls, and brand new appliances. Gregory places his hand on Tony's shoulder. "Well, it's not the Hilton, but I'm sure you'll like it just fine. Let's all get settled and meet back down here in a few minutes to talk about what our time here will be like."

"Think the rooms are nice?" Tony asks.

I look around the cabin again. "Maybe?"

He rubs his hands together. "Only one way to find out" he says, as he takes a step toward the stairs.

"No way, I call first dibs!" I race Tony up the stairs, and hear Ania and Gregory laughing from behind me.

My room is plain, nothing special, just your basic bed, dresser, and side tables. The view from the window is beautiful, however.

There's a small window seat that beckons me to come and sit for a minute. I look out at the trees. It's still a sea of green, and the sun setting behind them gives a golden hue to their tops. I struggle with leaving the seat, but I know that I have to go downstairs. After all, we're here for a reason.

We all sit down in the living room; an anxious feeling hangs in the air. Tony sits on the couch next to me, absently biting his finger-nails. Hopefully we'll get some answers now. Finally, Gregory sits down next to Ania. "I'm not going to beat around the bush with you guys. Why don't we just delve right into the facts of why we're here?"

Tony and I look at Gregory and nod our heads in agreement. The sooner we get down to business, the better I'll feel. He continues, "Some of what we're going to tell you is not going to be fair to you, Tony. Becca will get to learn about you and your abilities, but we can't tell you too much about her right now."

Tony's eyes flash in anger, but before he can open his mouth, Gregory keeps going. "I get that you're mad, but everyone's safety is at stake. Our main objective for being here is to train both of you for a covert mission. It'll be a retrieval, but even I don't know what we need to get. In order for this mission to happen and be completed successfully, secrecy is of the utmost importance. We had to leave in a hurry because Becca was being watched before she got to Project Lightning. No one can know what's going on if we're all to stay safe. You don't have to like it, but you do have to comply. Now Tony, do you want to explain your abilities or shall I?"

Tony gives Gregory a long, cold stare. It's not fair, but they have their reasons. What I don't understand is why they aren't telling him about the missing agents. "Even though I think this is a bunch of bull to be kept in the dark, I have no problem telling Becca what I can do. The short story is I have amazing vision."

Gregory huffs his annoyance at his response, and truthfully, I'm at a loss. That could mean a hundred different things. "What, do you have X-ray vision?"

Tony and Ania laugh. Tony leans back and puts his arm on the couch behind me. "No, if I had X-ray vision I would get nothing done because I'd be constantly distracted by women like you."

I can feel my cheeks getting redder by the second and I reflectively fold my arms in front of my chest. Gregory starts fidgeting in his chair, looking uncomfortable as well. He shoots an annoyed look over at Tony. "Why don't you elaborate for her and cut out the creepy crap."

Tony's smile falls. Pretty sure he just realized what he said. "I can see for miles. Not only can I see far distances, I can make out the smallest details miles away. I also can see every hair that is out of place on your head right now. Every flaw, imperfection, every small detail and *every* beauty mark is picked up by my eyes. It's sort of like using a zoom lens on a camera. I can turn it on and off. I've also been working on reading lips."

I subconsciously flatten my hair with my palm. "That's, well, kind of crazy, but cool. I have a question, though. If Tony and I are to train together, how is he not going to learn about what I can do?"

Gregory rubs his forehead. "You won't be exactly training side by side at first. As we get closer to the mission, things will change, but right now we need you to work on yourselves. You'll exercise together, but that'll be the extent."

"Well, when do we start training?"

"Tomorrow," Ania pipes in.

SEVENTEEN

Ania waits for me on the front porch with her running shoes on. "There's a path that leads through the woods and into a clearing about a mile from here. I thought we could jog out there."

I've always enjoyed running. When I would run in the woods for cross country, it was a place for me to clear my head and focus my thoughts. It's more mental at times than physical, and if you can master that, you can run far. In the past, I mostly thought about winning the race, but now as I examine my surroundings, I find myself thinking about our current situation. About Tony.

He's super charismatic, funny, observant, and charmingly arrogant. There's a likable, trusting quality about him. I don't like hiding my power from him, but wouldn't he be able to see us training? "Ania, if Tony has this amazing eyesight, can't he just look out the window and see what we're doing?"

"Luckily, Gregory and I have concocted a schedule that will keep Tony working in the basement while you're outside and vice versa. He won't be able to see what's going on."

"Why can't he know? And why aren't you telling him about the missing agents?"

"You're rare, and your power being different from your mother would scare most of us. We need to make sure that no one really knows that. When we're completely sure that we can trust Tony, he'll know about you. Don't forget that we still need to figure out exactly how your powers work.

"And as far as the missing agents, that's up to Mr. Smith. I'd tell him, but I'm under orders not to."

I don't like being left out of the loop. Ania and Gregory keep talking about this mission and the importance of its success, but I'm tired of being confused. I wish they would tell us already if we're going to rob a bank, steal plans for a nuclear bomb, or break into a building. Does it have to do with saving people? What is it?

The woods stretch out ahead of us. We follow a trail from the animals that lurk out here. The woods don't scare me now like they did yesterday, but they're still foreign. We wind through the trees, enjoying the crisp air. The only sounds, aside from us, are birds, the wind rustling the leaves, and the stillness it all brings. We've got to be miles from any other house or town.

After we reach the clearing, we stretch our legs and arms. My muscles protest from the constant worrying, not to mention the constant nightmares. Ania claps her hands together, bringing me out of the haze in my mind.

"Today's going to be a little different. I know you've been told that I'm like a killing machine, but there's something else I've found that I think will benefit you too. Now don't laugh, but we're going to do some yoga and some trust exercises.

"I think that when you 'flicker' or end up in another place, it's your emotions determining the effectiveness of that. You need to learn how to control your emotions and use them to your advantage."

I laugh. I was ready to come back to the cabin bruised and maybe a little bloody. "I never thought we would be doing yoga together."

She smiles and in a dramatic voice says, "You're going to feel mother earth flow through your legs and calm your soul."

I raise my eyebrow at her comment. "Really? Are we going to start chanting and dancing around a fire naked?"

We both laugh as we bend and stretch into different poses. My body needs this most of all. Apparently, nothing stretches you out like yoga.

After twenty minutes of contorting my body in ways I didn't think possible, we end up sitting across from each other on the ground. "Can I ask you something?" I ask.

She gives me a sincere smile. "Yeah. I'll do my best to answer."

I run my fingers through the weeds and grass surrounding us, not meeting her eyes. "Do you ever think about having a family?"

For a minute, she doesn't speak. And when I finally raise my eyes, she's looking into the trees, seeing something unseen. I must have touched on a nerve, but she doesn't wear a ring and she's old enough to be married. "I actually have a daughter. I never get to see her, of course— part of the job, unfortunately. A couple years after my mom died and my dad and I were living in America, I rebelled, *a lot*. I ran around with tons of boys, did things I was too young to do, and got pregnant. She lives with my dad. I never planned on having a family, even though Mr. Smith encourages it, but things changed."

She has a daughter? Whoa, didn't see that coming. "Why didn't you want a family? And how old *are* you?"

Her gaze stays fixed out in the woods. "Thirty." She says it almost absently. "Watching your mom be executed for treason changes you. I'm skilled in fighting and when I die, my daughter will be as well. It's not a glorious life. It's a dangerous one. I didn't want to pass that on."

I haven't given that much thought. I tend to agree with her, though. Do I really want my children to experience what I am experiencing? Maybe if my mother had prepared me more, this transition would have been smoother. Ania's powers are different from mine and a lot more dangerous.

"Did you know that I knew your mother?" she asks.

My face snaps toward hers. She knew my mom? I'm not surprised, though; it seems everyone knew her besides me. "No."

"Your mom was a friend and a mentor to me right when I got to the states. After my mom died and we found out I was pregnant, I was so angry, such a hateful young girl. She came to me and helped pull me from that. She was so funny, had such a contagious smile."

A soft look takes over her face. "She was devoted to me, and I'm so grateful to have had her. I hope I can have the same influence on you as she had on me. As angry as you have been with her all these years, she did love you and your dad fiercely. The day she found out that she was pregnant, her excitement poured out of her in waves. She told everyone she saw. I truly believe that she left you with your grandparents because she thought that was best for you."

Doesn't matter what she thought was best; you can't replace a mother or a father. How could she have been so devoted to one of her trainees, but not to her own flesh and blood? Drugs or not, she should have fought for a role in my life. But now with finding out she was sober for a year and carried a picture me around, things aren't adding up.

"Have you talked to her since she left?" I ask, because maybe she knows more.

Her gaze moves to the trees. "It's been a while. I talked with her a lot after your dad died, but that tapered off real quick."

Maybe she left me because she couldn't bear to look at me and be reminded of my dad. "Did you know my dad?"

"I knew him because of the FBI, but not as well as Linda."

"Something's been bugging me ever since I found out about where my parents met. What was my father doing at Project Lightning?"

She turns her head away, hiding her face. "I think the only one who could answer that question is Mr. Smith. I know your dad helped in coordinating missions, but I don't know how he got there or why."

She stands up and reaches out a hand to help me. I grab it and look into her eyes. I hope she's being truthful. But I've carried this anger and resentment for my mom all these years. She abandoned me and never bothered to help me know her or my father. I needed her to talk to me about boys, makeup and other things. Yes, I had my grandmother, but it wasn't the same. "Do you think you're doing the right thing for your daughter?" I ask her with some hesitancy.

She inhales sharply. Her eyes fixate on our shoes and her hands clench into fists. She takes a deep breath and relaxes her hands. "I don't know, but I'm trying to do the best for her I can. Let's head back to the cabin," she says, ending the conversation.

I don't know Ania well, but I definitely hit a nerve. And now I need a topic change. "So, uh, Tony's kind of cute, don't you think?"

What just came out of my mouth?

She lets out a small chuckle. "I guess he's not bad looking. A little too young for me though, and very arrogant. Besides, I thought you had a thing for Gregory?"

I blush. "I won't lie. I like him a lot— well, what I know of him. I haven't forgotten what you said about mixing work and pleasure, but I can't help being attracted to him."

"Just keep your guard up. I don't want to lecture you, but it's frowned upon to try to have relationships with one another. It's one thing to have a little fun, but it's another to fall head over heels for someone."

Does she know how attracted I am to him? Do *I* know how I feel about him? Does he? He probably dismisses it as a schoolgirl's crush, but there's something fascinating about him. I wonder what sort of training I'll be doing with him. I was surprised that Ania and I did yoga. I really thought that she'd be teaching me how to kill someone with my pinky. I may not be a killing machine like she is, but I am definitely far from being a delicate little flower.

As we leave the clearing for the cabin, my thoughts drift. I wonder what my grandpa Joe is doing. Has he been thinking about me or worrying about me? I haven't even been able to talk to him since I began this "internship." I shudder at the reminder of last night, when I woke up in the middle of another terrifying nightmare.

When I awoke, I closed my eyes, desperately wishing to be home.

When I opened my eyes again, I was back in my room at home, but it felt like a dream. I swore it was a dream. All of my trophies and awards, pictures with my grandparents, and stuffed animals were all around me. I dragged my fingers across the top of my dresser and walked toward the door. The house was dark and quiet, but I could hear the faint sound of the television below. I descended the stairs, feeling the soft pine railing under my palm as I went. As I walked to the living room, I saw him, Grandpa Joe, asleep in his recliner. I turned off the television and grabbed the afghan from the couch and draped it over him. Just as I was about to go back to bed, I felt his hand on mine. "Becca?"

That's when I realized that I wasn't dreaming. I was somewhere I wasn't supposed to be. Before I knew it, I was back in my bed at the cabin.

The shrill sound of a bird whistle brings me back to the forest with Ania. When we're a few yards from the front porch, voices drift through an open window.

We walk into the cabin and Gregory and Tony are sitting in the living room. They look like they're having a polite conversation, but you could cut the tension with a knife. The sight of Ania and me causes both of them to rise to their feet. "Good, I'm glad you two are back. Becca, I'm going to work with you down in the basement, and Ania, I was hoping you would work with Tony on hand-to-hand combat?" Gregory asks.

There's no complaint from her lips. It's not like she did anything with me but a warm up. She grabs a water bottle, and soon she and Tony are out the door.

Gregory ushers me down the steps into the basement. I haven't actually gone down here yet, and I was expecting it to be a dark, dank place, but I can see I was wrong. It's been finished with new furniture just like the rest of the house. The walls are painted a light yellow and the carpets are a cream color. It doesn't feel like a basement. He sits on a couch and I opt for a lounge chair across from him.

"Did you enjoy yoga with Ania?" he asks, laughter in his voice.

"I'm pretty sure my muscles aren't going to work tomorrow," I tell him.

He laughs. "It'll get better. The first time she had me do it, I totally split my shorts trying to do some of those moves."

I start laughing, and a snort slips out. And for a beat it's complete silence until he can't hold it in anymore. He bends over in his chair, loud laughs tumbling out of his mouth. "You just..." He can't even get the words out.

But I laugh right along with him. "I know! It's mortifying," I say.

He takes a deep breath, trying to rein in his laughter. "Nah, it's cute," he says.

I lean over and smack him on the arm. "Liar," I tell him.

"Not lying," he says, and I know I'm blushing now.

We both sit back in our seats. "All right, so today, I want you to try transporting to another room here in the house, like your bedroom, and then back down here. Sound good?"

"Sure," I say, and then take a deep breath. I got this. At least the pant-splitting and the snorting took away any anxiety.

But that soon comes rushing back, because my first few attempts are frustrating. I think about my bedroom and squeeze my eyes tight. When I open them back up, I see Gregory looking at me with a sad expression. This should be amazing because I could go anywhere I want, but it's turning out to be frustrating. After the sixth time of unsuccessful transporting, I'm close to picking up a lamp and chucking it. I pace back and forth, trying to ignore Gregory.

"Becca, you need to relax."

I shoot him a frustrated look. Like I don't know that. I'd like to see him try and do this. And I want this, even if it seems like I don't. I'm more frustrated with myself then anything else.

We work, I swear for hours, on manipulating emotions. I finally flicker in the chair, but that's about it. Apparently he can sense my frustration and tries another approach. He stands behind my chair and rests his hands on my shoulders, instructing me how to breathe and relax. It's hard at first to relax with his hands on me. He rubs my shoulders, his thumbs circling at the base of my neck, and I can slowly feel my body submit. I try to focus on my room in the cabin.

I close my eyes and picture it perfectly in my mind. I visualize the curve of my head board, the pattern of the fabric on the window seat, and the way my dresser appears to be so empty. I focus on the window seat. I enjoyed that so much yesterday.

I open my eyes and I'm sitting on my bed. Success. And seriously, how amazing is this? A wave of exhaustion and confidence washes over me, sending me all the way back to the basement. I jump up and throw my arms around Gregory. He freezes for a moment, but he doesn't push me away and lets me hug him as long I want. "You did it," he whispers into my ear, and I swear he tightens his arms just a little bit more.

EIGHTEEN

Three long, frustrating weeks have gone by, full of constant training at the cabin. Frustrating because I'm not any better at my powers. And some days being stuck here has turned this cabin into my own personal hell. And some days Gregory is my savior, but today he's my own personal warden.

He runs his hands through his hair, probably for the tenth time in the last thirty minutes of being in the basement. He closes his eyes and his mouth instantly grimaces. "This isn't working," I tell him, again.

He drops his hands and lays them flat on the coffee table in front of us. "No. We'll figure this out."

Well, at least he's sure, because I'm not. Last week I ended up transporting myself into the bathroom. Which would have been fine, but one of my feet ended up in the toilet. It was lovely. I burned those socks.

"Okay. Let's take a deep breath." Already tried that. "And imagine the kitchen." Doable.

"Kitchen. Got it," I say.

"Becca," he says, completely exasperated.

I raise my hands in surrender. "Fine, fine."

I chant the word *kitchen* in my mind.

"What the hell?" Tony shouts.

I open my eyes. Huh, pantry.

Tony stands in the open doorway, rubbing at his chest. "Did I scare you?" I ask.

He stares at me for a moment. "Uh, yeah. What are you hiding from?"

Internally, I'm thanking whoever is listening, because he didn't see me magically appear in front of his eyes. "Just felt like hanging out with the cereal," I say, patting a box of Cheerios.

He crosses his arms, totally not believing a word coming from my mouth. I let out a big huff. "Fine. Just wanted a little alone time." I kind of feel bad for lying, but what else am I going to say?

"Want some?" I ask, holding up the box of cereal.

He shakes his head and laughs at me.

"Becca?" I hear Gregory calling for me.

"In here!" I yell.

His face appears over Tony's shoulder. "Close," he says, but more to himself than either of us.

"Well, I'm going to head to the grocery store. Need anything?" Gregory asks. Guess training is done for the day. I look outside at the dark sky. I guess it is kind of late anyways.

"Can I come with?" I ask.

Any time I ask about getting away from here, I'm always told that it would be unsafe, but of course it's okay for Gregory to go to the grocery store. I'm an only child, and it's sad to admit, but I'm used to getting my way.

"You know you can't," he tells me.

Whatever. This is lame.

"Fine," I say.

He stares at me for a moment longer. Probably because when a woman says *fine*, she is anything but. He turns and walks away.

"Yeah. I'm fine. Don't need anything. Thanks for asking," Tony yells at Gregory.

The front door slams. Tony turns back to me and rolls his eyes. He opens his mouth, probably to complain about Gregory, but I throw up a hand to stop him. There's something more important on my mind.

It's time to break out of this prison. The only one probably willing to do this with me might be Tony. If his constant comments about cabin fever are any indication, he's been itching to leave too. And I get that some of the hundred are being kidnapped, and that should make me want to be cautious. But no one knows we're here.

"Is Ania down here?" I whisper.

He shakes his head no, and I motion for him to join me in the pantry. He walks inside, but still looks wary.

"I need to get out of here. We've been trapped like rats for weeks and I am going crazy. Gregory and Ania might be accustomed to this type of hermit lifestyle, but we aren't. What could be the harm?" *Wow, I'm probably going to jinx this whole thing...nah.*

"Do you want to come with me?" I ask him.

His eyes widen, but then he leans against the wall and his lips quirk. I've got his interest. "Where do you plan on going? We're in the middle of nowhere. How do you even plan on getting there?"

"Wait here," I say.

I race up the stairs to my room. I grab the bag on the window seat and race back down to him.

I pull out a map of the area. His eyebrows shoot to his hairline. "Yeah, I know. I found it inside the window seat in my room."

We're only about five miles from a town. I pull out the keys to a dirt bike I found in the shed out back. I've definitely been planning for days. "There's a bar, and granted, I'm not old enough to drink or anything, but maybe they have pool, music, a soda. I'll take anything right now."

He rubs his jaw for a moment. "All right, I'll go, but you do realize that we're probably going to get caught?"

I jump up and hug him, almost knocking him to the ground.

"Where did you get those keys from?"

"Out in the shed. There's a dirt bike there for emergencies. I figure we can push it until we're far enough away so it won't be too loud. I don't care if we get caught. I'm tired of being trapped here. I had more freedom at my prep school. We better hurry up and go before we can't."

We slip out the front door and head out back. I take the keys from my pocket and unlock the shed. We grab the bike and start pushing it down the dirt road we originally came in on. After about fifteen minutes, I stop, panting, and turn toward him. "I think you should drive since you've got the super eyes," I say, still whispering.

He puffs his chest out. "Hop on and hold on tight."

We speed down the road, making my legs and arms grip him tighter. The wind whips fiercely at my face and hair. We really should have considered helmets, but it's too late for that now. Luckily he can see where we're going, because I'm completely blind. Ahead of us is darkness and behind is a faint sight of the cabin. I rest my face on his back to block the wind.

We hit pavement, and street lights illuminate our path. It's only about another twenty minutes before we pull into the parking lot of the bar.

The bar is totally run down. It reminds me of the cabin, old and wooden, but the sound coming from inside tells me that it's a full house. I really could care less at this point what it looks like; it's civilization. Tony hops off and frowns at the sight of it. "Are you sure you want to go in there?" he asks.

I throw a teasing smile over my shoulder as I saunter in. "Yes. Stop being a pansy and let's go."

When we open the door, I'm pretty sure everyone in the bar stares at us. I'll just pretend not to notice. To my surprise, there are pool tables and even a jukebox in the corner playing tunes. I love this song. "What do you want to do first? Because I want to dance." I point to the crowded dance floor.

Tony just stares at me like I've asked him to punch some guy in the face. I know I totally don't look like someone who would want to dance. "Are you serious?" he asks.

"Yes! I guess I can dance by myself, but come on, this is a great song."

He reluctantly gives in, but I suspect it's only because we're not the only ones. As the music flows, I'm surprised that he actually dances. I laugh, not at him, but from the pure enjoyment of feeling normal for once. He laughs along with me.

Before we know it, a couple of guys get uncomfortably close to me. Tony notices and leads me away. I mouth the words *thank you* and he smiles. We don't need any problems tonight. This is the first time we've really let loose around one another. Everything back at the cabin revolves around training and secrecy.

After a couple more songs, he excuses himself to go to the restroom and I take the chance to grab a Coke from the bar. When I sit down on a stool, the vacant one next to me is immediately filled by a man in his late twenties. He's got a scruffy face, a little ragged in the clothes department, but otherwise cute. "Can I buy you a drink?" he asks.

"Oh, I was just getting a Coke."

"Well then, let me get you one." He winks. I didn't think people still winked.

He walks to the end of the bar where the bartender is and orders.

"You're not from around here, are you?" he asks when he gets back with our drinks.

Really, he's using one of the corniest pick-up lines ever, but maybe he's nervous. I can let it slide. "No, just passing through."

I take a sip of my drink and it's extremely sweet. "In college?" he asks.

"No, uh, just taking a break from school." It's not really a lie, but what am I going to tell him, that I work for a covert government agency and I have powers? That wouldn't go over well, plus it's a little fun to pretend to be someone else.

The guy—apparently his name is Zack and he's a local—is chatty. Several minutes go by of him talking about his job, his truck, his dog. Every. Freaking. Thing. I know more about this guy than my best friend from elementary school.

I turn from him for a moment, searching for Tony. He's playing pool, not bothering to watch me. His gaze is planted firmly on the beautiful blonde playing at his table. For some reason I'm not surprised.

I'm finishing my Coke and still talking with the stranger, but I'm starting to feel weird. Like fuzzy and light. "Is there something wrong with this soda?" I ask.

Zack smiles and a troubled feeling goes through me. I don't like his smile; there's something wrong with it. "It's just a Coke, sweetheart," he says with a thick drawl.

I blink my eyes to get them to focus, but it just causes me to stumble off the stool. The room starts to spin and things seem to be teetering like a seesaw. He puts my arms around him and I can't quite make out what he's saying, but we're heading for the door. "No," I try to say, but actually slur the word.

He laughs at someone and says, "She just had too much. I'm going get my girl home."

His girl? What?

We reach the parking lot and I'm panicking, but the spinning won't stop. "I've got to get back inside to my friend Tony," I manage to say.

His grip around my waist tightens. He leans in and sneers at me. "No, you don't. I'm going to take care of you."

Awful thoughts begin running through my mind. I need to get away. I want to run, but my legs won't work. Did he put something in my drink? I try pushing myself off of him, but he has a tight grip on me. Now would be an awesome time for me to transport. But whatever is affecting my body isn't even allowing me to flicker.

He pushes me up against a truck and a sharp pain rushes up my back. His face hovers right above mine and I can smell the rankness coming off of him. He forces his lips to mine, and I manage to shove him in the shoulders. He slaps me hard across the face, making me fall to the ground. He bends down and grabs me by my arm, forcing me up against the truck. Just as he opens the door and tries to get me inside, Tony *finally* comes running out. Zack shoves me hard into the driver's seat. "Hey, where do you think you're going with her?" Tony shouts.

"Sorry, man, she's coming home with me," Zack answers.

"I don't think so. She's seventeen. I came with her and I'm leaving with her." Tony gets right up in his face.

Suddenly I hear a car horn honking close by. I crawl over to the passenger side and manage to get the other door open and fall out onto the pavement. From the ground, I see Gregory coming over to me. He scoops me up and carries me to the car. Before he puts me in the back seat, I see Ania getting in between Tony and Zack. When Zack goes to throw a punch at Tony, she blocks it and knocks him on the back of the head. He slumps to the ground, unconscious. She picks him up and tosses him into the truck like he's nothing more than a sack of groceries. Then she takes his keys and chucks them far into the woods. Gregory lays me in the back seat, climbing in beside me as Ania gets in behind the wheel. "What were you thinking?" Ania screeches.

"I just wanted a soda and maybe dance. Where's Tony?" I mumble.

"He's driving the dirt bike. But honestly, what was going through that head of yours?" Huh, she sounds mad.

"I wanted to...why is there water coming out of my face?" I swipe at my cheeks.

"You're crying," Gregory tells me.

"But why?"

"Probably because you're drunk. And I think he slipped you something."

Oooooh, he's pissed.

"Of course I am," Gregory says. Guess I said that out loud.

"Hey, can you tell whoever is whining to shut up?" I ask. It's freaking annoying.

A bark of laughter slips out of Gregory's mouth.

"I'll try," he tells me.

"Good, because they're being super dramatic."

"Maybe she just wanted to dance too," he says.

"Ania?" I ask.

"No, not Ania. Just close your eyes. You're going to be feeling really bad in a couple of hours. But I need you to sleep. You're flickering." The last part is barely a whisper.

Before I pass out, all I'm able to get out is a mumbled laugh as I say "Flicker." Such a fun word.

THE TILE of the bathroom floor is freezing, but it feels great against my skin and head. If only the room would stop spinning and my stomach would decide it's already emptied itself. Four times seems plenty enough to me.

There's a knock at the door and Gregory lets himself in. He grabs a washcloth and towel from the linen closet and then soaks the washcloth in the sink. He places the towel on the ground. "Here, lay your head down on the towel."

I do as he says, then watch as he wrings out the excess water from the washcloth and sits beside me on the floor. He brushes the hair back from my forehead and lays the cold, damp cloth on my head. "Still happy that you got to dance?" he asks.

I do my best to smile, but it quickly turns into a grimace. Facial movement is making this headache worse. "That part was at least fun," I reply.

He frowns at my answer. "Tonight could have ended differently. It could have been a lot worse, and I'm sure you know that. But why sneak out?" His disappointment is like a living thing, filling the space between us.

I lie there, completely ashamed. I didn't think it would be that big of a deal, but I was wrong. "I'm not usually the rebellious type." My stomach lurches and I close my mouth.

False alarm.

"I had a lot of freedom by my grandparents. It's just that I was going crazy here. I needed to get out."

He flips the cloth over so the cooler side is now on my forehead. "Do you trust me?"

I manage to sit up and stare at him straight in the eyes. Do I trust him? Why wouldn't I trust him? He's never given me any reason not to, except I still don't know what his power is. I wish I knew how he felt about me. Sometimes he seems to care for me, more than just being my mentor, but other times he pulls back.

His gaze seems more intense. "What would have happened if you'd revealed yourself at the bar tonight? What if your emotions had gotten the best of you and you began to flicker?"

I hadn't really given it that much thought.

"Sometimes the decisions we have to make aren't always what we want, but it's important to look at the bigger picture. It's like chess; you need to look a couple of moves ahead before you make that first move."

I laugh at the chess reference. My laugh is quickly stopped as my stomach begins to gurgle. His facial expression seems to relax a little bit. "Okay, I know the chess reference is a little nerdy, but it makes my point."

It did make his point clear, and just because I'm seventeen doesn't mean I'm dumb. "I trust you, Gregory, but you're already hiding things from me. That makes it hard to completely trust you."

His eyes look toward the floor. "I am hiding things from you, but only because I have to right now."

His honesty is refreshing, but at the same time I feel so unsure. He gets up and walks over to the medicine cabinet. He pulls out a bottle of aspirin and a bottle of Tums. "Here, you're going to need these," he says and tosses me the bottles.

"I'm sorry for disappointing you," I say with my eyes downcast.

He stops at the door before leaving, but doesn't turn back to face me. "I was disappointed in the situation, but not you. Never you." My heart beats wildly at his words.

I smile at the door, even after he's closed it. I lie back down on the cold floor with the towel as my pillow and drift off to sleep.

NINETEEN

Waking up on a bathroom floor sucks. As I try and pull myself together, I catch a glimpse of myself in the mirror. Not only do I have the octagonal imprint of tile on my face, but my hair looks like a rat's nest, and my eyeliner has smudged, giving me that lovely raccoon look. I wonder if I looked this awful last night when Gregory came in. I can only guess that I smell just as pleasant.

After a long, hot shower, I make my way downstairs to the kitchen. I need something to keep this queasy feeling in my stomach at bay. I stumble down the stairs and grab on to the railing for support. Tony peeks his head around the corner from the kitchen. "Morning, sunshine!" he says, sounding way too chipper.

I try to smile, but all I can get out is a pained grimace. The kitchen table is filled with pancakes, bacon, and some fresh fruit. "What's with the spread?" I ask.

Tony goes back over to the stove to finish cooking some eggs. "Thought you might want some pancakes to help sop up whatever is still left in your stomach."

"Oh...well, thank you." He shoots me a corny smile in response. "Hey, Tony, I'm sorry about last night." My voice catches, but only slightly. "Never in a million years did I think anything would happen. I'm sorry if I put you in a rough spot."

His whole body changes and that carefree expression is gone as his eyes roam my face. "Don't worry about it." His eyes study me.

"You're safe. You're safe." He says it twice like he needs to remind himself as well as me.

He shakes himself, and his body goes back to his usual relaxed posture. "I got to watch Ania knock some guy out, and at least you got to have some fun. Not to mention, you got to experience my awesome dance moves."

I give him a small smile. We did have fun before that creep Zack crashed our party. The memory of his cracked lips sends a wave of deep revulsion through me. I let out a slow, steady breath. Nothing else happened. I'm okay. Maybe if I tell myself that ten more times, I'll believe it.

We shouldn't have been there in the first place. "Yeah, but it was a bad move on my part to have you sneak out with me."

He gives a little shrug. "You gotta live a little. Life would be boring if we didn't."

Gregory comes around the corner, stopping next to me. "And that's why you're not going to be a mentor for a long time. Good morning to both of you."

Gregory's entrance catches both of us by surprise, but Tony's eyes flash in annoyance. "I don't want to be a mentor, because then I'd have to become boring, lame, and basically worthless."

The tension in the room skyrockets along with their over-inflated egos. This could get out of hand real quick. "Now, boys, play nice," I say, trying to defuse the bomb.

Gregory keeps his eyes locked on Tony's for a moment longer, but then he nudges me. "Are you feeling any better?"

"Well, my stomach is a bit more settled, but I feel like an idiot."

Tony puts a plate in my hands and then pushes me toward the table. Ania joins us in the kitchen. "Well, how is our little damsel in distress doing this morning?" she asks.

I plop my head on top of the table. "I'm never going to live this down, am I?"

Everyone laughs.

Gregory's cell rings inside his pocket, and the smile on his face quickly disappears. He leaves the table and answers it. He nods his head to whatever is being said. "We'll be there by tonight," he says, then hangs up the phone.

We all stare at him, waiting for some type of explanation. He rubs his temples and then says, "Becca, finish your food and then go get a bag. Pack enough for a week. That was Mr. Smith. We need to return to headquarters immediately."

"Should I go pack a bag too?" Tony asks.

"No, just Becca and I will be going. You're going to stay here with Ania and work more on your combat skills."

Tony crosses his arms over his chest and glares at Gregory, but there's nothing he can really do about it. I stuff some food into my mouth and then head upstairs to grab my things. Why do I need to go? Could Mr. Smith know about last night? There's no way, though; it just happened, and I doubt anyone here told him.

I race down the stairs and Gregory's waiting for me at the door. Ania and Tony are still sitting at the kitchen table. "Hopefully we'll see you guys soon," Ania says. "Be good and don't get into any more trouble." I wave goodbye and walk out the door.

THE CAR RIDE back is a lot longer than I remember, probably because last time I slept for most of it. It also doesn't help that Gregory hasn't said a word since we left. He just keeps tapping the steering wheel. "So...can you tell me why we're going back to head-quarters suddenly?"

I can see him debating with himself before he finally answers. "Mr. Smith knows about last night and he's pissed."

"How is that even possible? It happened less than twenty-four hours ago. Did you call him?"

"No. He's been having the police scanner monitored. The bar owner called the cops after he realized you left with Zack. Apparently this isn't the first time he's walked out with a drunk girl. But it wasn't just the bar owner."

His hands briefly strangle the steering wheel. "Someone saw Ania lift the guy like he was a toy. He told the cops and they found him still unconscious in the bed of his truck. Mr. Smith knew all about this before we even woke up this morning."

Going back is all about me, then. Wonderful.

He glances at me quickly. "How are you feeling today?" he asks.

"Like crap."

He grips the steering wheel. "How are you...dealing with everything?" he asks.

Do I tell him that I'm not really? That that's a moment I'd rather have erased from my memory? That the idea of not being in control of my body, the one thing I should always be in control of, is terrifying? That even a hint of an idea of what he could have done to me makes me break out in cold sweat?

I settle with a simple truth. "I'll be fine." And I will, at some point.

And Mr. Smith definitely knows what happened, that I disregarded all of his warnings. "He's bringing me back to teach me a lesson, isn't he?" I ask.

He sighs deeply. "I would assume so, but let's just see how it goes. It's very important that you listen to him and do what he tells you to do."

He never speaks badly about Mr. Smith and is always firm in his devotion toward him. "What's with the unwavering loyalty to him?"

He shrugs his shoulders. "Mr. Smith has been my mentor for the past ten years. He was there for me right after my parents died. I wasn't even aware that I would have powers before then. He's someone I trust wholeheartedly."

"Nobody said anything?"

His body deflates a little. "My parents never told me that one day I would inherit powers. Unlike most of you guys, who had an idea, I didn't. They might have been waiting until I got a little older, but they never had the chance.

"When I first realized that something was different, I was scared. Imagine having your parents die and then having powers appear. I thought I was going crazy, that I was a freak. It scared my grandparents, too. Mr. Smith showed up at the funeral and from then on, every summer until I was done with school was spent with Mr. Smith."

"Are you ever going to tell me about your power?"

"Just like Tony doesn't know what you can do, you can't know what I can do."

I roll my eyes. This is so ridiculous. "Seriously, that's such a lame rule. You're supposed to be my mentor and we're supposed to be this team. But you get to keep all the important information to yourself?"

He breathes a heavy sigh. "Someday, Becca, you'll know what I can do, but it's better if you don't know right now."

He places a hand on my arm. "Soon," he says.

I don't really care whether or not it's safe for me. I'm just tired of being treated like a child. I realize that I am only seventeen, but I'm *seventeen*, not five. Harping on it, though, won't get my anywhere. And I don't want to waste this little slice of freedom before we reach headquarters.

The rest of the ride I pester him with questions about growing up on a farm, and what it was like being so young at MIT. And for a few hours we laugh and joke, trying our hardest to reach for that normalcy we can't get with how our lives are now. The fact that Gregory's laugh is infectious is just an added bonus.

The more time I spend with him, the more I like him. And that's only going to lead to heartache.

TWENTY

We're back to the sterile, hospital-like rooms, walls, and even people. We waste no time, walking to meet Mr. Smith in his office as soon as we exit the elevator. When we enter, he's seated at his desk. It's still cluttered with paper and folders, so I assume this is just the usual state of it. His face is hard and cold. It's going to be an unpleasant visit.

I walk toward one of the chairs and Gregory shuts the door. Before I even have a chance to sit, Mr. Smith stands. I swear time slows as his arm raises from his side. And in his hand, a gun, pointed right at me. "Transport yourself. Right. Now," he demands.

Time stops. The air in my lungs turns to lead. I need to run.

I stumble back into the chair, my eyes wide. He's gone insane. Totally freaking insane.

Gregory rushes forward, his hands raised in a helpless gesture. "This is a little drastic, don't you think?"

Drastic? This is freaking terrifying.

Without taking his eyes or the gun off of me, Mr. Smith snaps back at Gregory. "Stay out of this! Becca, I am ordering you to transport right now, or I will shoot you!"

Gregory doesn't move from my side. My fingers grip the chair and I stare at Mr. Smith, paralyzed with fear. "I...I'm trying," I plead.

"Not hard enough. You have until the count of five," Mr. Smith says as he pulls back the hammer on the gun and my whole body flinches at the noise.

I try. I try so hard to focus on another place: the cabin, my grandparents', even the room I used to sleep in here, but my heart is pounding and I feel as if there isn't enough air in the room. Why can't I do this? What's wrong with me?

"One."

I squeeze my eyes tight. *Please.*

"Two."

A sob rips out of me. *Come on.*

"Three." I grip the pocket of my jeans, and try to feel for the outline of the coin, but it's not there.

The tears start pouring out of my eyes like a rushing river. "Please, I'm trying...I swear I'm trying," I manage to get out between sobs.

"Four..." Mr. Smith says, no emotion in his voice.

My grip on the chair tightens and I pray to whoever is listening to help. *Just do it.* The clock ticks, its sound blaring in my eardrums. Drips of sweat slide down my temples.

"Five," Mr. Smith says in a soft, menacing voice that's so much worse than if he'd screamed at me.

I bolt from the chair when nothing happens. My heart thuds and the click of the trigger echoes through the room. I wait, but there's nothing. No pain. No loud noise. Silence.

Am I dead?

"Open your eyes, Becca."

I do, and he waves the gun in my face. "There are no bullets in the gun," Mr. Smith says coolly.

It takes a minute for his words to register. I storm around his desk and march up to him and get right up into his face. "What the hell is wrong with you?" I scream.

He barks a harsh laugh and crowds me with his body. "What is wrong with me? Nothing. You, on the other hand, could have been raped, killed, tortured, or discovered last night. You could have been *taken*. I think the question should be *what were you thinking?*"

I stare at him, dumbfounded.

"You put yourself and everyone else in jeopardy so you could have a night out. Do you know why I pointed a gun at you?"

I can't think of anything to say to him in return. Who the heck points a gun at someone in the first place? Some psychopath, that's who.

"I did it to prove a point. You still need a lot of training, not to mention that you're unpredictable, non-compliant, and unreliable. I put you in a life-or-death situation and you couldn't budge. What would have happened last night? What would you have done if he'd raped you in that truck?"

"Enough," I whisper, my voice hoarse, my stomach churning as he says the words out loud that have already gone through my mind. I stumble back to the chair.

He swipes a hand through the air. "Do you think that when you're out on a mission, the enemy is going to forewarn you that they're going to kill you? Don't you want to be able to get away if someone kidnaps you? I forget how naïve you are sometimes."

His condescending tone makes me want to punch him, preferably in the balls.

I've only been at this a short time, and he already expects the world from me.

Mr. Smith turns on Gregory. "And you! You're supposed to be working with her on this, and you're clearly doing an awful job. I don't care what it takes, but she needs to work through these emotions."

Gregory drops down into the chair next to me. "She's getting a lot better, but she's still new to this. We'll work harder."

"Good. And you're going to be working here for the next week. I want you to see, Becca, how much of a privilege it is to be working outside of here. You could have ruined everything for a night of dancing and pool, you thoughtless girl."

With those lovely words of encouragement, I get to my feet and storm out of his office. Gregory follows me out and once the door closes, I unload on him. "Is he psychotic? What am I saying? Of course he's psychotic. What sane person points a gun at someone to prove a point?" I ask as I slump down the wall.

Gregory joins me on the floor. "That was a little extreme, but do you understand why he did it?"

I can't believe he's siding with him on this. "Well yes, but come on, he pointed a gun at me and threatened to kill me."

"I would never have let that happen," he says, his voice conveying his promise.

My heart is still pounding in my chest and my limbs feel weak and wobbly. "I don't even know how I'm going to sleep tonight. My anxiety level is through the roof."

He pulls me to my feet. "Let's see if we can get some food into you and your mind off what just happened."

"Fat chance of that."

The dining hall is full of the other trainees. The presence of Gregory and me causes quite the commotion. What is normally a room full of talking and the clanking of utensils is now quiet and still. People start talking in hushed tones, sneaking quick glimpses of us. I feel like I'm back at school walking into the lunch room. I look around for Dex, but he's not here. It would have been nice to see a friendly face.

We grab some dinner and sit at a table by ourselves. "Apparently we're the talk of the dining room," I say.

Gregory looks around like he hasn't noticed yet. "Well, we did leave in the middle of the night unannounced. And all of a sudden we're back here, but Tony and Ania are nowhere to be seen. Plus, they haven't gotten to leave this place, so any news is big news."

I haven't even thought about that. I wonder what everyone thought when the four of us abruptly left. Has anyone told them what we're doing? "What am I allowed to tell anyone if they ask questions?"

"Just tell them that we've been training out in the field and came back for some further instructions from Mr. Smith. That's all they need to know."

Well, at least we won't be lying. As we eat, we're approached by a girl. It takes me a minute to place her name, but I remember that it's Sariah. She's the one who wanted Tony. So much for that now.

Her facial expression is stern and uninviting. Gregory and I both stare at her, waiting for her to speak. "So I see you've returned," she says in a matter-of-fact tone.

"Yes, we have." I say. Would it be rude to roll my eyes? Who cares, I do it anyways.

She immediately puts her hands on her hips and gives a disapproving sigh. I guess she expected a little bit more of an explanation. "Is Tony back with you?" she asks.

"Obviously not," I say pointing to the empty seats near us.

I don't know why, but I feel the need to challenge her. Maybe it's because she marched right over to us, or it could just possibly be that she's foul. Or maybe it's because I don't want to feel weak like I did back in that parking lot of the bar.

Apparently, my challenging her hasn't gone unnoticed by the other trainees. Some of them sit with their jaws hitting the floor while the others whisper to each other.

"So I guess time out of here has made you feel superior?" she asks, her voice dripping with arrogance.

"And I guess still being here has made you obnoxious?" I counter.

She does a mock laugh and tosses her head back. "You know, you might want some friends now that you're back. So I wouldn't try to go up against me."

I can't believe she just said that to me. Have I walked into *Mean Girls*? "I thought you'd already graduated high school. Maybe I was wrong."

She sneers at me and walks away to her little band of followers. "What was that?" Gregory asks.

I forgot he was even sitting next to me for a minute. I rub at my forehead. "I don't know. I'm not myself right now. I don't tolerate bullies, but I'm not usually this defensive. The thing with Mr. Smith has me all screwed up right now. I should probably apologize to her, but I think she'd just turn her nose up at it." This isn't me.

"Well, this should be a fun visit back," he says in a sarcastic tone.

I look at him and laugh. "I might only be training with you, because I doubt anyone is going to volunteer to be my partner now."

"I don't know, I think Sariah might want to be your sparring partner."

"Very funny. Maybe you should partner with her." I flick some mashed potatoes at him and leave him chuckling at the table.

TWENTY-ONE

So I guess I have the plague. Or I'm invisible. Either way, the other recruits ignore me as we assemble for group exercises the next morning after breakfast. Maybe Sariah has a point about me being superior. I do feel different coming back. It's like when you return to see your elementary school teachers—that feeling of being older, even a little wiser. I also doubt that Mr. Smith has pulled a gun on any of them. I wish Ania were here, because she always seems to know what to say.

We begin routines of cardio and weight training. Even though I've been constantly working out at the cabin, I see how much I've been missing by not having this equipment. I know I can outrun anyone in the room, but as far as brute strength goes, I'm sorely lacking. It appears that I'm not the only one who notices it, because I can feel her eyes on me the whole time.

Sariah watches me intently. It almost seems like she's keeping score of what areas I can beat her in and in what area she'll wipe the floor with me. We're the only two in the room who realize this, though, because she's surrounded by other trainees who seem to hang on her every word. There has to be something about her that I just don't see. She's pretty, but her physical build is small and skinny. Half of the other trainees could snap her like a twig over their knees. She seems to be silently in charge, though, because when she moves, the rest of them move.

Man, I'm super judgy right now, but she just rubs me the wrong way. I usually just ignore people like this, but apparently she's the exception to this rule.

Gregory walks up behind me. "I see you're being sized up," he tilts his head toward Sariah.

"Yeah, but she and I both know what's really going on. It's strange, really, how she's already placed herself as queen bee."

He looks her over. "I don't think it's that strange. Put all of these trainees in the same area for a while and cliques, leaders, and followers are bound to emerge."

"I guess, but everyone here has powers. Everyone should be a leader."

"True, everyone should lead, but that's not how the world works. Out on missions, there will be times when you'll lead, but there are times when you need to follow. It's vital to learn how to follow someone else. It can mean life and death."

Sometimes I forget that Gregory is my mentor, and then a moment like this happens. He's only a few years older than me, but his maturity level is that of a forty-year-old man at times.

"Secrecy about what you can do is still important, so you and I are going to break off from the group and train alone."

We go into another room with mats on the floor. He tosses me a pair of boxing gloves and ear protection. "I think Mr. Smith's tactics were a little rash yesterday. I suppose I could keep putting you in terrifying situations until you finally learn to transport yourself, but that won't work for long term. I think that if we can build your confidence and give you better fighting skills, your powers will be more manageable."

I don't know if he's right or not, but I need something to take me out of my thoughts. I'm annoyed with Sariah and completely furious with Mr. Smith. Yesterday proved that even when my life is on the line, I can't focus.

I start punching at Gregory's hands, but my heart isn't in it. My mind is too frazzled and my self-respect is at an all-time low. He puts his arms down. "This isn't working, is it?" he asks.

I bite my lower lip and look down at the floor. "I just don't know how I'm supposed to succeed at this mission when I can't even save myself. It would be like a suicide mission, because there is no guarantee that I'm going to be leaving alive. I don't want to disappoint everyone. I don't want to get anyone killed."

He takes my gloves off and sits on the floor, patting the space next to him. He rubs his face with his hands and seems to be racking his brain for an answer. "Does working with Ania help?"

I plop down onto the floor next to him. "I've built a great relationship with her over the last few weeks. We talk while we do yoga, stretch, run. Any time we're together, actually, we have a good conversation."

"Why don't we take this time to just talk, and maybe you can become more comfortable with me."

If only I could be more comfortable with him, but at times he makes me sweat and my heart race. "What do you want to talk about?" I ask.

"Anything. Go ahead and ask me some questions."

What do I want to ask him? There's still so much I don't know. He has told me some. When Tony asked him what he looked for in a woman, he was annoyed at the question. He seems like such a private person. "Do you have a girlfriend?" I ask, and as soon as the question leaves my mouth I feel like an idiot.

He squints his eyes and tilts his head. "Of all the things to ask me, that's the question you pick?"

I shrug. "I was on the spot and couldn't think of anything else to ask."

He shakes his head at my response. "I don't. I would probably make an awful boyfriend right now, considering I'm gone for months and living in a cabin with two other women."

I have to fight the smug smile threatening to take over. I'm like a twelve-year-old with my first crush. "All right, your turn to ask a question," I say.

We sit there in silence for a moment. "Anything you're missing out on during your senior year?"

I don't know if he realizes the complexity of that question. I'm missing *everything* back at school. Friends, grades, sports, not to mention graduation, getting into college, and living out the rest of my *childhood* before I become a legal adult, but there's one thing in particular.

"There are a lot of regrets with what I am missing out on, but you can't make fun of me for what I'm going to tell you." I take a deep breath and rush out the words. "I really wanted to go to prom."

Okay, it sounds lame, but I want that Cinderella night where I get to be in a beautiful dress and have a handsome guy escort me across the dance floor. It's a part of me that I don't ever let out, but the idea has always appealed to me.

He stares at me, blinking those green eyes, and then starts to laugh. "I would never have imagined that coming out of your mouth."

"I know, I know...but for a girl, there's something about transforming into a beautiful woman. I usually only do it once a year at homecoming, but I like doing it regardless." I would do it all: makeup, hair, dress.

He looks me over. "You've already transformed into a beautiful woman."

My face turns bright red, and his does as well. "I'm sorry, that was out of line," he says.

I place my hand on his shoulder, but only for a moment. "It's okay, thank you. It made me feel a lot better."

If I could jump up and down right now without looking like a complete idiot, I would. I don't care how silly and dorky it is, because he called me beautiful and that's amazing.

Awkwardness follows for the next few moments, because neither of us is saying anything. It's like we're both trying to think of ways to break the silence. "Soooo...do you want to try boxing again?" I ask.

He jumps up. "Oh yeah, definitely. That sounds like a great idea."

I don't know if it's because he said I was beautiful, but my confidence level definitely just got a boost.

After a while of me throwing punches into his hands, he decides to actually spar against me. He's a lot quicker than I imagined and it causes me to work harder, but I'm able to keep up with him. Working with Ania has given me an edge. We trade blows and blocks. An abrupt voice from behind me interrupts us. "It looks like you two are dancing."

I turn and find Sariah standing at the door. "It's time for lunch," she says and then walks back out the door. Okay, because lurking by the door isn't weird or anything.

We head for the dining hall, and when we enter, the feeling is the same as the night before. At least this morning I avoided all this, when I grabbed breakfast and raced back to my room. Gregory and I sit alone at a table, but we're soon joined by Sariah. "What is this, round two?" I whisper.

She puts her hands on her hips. "Are you really not going to tell us about where Tony is?"

I turn and look at Gregory, and thankfully he answers for me. "He's with Ania at a different location, training for a mission. That's all I can tell you right now, and that's all you need to know."

She wrinkles her nose. "So then, why are you two back?"

Instead of letting him answer this time, I look her straight in the eye. "Some additional training."

She stares at me, probably waiting for more of an answer, but that's all she's going to get.

She stamps off to her table and quickly starts whispering to the other trainees.

I turn back toward Gregory, and he has a small smile on his face. "What?" I ask.

He's got a dorky smile. "Way to rise above."

Seriously?

"So when are we leaving here?"

"I really don't know. Mr. Smith is the one who's going to make the decision. I bet you're wishing that we were back at the cabin rather than here."

I shoot a disgruntled look at him, because I know he's right and that Mr. Smith is right. I've taken for granted the opportunity of being away from this place. Sucks being wrong.

MY CHEST FEELS heavy and it's difficult to breathe. It takes me a minute to register what I'm staring at. There are at least a hundred pairs of eyes looking back at me, but they're looking at me like I'm an intruder. I hear screams in the distance, but I can't seem to make them out.

The ground I'm standing on starts to tremble. I feel my feet moving, almost of their own accord. Dirt is flying through the air near my face and I hear the roar of an engine. I see a vehicle pulling away from me at a fast pace. My body hurdles toward the open door of the car, but no matter how much I try, I can't reach it.

Tears are streaming down my face and I can hear someone crying. Wait...I'm crying. This is all so confusing. It's as if my mind and body are not working together. The sound of an explosion echoes in my ears. I smell the smoke behind me.

I'm inches from the handle of the car door. Just a few more steps. If only my body would move faster. I close my eyes and my body lunges forward.

When my eyes open, I'm not in a car or running down a street. There are no explosions or vengeful eyes. There's only darkness. I can't make out any shadows or shapes. It's a complete and utter void. All around is nothing, encircling me. I reach my hands around and feel something hard above me. And that's when I hear the sound. At first I think it's rain. I move my hands to my sides and underneath me. I must be in a box. I listen more closely to the sound above me. Definitely not rain.

The smell of dirt hits my nose. "You should have prepared better, like I told you," a voice says from above.

It hits me like a ton of bricks...I'm being buried! I kick and scream, but no sound comes from my mouth and there's not enough room for my kicking to help. I keep hearing the dirt pound above me. The smell of it is nauseating. I try pounding my fists, but more dirt falls and suddenly the top of the box collapses, engulfing me.

I try to move, and the shaking and screaming snap me back to life. Gregory is holding my wrists and Sariah stands there with a pitcher of water ready for another round. It's not only them in my room; the door is filled with other trainees and mentors staring at me like I'm a lunatic. I take a deep breath. "It's okay. I'm fine now."

Gregory tells everyone to go back to their rooms as I grab a towel to dry myself off. "Fantastic, now everyone is going to think that I'm back here because I went mental while we were training."

"What's going on with you?" he asks.

"I was having a nightmare. Didn't realize I woke up everyone." I try to shrug it off.

"Becca, we couldn't get you to wake up. You were flinging your body all over the place, screaming, crying...it was pretty intense."

I wipe off my face. I don't want him to see how embarrassed I am. I walk back over to my bed and suddenly realize that he's standing there with no shirt on. It's like a car crash: as hard as I try, I keep looking down at his well-defined abs. I can't cover my face fast enough, because he can see I'm blushing. "Oh sorry, I didn't have a chance to grab a shirt. It sounded like you were being murdered," he says sheepishly.

"I'm okay now, so you can go back to your room."

"What's in your hand?" he asks.

I look down at my clenched fist. I know the freaking coin is in there, but instead I tell him, "Nothing."

He excuses himself and I plop back down on the bed. Great, everything is wet and has to be changed. These nightmares are getting out of control. I'll bet tomorrow everyone will be staring at me like I'm a freak.

TWENTY-TWO

At breakfast I'm met with a lot of stares, hushed voices, and avoidance by anyone and everyone. They all got to witness my night terror, and who knows what horrible things they're all thinking about me right now. I understand now how lucky I was to be able to leave this place. I can truly call Ania and Tony my friends, but here I'm just the crazy girl who woke everyone up with her screaming.

A head pops in the door of the cafeteria. Dex finally sees me and gives me a bright smile. He walks over and everyone stares. I give him a big smile in return and my body finally relaxes.

"How you doing?" he asks.

"Were you there last night?" I ask.

He winces. Guess that answers that. "Just a bad nightmare," I tell him.

He nods his head in understanding. "I've got to get going to a meeting, but I wanted to say hi."

And man, do I appreciate that. More than I think he knows.

"Meeting, huh?"

He cheeks redden a bit. "Been to a couple of them lately, nothing too exciting. That's why you haven't seen me around."

"Well, good luck," I tell him, and he smiles at me and then turns and walks back out.

A few minutes, and lots of stares later, Gregory finally joins me at the table.

"Are you sure you want to be seen with me?" I ask. "Everyone is looking at me like I'm a zoo exhibit."

"Maybe you should act like a monkey."

We both start laughing hard, causing more stares and whispering.

"I'm glad you're here with me. I don't think I could do this alone," I say reluctantly.

"Starting to understand the value of life on the outside?"

I give him a rueful smile. I wonder what it would be like to be trapped in here for months. Do they even get to breathe fresh air? I've definitely taken my little bit of freedom for granted.

Gregory's voice snaps me out my thoughts. "Instead of training after breakfast, Mr. Smith wants to meet with you...alone."

I sink a little lower in my chair. Maybe if I play possum he'll go away.

We haven't really worked on my ability to transport effectively, and I'm praying that he's not going to try to force me to do it again. If that's not the reason he wants to see me, though, then I have no idea what he wants. Maybe he's heard about Sariah and me not getting along so well. Or maybe he's going to tell me that I'm going back to the cabin.

We finish up breakfast. "I'm going to wait for you at the training center. Meet me there when you're done," he tells me.

I walk down the hallway like I'm walking to my doom. Just the other day Mr. Smith pulled a gun on me; who knows what he's going to do now? I can't really figure him out, but then again, I don't really know him.

I knock on his door, my heart screaming in my chest. My mind is telling me to turn and run. But I have to believe that all of this craziness stems from losing so many agents recently. "Come in," he calls out.

When I enter, he's sitting at his large oak desk. His eyes are fixed on me, but he's like a master of emotion; I can't read his face. He motions for me to sit down. I feel sweat dripping down my back and my palms feel like they could be wrung out.

I sit cautiously, since our last greeting was anything but normal. He studies me, my uneasiness. "Don't worry, Becca. I'm not going to be pulling a gun on you this time."

Even with that assurance, I can't relax in his presence. Everything in my body and mind is telling me to book it for the door. He folds his hands and places them on the desk as if to show me he's unarmed. "I want to know the nature of the relationship between you and Gregory."

His question catches me completely off guard. "What?"

He takes a deep breath, sighs, and gives me an annoyed look. "I guess I'm going to have to be blunt. What are your feelings toward him?"

The question rattles me. What *are* my feelings for Gregory? I'm attracted to him and I enjoy being around him, but is there anything more to that? "I will admit that I do find him attractive, but beyond that, I don't know."

He scratches his chin and seems unsatisfied with my answer. "You do remember the rules, don't you?"

"Yes, of course I do. Why are you asking?"

He straightens up in his chair, and it's almost as if he's surprised by me questioning him. "My job is to know your business and keep you alive. I'm glad that nothing has transpired between the two of you. Let's keep it that way. Remember, no improper fraternization."

There is such a ring of arrogance in his address. Apparently as long as he has my best interests at heart, then nothing I think matters. "Is that all?"

"Unfortunately not. I called you in here to give you some bad news."

I grip the arms of the chair.

"Your grandfather is very sick. It's vital that you work hard, harder than you have been. The sooner you're ready for this mission, the sooner it can be executed and the quicker you can get home to him."

I don't even let the information sink into my brain. "Wait, you aren't even going to let me see him right now?"

Mr. Smith blows out a harsh breath. "It's too dangerous for you to go see him now. How many times do I need to reiterate that to you? Did you forget about being followed before you came here?"

My hands clench into fists. It would give me the greatest pleasure to get up and storm out of here, but I know that's not realistic. How can they keep me from the only people who have ever loved me? "You know I didn't ask for this life, and now you're keeping me from my own grandfather. What's even wrong with him?" I ask.

He leans forward in his chair. "He has a bad case of pneumonia. Now, are you going to keep acting like a child, or can I address you as an adult?"

I cross my arms and motion for him to proceed.

"You were born this way, as we all were. I gave you the opportunity when you came in here with your grandfather to back out, but you chose to be here. And I am so glad you did. You have this power for a reason, just like your ancestors. You aren't the only one here who is missing loved ones. We've even taken in some of the children of the missing."

I haven't even thought about them. He's right, as much as I don't want to admit it. I sometimes forget that all of us trainees are in the same boat. None of us have had the chance to talk to family or friends. I can feel the anger and tension leave my face and then my shoulders.

"I understand this is hard for you. This is why I need you to work harder with Gregory."

All I can do is nod my head. The past few days here have been nothing but insanity and constant curve balls.

I get up from the seat and head toward the door, but he stops me before I can leave. "Becca, don't forget what I said to you about Gregory. Keep it friendly and professional, understand?"

I don't even bother turning back to look at him. I dip my head in acknowledgement and walk out the door.

Instead of meeting Gregory, I head back toward my room. I didn't really get good sleep last night, and the news that Mr. Smith has given me makes me feel drained. I don't get to relax for that long, though, because soon Gregory is knocking at my door. I let him in and lie back down. He joins me, sitting on the foot of my bed. "Forget that you were supposed to meet me?"

"Honestly, no, I didn't forget. I just really needed to lie down."

I can feel him shifting on the bed. "Do you want to talk about it?"

I relay everything that Mr. Smith told me about my grandfather. I decide to leave out the conversation concerning him, because it would be too embarrassing to talk about. "It's just so hard being here and not at home, helping my grandma or being with my grandpa."

He starts playing with the blanket on my bed, his eyes looking down, but it's like he's seeing something else. "I came here rather young. As soon as I knew what was going on with my powers, I went back to my grandparents. I love them. And there was never a doubt that they loved me. A year ago, though, I lost my grandmother."

His face emits such vulnerability at this moment, as if he still hasn't dealt with her death. I sit up and lean in closer to him. His eyes reveal honesty and pain. "I didn't get to be there when she died, and I regret that every day. My grandfather told me that she knew whatever I was doing was important, but it doesn't take away the guilt."

His words strike pain into my heart. I can feel the tears welling up in my eyes. I lie back down. I don't want him to see me cry. I can't hold the tears at bay long. I feel his strong hand on my knee. "I'm sorry that these are probably not the words you want to hear, but I would have moved heaven and earth to go back and make sure I saw her before she died. There's a simple solution, Becca. Work harder."

I don't know why, but I sit back up and wrap my arms around him. Slowly, his arms encircle me and he strokes my hair. Life has gone from zero to sixty over and over again. This path is just too hard sometimes.

I pull away from him and wipe my tears. "I'm sorry, I...I just needed a hug," I say.

He smiles so sweetly at me. "It's okay, as long as you remember that I am here for you. Always."

TWENTY-THREE

It's been two days since Gregory told me to work harder. I've pushed my body and mind harder than ever before. I finally see light at the end of this tunnel. Gregory has been working every single muscle group in my body. I've been running, boxing, weight lifting, swimming, and doing martial arts. I've been doing it all. With every pound of my fist, step of my foot, and drop of sweat, I've accomplished what he thought would take a week.

The hardest thing, though, has been perfecting my powers. To try to catch me off guard, Gregory will scare me on purpose to make me transport. Sometimes it works, and I end in my room, and sometimes I start laughing. The real challenge has been making sure to keep my powers a secret. I still don't understand why that is, but we are under strict orders to be careful. It's been extremely hard to follow through on those, because Sariah keeps lurking around every corner. I can't figure her out, but Gregory seems not to pay any attention to her.

Her glances are still challenges, though. Luckily, there haven't been any more encounters during mealtimes or otherwise. I can still tell that she talks about me from the way conversations stop when I walk by, and by the looks from across the dining room.

Today, though, feels different. After breakfast, Gregory and I are summoned to see Mr. Smith. I'm afraid he's going to pull some ridiculous stunt to see how well I've been doing.

As we enter, an eerie smile spreads across his face. I hesitantly sit down. Gregory seems unfazed by the smile. "I must say, Becca, that I'm impressed by the effort you've put in these past few days."

A puzzled look settles on my face and he continues, "I've been watching you since we had our last little chat. There are cameras everywhere. Anyway, that's beside the point. You two are going back to the cabin."

This news makes both Gregory and me sit up a little taller in our seats. Ever since that first night in Mr. Smith's office, I've been praying for the day when we could leave. I miss the outdoors, the small sense of freedom we had there, and Ania and Tony. We begin to stand.

"I'll come visit you at the cabin soon and see how much further you've come."

I follow Gregory to the door, but I'm stopped again by Mr. Smith. "Oh, and Becca, your grandfather is doing fine and is on the mend."

This information at first makes me so happy, but something doesn't make sense. He made grandpa's sickness sound so bad. How could he have recovered that fast? I turn back and look at him. "He recovered that quickly?"

He shuffles some papers on his desk, avoiding eye contact. "Yes, it seems it was a case of the flu."

I can tell that he's lying to me. I walk back to his desk and Gregory starts fidgeting in the doorway. "Was he actually sick or did you lie to me?"

When he looks up from his desk, I can see the deceit and manipulation written all over his face. His mouth begins to lift into a slight grin. "You're too smart for your own good. Yes, I did lie to you. It got you to work harder, didn't it?"

I slam my fist down on his desk, but it doesn't rattle him. "Is this what your covert operation is built on—lies? You manipulate the feelings of a seventeen-year-old girl to get the results you want?" I yell at him.

He pushes to his feet so he can tower over me. "I could care less what you think or feel about me, because if I didn't care about your success I wouldn't push you. I would just let you die in the field. I needed you to work harder, and I found a way to get it."

My breath rushes out of me. Rarely do you get such honesty from anyone.

I storm out of the office, not even bothering to acknowledge Gregory's attempt to talk to me. What the heck have I gotten myself into? Grandpa seems to think this is where I should be, but seriously? If it wasn't for the fear of people finding me and hurting my grandparents, I'd totally be out of here.

On the way to my room, I pass some other trainees and they stare at me like I have smoke coming out of my ears. As I'm about to reach my door, Sariah is leaning against the wall with a smug look on her face. I can feel my heart pounding even harder and I begin breathing deeper. "Look, if you're here for some ridiculous verbal sparring match, I am not in the mood," I say.

She saunters over to me with the same stupid grin on her face. I would give anything to slap that off her. It's taking everything in me not to go at her. I'm already on edge because of Mr. Smith; one small thing is going to make me explode.

"Poor Becca, did you get into trouble? Are you going to be stuck here with us for a little longer? Did Gregory reject you?" she asks in a patronizing voice.

My fists ball tightly and they start to shake with the rage that is rising up in me. All I want to do is knock her on her butt, but I know that won't accomplish anything. I take a deep breath. "You know what, Sariah? I actually get to leave this place."

I step right up to her, forcing her to take a step back. "I get to go back into the real world and work on a mission, because I show promise, talent, and obviously a lot more skill than you do. And you get to stay here because you offer nothing to Mr. Smith, or anyone else for that matter."

She's pinned up against the wall now. "So go run along and tell your little minions about how much of a loser I am. Just remember that we both know who has what it takes to succeed and who is more valuable to Project Lightning," I say.

I don't give her a chance to respond. I really don't want to hear it. I rip my door open, enter my room, and sit down heavily on my bed. I swear this place is making me into someone else. Having this anger is exhausting. But she just pushes the right buttons, making me snap. I don't want to apologize. It'd be wasted on her.

My door slowly creaks open and I'm ready for it to be her, but it's Gregory. "What just happened with Sariah? She seems pretty mad."

"Don't worry about it." I stare at him, wondering why he came to my room. "Look, if you came in here to talk about what happened in Mr. Smith's office, I'm really not in the mood right now."

"Oh...I was just coming to tell you to hurry and get packed so we can get out of here," he responds.

I smile and start grabbing my clothes, throwing everything into my bags.

"I'll meet you in about ten minutes by the elevator," he says.

I don't even bother to respond. Forget folding. I want to get the heck out of here.

As I walk to the elevator, I notice some of the other trainees staring at me from their own rooms. I hold my head up high. Last time we left like thieves in the night, but now I'll leave with dignity. They can stay here in this awful place, and I can see Tony and Ania again. Gregory's waiting for me at the elevators. He gives me a disapproving look. "Why don't you smile a little bigger? You know, just pour a little bit more salt into their wounded egos."

"Sorry. I can't help smiling," I shoot back at him. "Because we get to leave."

OUR DRIVE back seems to take forever. I try to pass the time by finding music on the radio, but I'm so anxious to get back to cabin. "All right, I can't take the radio anymore. Entertain me, Gregory."

His brows quirk in amusement. "Excuse me? Since when did it become my responsibility to entertain you? What about me?"

"You know, let's play twenty questions....Wait. I have a great idea!"

"Oh, I can't wait to hear what this brilliant idea is. Just keep in mind that I would like to get back to the cabin in one piece."

I flash him a devilish smile. "Have a little faith. We're going to play truth or dare."

Silence fills the car and his mouth dips down into a frown.

"Come on, Gregory. It'll be fun, I promise. I'll even let you ask me first."

He sighs deeply. "Can't we play like 'I Spy' or something like that?" he asks.

I stare blankly at him for a minute. "Really? What are we, six? Don't worry, I won't do or say anything that will make you blush... that much." I start laughing because his face is already turning red.

He heaves a huge sigh and I know I've succeeded.

"Fine, I'll play. Okay, Becca, truth or dare?"

"Truth. And nothing is off limits to ask me."

I know that he's going to be a complete gentleman, but I get a thrill out of making him uncomfortable. It's not like I'm some crazy vixen or anything, but he seems a little prudish. "All right, I can do this," he takes a deep breath. "What do you really think about me?"

I pause for a minute. How much do I really want to tell him? I told him that I wouldn't hold back, though, and we're just playing a game. I can just rush out the answer and we'll move on. "Well, I think that you're really cute, intelligent, and somewhat of a mystery, and I enjoy being around you."

A huge smile appears on his face. "So, you think I'm cute, huh?"

I start to blush. "Yes, but let's try to keep our egos in check. It's my turn. Truth or dare?"

He hesitates before answering. "Truth seems safe enough."

I can't resist. "What do you really think of me?"

His face goes stone cold. You wouldn't be able to tell that only a few short moments ago he was smiling from ear to ear. I don't know what the big deal is. He just asked me the same exact question. "I think...I think you're amazing," he says in a subdued tone.

Mr. Smith's words echo in my mind. *Keep it professional and friendly.* Maybe it's because it's forbidden or maybe its destiny, but I can't help myself. Here, sitting right next to me, is a guy who must be fighting the same feelings that I am. "Well, thank you. At least someone notices," I say, trying to put a little levity into the sudden seriousness.

He tugs at his hair, and then takes a deep breath. "I think it's amazing how hard you're working, and you're really coming into your own." He hesitates, and nods to some unknown conclusion he's come to in his mind. "One day, you'll make some man very happy. Luckily, he won't have powers so you won't have to worry about him being on missions."

Knife to the gut. It feels like he's ripped my heart out, thrown it out the window, and left it for the birds. We keep driving, but my mind is racing miles ahead. Maybe I'm wrong about everything. I thought he looked at me differently. He always compliments me, and it seems like he feels like I do, but apparently I'm wrong.

Too embarrassed to look at him, I lean my head against the window. For the rest of the trip I pretend to be asleep when he tries to talk to me. I doubt he believes it, but as we turn down the dirt road to the cabin, he starts talking freely. "If I could, I'd take you to your prom. I'm sorry I can't."

My throat seizes up and I can't respond. No normal guy could ever understand the life we live. How could I be with a normal guy and face lying to him about where I was going and who I was going with, or face the fact that I might not come home alive? No normal guy would want that in a girlfriend, never mind a wife, and I wouldn't blame him.

I feel his hand touch my knee. "Becca, wake up, we're here."

His hand lingers for a minute. I let it, but it breaks my heart. I turn and look him straight in the eye. "Gregory?" I ask.

"Yeah."

I push his hand off my knee. "Don't touch me anymore." Because it hurts too much to want something I'm not going to have.

TWENTY-FOUR

The tension at the kitchen table is thick. "Something you want to fill us in on?" Tony asks.

I stand up from the table. "I'm exhausted; it was a long trip. I need to lie down. I'll see you all in the morning."

Ania follows me up to my bedroom. I drop face-down onto my bed and she sits beside me. "Long trip?" she asks.

I roll my head to the side. The concern is plain on her face. "You have no idea. It might have been only for a week, but it was the week from hell."

"Well, why don't you fill me in?" she asks gently.

Really, I just want to explode all over her with what's been going on. Between Gregory, Mr. Smith, this ridiculous operation, and life in general, I've just about had enough. "Where would you like me to start, with Mr. Smith pulling a gun on me, getting into fights with the other trainees, my terrifying nightmares, or the absurd relationship between Gregory and me?"

Her eyes widen in response. I just threw the gauntlet at her feet with that loaded question. "What do you want to talk about first?" she asks tentatively.

I bury my face between my pillows. "Let's talk about Gregory first because that's why I'm in such a pleasant mood right now," I say.

She sits waiting patiently beside me and I peek out at her from my cover and spill all that happened between us. "I don't know, Ania. I realize that I can't be with him, but this it too hard. He lets his guard down with me, tells me I'm beautiful and amazing. He does all these great things for me, but then he puts up the road blocks."

Her eyes stare off into nothing. She opens her mouth a few times, but no words actually form. It's like she's afraid to speak. "There's no easy answer, Becca. I wish I could say screw the rules and just be with him, but I can't. You have to try not to let your heart rule you. This business we're in, it can bring a lot of heartache. Don't you think Gregory is having a hard time too?"

Well, that wasn't the answer I wanted to hear.

"Now, what about this business with Mr. Smith?" she asks.

I tell her all about the visits with him, how he pointed a gun at me demanding I transport, and the lie regarding my grandfather. All the while Ania has a severe look on her face. "You must be really important to him."

That makes me sit straight up. "Are you crazy? He has no regard for me or my feelings. I'm just a meal ticket."

She sighs in exasperation. "Becca, he wouldn't put so much emphasis on your success if he didn't care. I know his approach seems wrong, but I trust him."

I can't decide whether this is a comfort to me or not. I trust her, so I should probably trust him as well, but I can't help that feeling in the pit of my stomach. His methods are ridiculous.

She tries to lighten the mood. "So you weren't welcomed with open arms upon your return?"

I bark a harsh laugh. "You have no idea. It was like I was back in high school and I had just stolen the head cheerleader's boyfriend."

She lies back on my bed, laughing.

"No, I'm serious! I got bombarded with demands about where Tony was, and this little snot Sariah was like the ring leader."

"Make any new friends?" she asks, half laughing.

"Quite the opposite. I managed to single myself out and make enemies with the queen bee. Not to mention that I humiliated myself when I wouldn't wake up from a bad dream and they had to douse me with water while everyone watched."

She starts laughing even harder, holding her stomach.

"I'm glad that you find humor in my pain," I say, shoving her off my bed, trying to hide my own smile.

"I'm sorry....I'm sorry I didn't get to witness all of this," she says from her place now on the floor.

"I really don't think I'll take for granted being out here in the cabin anymore. I hated it there," I tell her in all seriousness.

She stands and places her hand on my shoulder. "I'm really glad that you're here. Being alone with Tony for this long has just about killed me. Not to mention his constant nagging about when you'd be back."

"Come on, he can't be that bad."

She places her hands over her face and shakes her head. "Well, if you don't think he's that bad, you two can work out tomorrow while Gregory catches me up on the trip."

TONY'S WAITING for me at the kitchen table the following morning. "Eat or run, which one do you want to do first?" he asks.

My stomach rumbles at the sound of his question, but I realize if I eat now I'll just be inviting my breakfast to join us all over the path in the woods. "Let's run first. I'd rather not eat breakfast twice."

We head down the trail. Our feet are a chorus hitting the hard dirt. Rays of sun stream through the trees, hitting my face. The warmth from it caresses me, making a smile tug at my lips. I'm so glad to be back. Headquarters was just a sea of white, but now color and sound fill my senses. The air is still heavy with the scent of the morning dew lingering on the leaves. I take a deep breath, savoring the moment.

Tony leads the way deeper into the woods. The sun hits the side of his face. Man, he's cute. He knows he looks good, but being away for a while has given me a chance for a second look. His features are well defined with his distinct jaw line, full lips, and perfect teeth.

He wets his lips ever so slightly with the tip of his tongue. "Like what you see?"

Apparently my gawking hasn't gone unnoticed. I try to brush it off. "Don't flatter yourself."

He smiles and his eyes seem to become even brighter. "Oh come on, Becca, you know you missed me and my devilishly handsome face."

He has such a way with words. He must have been quite the ladies' man at school. "Yup, you've figured me out. I could barely be away from you as long as I was. Only the hope of seeing your beautiful face again kept me going," I tell him.

"I kind of figured you felt that way about me. I can hear you say my name at night when you dream."

I wrinkle my nose at the suggestion. "And I suppose you just imagined my face on Ania's body. I mean, how else could you pass the time without me?"

A huge grin spreads across his face. "No, Ania is perfect just the way she is. I think I drove her crazy while you were gone, though." I laugh at the thought of Ania and Tony stuck in the cabin alone.

We swerve to the left and a clearing opens ahead of us. He stops without warning and I follow suit. We plop on the ground, and stretch in silence. Ever since he caught me staring I can't seem to stop myself. He finally breaks the awkward silence. "Anything interesting happen while you guys were back at HQ?"

Instantly Sariah's face comes to mind. "Funny you should ask, because everyone wanted to know where you were."

The comment piques his interest. He scoots closer to me and

leans in with anticipation. "Really? Anyone in particular asking for me?"

I can see the smug expression on his face growing by the second. "Apparently, Sariah is very concerned about your whereabouts. I told her I had you chained in the basement, begging Ania to have me return."

He slaps me on the back and shakes his hair out of his eyes. "Very cute. Have me as your slave now?"

I playfully punch him in the shoulder. "Well of course, what else would you be good for?"

We both smile and his reaches his eyes. "So, I was being honest when I asked if anything happened while you were there."

I leave out the parts with Mr. Smith. I like Tony and all, but I don't know him well enough to unload all that baggage on him. Instead, I tell him all about Sariah and the interaction, or lack thereof, with the other trainees. I let him know that it seems she has become the one in charge with everyone following her. "It's really weird how without hesitation they follow her. Makes me wonder what kind of dirt she has on everyone else."

Tony stands and extends his hand to help me up. "Well, she seemed super intimidating."

He brushes the dirt off his shorts. "We'd better start heading back. I'm starving. Look at me, I'm practically wasting away to nothing," he says, patting his perfectly flat stomach.

That couldn't be any further from the truth. I shake my head in disapproval at him and roll my eyes. "Race you to the house?"

I take off like a flash down the trail, not even bothering to look back and see if he's coming or on my heels. But I track my speed. Too fast and I'll flicker.

I reach the stairs and collapse on the top step. Tony brings up the rear. He stops at the bottom of the steps, grabs the railing, and leans forward. His breathing is fast and heavy. "You said *race*, not *all-out sprint the entire way back*. My eyes were like going out of focus because we were running so fast. Half the time I couldn't see you."

A loud choking sound comes from behind me. I turn, and there's Gregory with wide eyes. "Becca," he says. That one word—full of reprimand.

"What's with the tone?" Tony asks, coming up the stairs to slightly block me from Gregory.

"None of your concern," Gregory says.

And that was the wrong thing to say.

"Man. I don't know what your deal is, but—"

I step between them. "Enough. You guys need to knock it off."

"He's the one acting like a little b—" I slap a hand across Tony's mouth.

"Please, just go inside before something is said that can't be taken back," I plead with the both of them.

They both stare each other down, but thankfully Tony raises his hands in surrender. He pushes past Gregory and me into the house.

"Really, you couldn't think of anything better to say to him? Bad move on your part," I scold him.

I know that he was only trying to make Tony forget about how fast I'd run through the woods, but he definitely struck a nerve. I follow Tony into the house and find him in the kitchen pouring two bowls of cereal. "One of those for me?" I ask gently.

He nods his head yes, but his face is still hard and angry. "Maybe. Are you going to act like a d-bag too?"

"Don't judge him too harshly. If it wasn't for him, time at HQ would have been awful. He cares about all of us."

He scoffs at my comment. "I think he cares more about some of us than others."

His gaze bores into mine, like he knows there is more to my relationship with Gregory. "I can assure you that he cares the same for you as he does for me," I say defensively.

"I would hope not," he shoots back at me as he starts backing out of the kitchen. "Because I definitely don't want him looking like he's about to kiss me."

I stare at his retreating back, completely speechless. Gregory doesn't look at me like that. Does he?

TWENTY-FIVE

"This is getting ridiculous," I whisper to Ania. It's been two days, but these guys are holding grudges like they're competing for some Guinness World Record.

She looks across the living room to Gregory and Tony sitting in the kitchen, the frustration plainly written on their faces. "You've made quite the mess, my dear."

My jaw drops. "What do you mean *I* made a mess?" This is their own making, not mine.

She rolls her eyes at me. "Let's go outside and have a little chat."

We walk out the front door and we're met by a cold chill in the air. It seems fitting, because the feeling in the house is not much different from outside. Ania sits down on the porch swing and pats the spot next to her. "Have you ever watched two lions competing to be the leader of the pride?"

Seriously, is she really talking about lions? "I don't watch much television involving lions."

"Well, they want to be the lead man, the leader of the pride. And what comes with being the lead man? I'll tell you: the lioness."

I stare at her dumbfounded. Are we really comparing them to

lions? "Now, I know there is more than one lioness in a pride, but that's not the point. These two are vying for your attention and affection," Ania says.

I finally close my gaping mouth. "You're being absurd."

"Oh, am I? It's warmer out here than in the cabin. Just be careful—"

I cut her off before she has a chance to finish. "Don't worry, we don't need to go over this again."

She makes a *hmm* noise. She doesn't believe me. "Good. I think you and Tony should work together today. I'm going to have a chat with Gregory, to remind him what it means to be an authority figure and your mentor."

I walk into the cabin and both sets of eyes meet mine. All I can picture is two lions looking at a fresh piece of meat. *Thanks a lot for that, Ania.* They're both waiting for me to speak, but there's this unspoken question just waiting for me to choose. There's no real easy way around this. "Gregory, Ania wants to talk to you while Tony and I go for a run."

A grin creeps across Tony's face. What is he so giddy about? Gregory just shakes his head at Tony. No one is going to win in this grudge match, but there's nothing I can do about that now. As Tony gets out of his chair he stands tall and proud. *Boys.*

I follow him out the front door. He's still grinning as we stretch a little before we run. "You'd better wipe that grin off your face."

His eyes go wide in mock innocence. "What, am I grinning? I didn't even feel it."

I shake my head at his smug tone. Instead of giving him the satisfaction of a reply, I head off the dirt path into the woods without him. He's soon biting at my heels. He pulls up alongside of me, panting as if out of breath. "Does Ania really want to talk to him or did you want me all to yourself?"

I look to the sky, praying for an ounce of patience. "You think way too highly of yourself."

I pull ahead of him, picking up my speed. He pushes himself to keep up the pace. His feet pound the dirt viciously, while my steps seem sweet and light. I do have the advantage here, but I'll never admit that to him openly.

I decide to make a quick turn off the path into the woods. I want to have a little fun with him, see if he can keep up. Without a clear path, I forge my own, darting around the tall pine trees and ensuring not to snag on any roots. The forest floor is littered with pine needles, acorns, and other debris. He follows behind, but at a slower pace. I must look like a deer, running, turning, leaping over fallen tree limbs.

I turn my head and smile at Tony. He's got sweat running down his face, and judging by how hard he's breathing, he's going to be hurting later. His eyes, however, are determined and fixed on me.

We reach an unfamiliar clearing. The ground is covered in clovers and moss and the sun's beams cut a path through the pine trees' branches.

I stop to marvel at the beauty of the space. It's only for a moment, though, because soon Tony's bent over next to me, gasping for breath, interrupting the silence. "Do you ever get tired?"

If he only knew how fast I could go—and that, in reality, I shouldn't even need to run anymore if I could transport at will. "I'm a runner. This is what I do," I tell him in a matter-of-fact tone.

"I feel like an old man when I run with you." He collapses to the ground in a loud huff. "I think I'm dying."

I sit down next to him. The moss and clovers make for a comfortable cushion. "You're not dying, you're just...not as young."

"By like two years!" He holds up two fingers for emphasis.

He looks at me and grins mischievously. Oh man, what could possibly be going through that mind? "Okay, tonight I get to showboat. We're going on the roof and you'll see how amazing I am."

I shove him in the shoulder. "Deal."

He plops down and closes his eyes for a minute. "What now?"

"Do you want to race back?"

His eyes widen and he looks like I just asked him to kill his dog.

"*You* can race back. I'm going to lie here and wait for my lungs to catch up with me."

I start stretching my legs and arms. Crunches and push-ups come next. He pushes himself up onto his side and gives me a wolfish smile. "Are you trying to make me look bad?"

I look around at the trees standing sentinel. "Who am I making you look bad in front of: Mr. Birch or Mr. Pine?"

His loud laugh bursts out at my question. "You make me feel out of shape."

My tone becomes very serious. "I need to be in the best shape possible, to make sure I'll be able to see my grandparents again. And to deal with whatever missions we have."

In that moment, the reality of the situation hits us both. He sits straight up and begins stretching. As I practice some martial art moves that Ania taught me, my mind drifts to the last time I saw my grandpa.

He pulled me close and whispered into my ear. "Just remember to always do what's asked of you. I want to make sure that I see you again, whole and strong."

His words never rang more true than right now. I need to be whole and strong. I need to make my own path and not let these two guys affect my outcome. I hate being a girl sometimes, hate the constant struggle of my heart. Stupid boys, stupid crushes, stupid Mr. Smith, and stupid me for constantly forgetting what I'm doing for so many reasons. I will harness these powers, protect the only family I have left, and maybe find a life within all of this. These powers aren't going anywhere. This is something I need to embrace.

Tony interrupts my thoughts. "What do you want to do now?"

I turn and look back down at him. He's sprawled on the grass with his legs out, leaning back on his hands. He looks tired but strong. He's just another guy, no more special than any other. He's not Gregory by any stretch, but it doesn't matter regardless. "Actually, I want to go back and work with Ania on technique."

He shakes his head in disbelief. "What, I'm not good enough for you?"

I know he's joking, but sincerity shines in his eyes. Should I joke with him or be honest? Partial honesty will have to work. "I'm lacking in a lot of areas, and I really need her to correct me. Maybe later I can take you on."

"I bet Gregory would come running to your rescue," he mumbles under his breath.

"Maybe he'll need to come to your rescue," I tell him.

His eyes widen at my response, but then he laughs. "Fine, I'll run back with you, but no more sprinting through the woods like a madwoman."

"Okay."

He spins around in a slow circle. "Do you even remember how to get back?"

I glimpse back through the woods. I hadn't really paid that much attention to where we came from. "You pounded your feet so hard I'm sure we can just follow your tracks back to the path."

"Ha ha, very funny." He stands and brushes the dirt from his tired legs and then his eyes widen in amusement. "I almost forgot that I can just look for the cabin. It's kind of funny how I forget we have powers at times."

Within a few moments we're on our way back. Hopefully the mood in the cabin won't be so cold, and if it is, at least I'll get to see Tony use his power to look at stars tonight.

TWENTY-SIX

The night sky seems different to me now. When I was little, I used to wish hard on shooting stars. My wishes would range from my mom coming back, to getting a puppy for my birthday, to eventually wishing that a boy I liked would notice me. Now, when I look up at the sky I marvel at it. What small specks we are here on this earth. What does my future hold? How can I make a difference on this earth? So many questions, especially now since my entire world has been turned upside down. Is this what my ancestors thought? Or did they grow up thinking that they were normal?

Tony breaks the silence from our stargazing. "So, when are you going to tell me what your power is?"

I tilt my head in his direction. "When Gregory gives the okay."

He shakes his head as if he's displeased by my even mentioning Gregory's name. "Well, what can you tell me?"

I think for a minute. What information do I want to divulge? "I have a wicked 3-point shot from the left side of the hoop."

We both laugh as we lie sprawled out on a blanket up on the roof. I shift onto my side to face him. "Your turn."

He lies there, flat on his back, looking straight up at the stars. His chest slowly rises and falls with each breath. The wind gently moves his shirt. His hands are clasped above his head, and for the first time, I see the strength in them. "I really wish my dad was here to fill in all the gaps, you know?" Tony finally answers.

And sadly, I do know. And then it hits me again, the thought that we somehow seem to forget that we've all lost at least one parent. That's the reason why we're all here: our parents died and we filled their spots. I've always felt like my mom died right along with my father. I don't even have a concept of what a real mother is, except for what I've seen on television, but of course those aren't real depictions. What could my dad tell me about all of this? They're so vague on what his position was in Project Lightning.

Tony grabs my hand and tries to coax me back out of my shell. "Who did you inherit from?"

"Oh, um, my mom, but she didn't raise me. My grandparents did."

He gets that pity look in his eyes and I hate it. "Oh, I'm sorry."

I'm not surprised by his response, or lack thereof, for that matter. What do you say to someone who really has no parents? As a child, I used to lie to people and tell them all these wonderful stories about my mom and how she traveled a lot for work. I would pretend that she brought me great gifts from far-off places. Around the age of eight, I realized that I had to stop lying to myself and other people. My mom *was* in some far-off place, but that was of her own making, and she didn't care if she came back or not.

He flips onto his side and stares into my eyes, making me blush. "What about you? Did you inherit from your dad?"

His eyes finally look away, allowing me to relax slightly. "Yeah, he always told me the day would come, and he would give me clues about what I would be able to do. It was as if he couldn't tell me everything, no matter how much he wanted to."

"How...do you..."

He lets out a low chuckle. "Spit it out," he tells me.

"Do you know how he died?" I ask, and I'm probably crossing a line, but was his dad one of the agents taken?

He looks up at the night sky. "A car crash. He was hit by a drunk driver."

I touch his arm lightly. "I'm sorry." Part of my wants to ask more questions. Like how does he know? Who told them? Could his death be a cover-up? But the wound is too fresh, and I don't think it would be wise to push.

He clears his throat, and I know he wants to talk about something else. "Have you ever thought about what the others we haven't even met can do?" he asks.

I have been really curious about Gregory and Mr. Smith, but I sometimes forgot about the others we've never even see. What was it that Mr. Smith said back during training, that people would seek to destroy us? Does that mean people like us could actually be against me? So many questions keep floating around in my head. "You know, I haven't really given it much thought. I've just been trying to figure out what I can do."

"I get it," he says like he completely understands. "I've thought about the others a little. I wonder if someone could read my thoughts, fly, change their appearance like shapeshifters...I guess the sky is the limit."

I guess the possibilities are endless. Shapeshifters? I'm totally living in a sci-fi book. "I had no idea what I was going to be able to do until I got to training and Mr. Smith filled me in."

The tone in the air turns serious after I mention Mr. Smith. Sometimes I feel as if he can hear everything we're saying. A smile creeps across Tony's face. "Why don't we stop the shop talk and see what I can find in the sky with this nifty ability I have?"

I laugh as he waves to the sky like a beauty pageant contestant. "Any alien spaceships strolling around up there?"

He looks straight up into the sky. I wonder if he can see the heavens. "No, sorry, just an astronaut picking his nose on the space station."

We both laugh, lightening the mood of talking about our dead parents. Tony looks back toward me, a soft smile stretching across his handsome face. If my many hours of movie watching are anything to go by, it looks like he's going to kiss me. Nah. It's just the setting. We *are* alone, on a roof, looking at stars, and sharing secrets. I couldn't go there with him anyway. He's cute and funny, but those feelings, those stupid butterflies (which I swear exist), aren't there.

Gregory's sharp voice from the nearby window startles us. "Becca, can you come back inside for a minute?"

My body goes rigid at the sound of his voice. "Yeah, just give me a second."

Tony lies back, looking up at the stars. "I'll be here waiting for you."

I slink back through the window into my room and follow the sound of pacing feet.

He stops in the middle of the hallway.

He stands rigid at the end of the hall, his eyes staring straight into mine. His body is tense and I can see his muscles working against his shirt. Man, he looks amazing even when he's pissed. And I can't believe I'm thinking this right now. But why is even he mad? Because we were on the roof?

He looks ready to pounce or maybe flee. His beautiful green eyes pierce into mine. He shakes his head and turns to walk away, but then stops.

He stands there facing away from me, his shoulders rising and falling from deep breaths. He's fighting something, but what? He turns his head toward me and looks into my eyes. Could he be fighting the pull, the one I feel between us that is ever increasing the longer we're around each other?

Those striking eyes of his seem to soften. He nods his head as if answering a question only he can hear. He marches up to me, not breaking eye contact. His hand lifts, tracing up my arm, and that familiar jolt only heightens the tension already in the air. His hand moves farther up until he caresses the back of my neck. He slowly leans in, and his lips barely brush mine. He brings his head back a fraction of an inch. A look I don't understand flashes across his face.

He leans in again and his lips firmly land on mine. There's a surge of warmth and hunger that begins to fill the pit of my stomach, races through my fingers, and washes down my legs. I want more, I need more. This is amazing.

His other hand drops and grips my hip in a tight caress. I grip his arms and then slowly move them along his shoulders to his neck. His tongue lightly licks my bottom lip. Such a different sensation then I've ever felt before. I wish this moment in time would stop, or slow down, so I can continue living within it.

He pulls back and rests his forehead against mine. His warm, minty breath hits my still- tingling lips. He looks into my eyes and the softness suddenly fades. Soon fear takes over and he lifts his head quickly away from mine. "I just wanted to do that first," he says, and steps away from me, walking back down the hall.

Huh? Do it first? And what was he suddenly afraid of? I stand there in complete silence as I watch him walk down the hall into his room. Peaking around a bedroom door, however, is Ania, and her jaw is on the floor. She starts motioning me to come into the room, but Tony. He's waiting for me on the roof. I hold up a finger to tell Ania that I'll be there in just a minute and head back out to the window.

He's still lying on the blanket looking up at the sky when I poke my head out. My hands are shaking and my knees are trembling, but I do my best to play it cool. "Hey, Ania needs me to come and talk with her for a minute in her room."

He scoots toward the window, looking concerned. "Everything okay?"

Maybe he doesn't suspect what just happened; at least I pray he's ignorant. I look away from him, just so he can't read the look on my face. "Yeah, everything's fine. Ania just really needs to talk to me about something private."

I can see him trying to get a look at my averted face. "All right, I guess I'll just see you in the morning then...unless you want to join me back out here later for some more stargazing?"

All I can do is smile and shake my head at him and his presumptions. "See you later, Casanova."

I try to leave the room in a calm manner, but I end up racing down the hall to Ania's. She's sitting on the edge of her bed with her knee bobbing up and down. I walk in and sit next to her and stare at my shoes. I don't even know what to think about what just happened. I don't even know what to tell her.

The silence becomes too much for her. "Okay, I can't take it anymore. What just went down out there in the hallway, and weren't you just on the roof with Tony? And what did Gregory mean that he wanted to do that first? And, man, I'm getting too old for this stuff."

My head spins from all the questions. She just keeps staring at me, perplexed. I start laughing uncontrollably, and her eyes widen at me like I'm a crazy person. Maybe I am. "This has got to be the strangest and most exhilarating night of my life."

"Well, start from the beginning."

I take a deep breath. "Tony and I were just hanging out on the roof."

She makes a 'keep going' motion with her hand.

It's like front row seats for a soap opera. I tell her all about our conversation on the roof, talking about our parents, the astronaut picking his nose... "And there was this moment, where he seemed like he was going to kiss me, but I think that's because I've read way too many books."

She taps her fingers on her knees and her eyes are looking at me, but really through me. "Did you want him to kiss you?"

"No." My answer is swift and firm. "He's fun and I love hanging out with him. But that feeling you get in the pit of your stomach when you're around a guy you like, it wasn't there. I bet he's a good kisser, but it would just be attraction. Nothing deeper. Just surface feelings."

She just blinks at me for a moment. I might have broken her.

"Wow. Yeah, I totally wasn't like that as a teenager. I'd make out with whoever was willing. Well, within reason. Some guys are gross, even if they look gorgeous."

We both laugh at her sudden bluntness, but she sobers quickly. "But, Becca, what are you doing? I'm actually disappointed more in Gregory. He knows better. And I don't mean to sound like a mom, but these rules were put in place for a reason. You're skirting a real fine line."

What am I doing? What's *he* doing?

"I'm not going to tell you what to do. But, are the consequences worth it?" she asks.

"I don't even know what the consequences are."

A shadow passes in front of her eyes. And I just know that whatever she's about to tell me is a lie. "I don't know either. But I can only assume it's bad."

She knows, but for some reason, she isn't going to tell me.

I bid her good night and walk back toward my room. The window is open. Tony must still be on the roof. I stick my head out and see he's still lying on the blanket staring at the sky. "Find anything else interesting trolling the skies?"

He looks over and a smile lights up his face. "No, just seeing what satellites are out there. Want to come back out here and I'll show you?"

Somehow the past ten minutes have exhausted me more than any workout we've done so far. "I think it's getting a little late and it's about time for bed."

He sighs like he's disappointed and crouches back through the window. "All right, so do you want company in that bed?"

That same ever-present, smug grin is on his face.

"Very funny, but no one is spending any time in my bed but me."

He snaps his fingers in displeasure. "It was worth a try."

I smile at him, because he's just so charming and smooth. As he heads toward the door, he yells over his shoulder, "Sweet dreams, Becca."

Tonight has been so unreal, I can't even begin to figure out how I feel about it. I just need to go to sleep and figure this whole thing out another day. There is one thing that I can't deny, though. I would give anything for Gregory to kiss me again.

TWENTY-SEVEN

Sitting at a desk across from me is Mr. Smith. His eyes are fixed on me and he looks pissed. My hands begin to sweat, but no matter how much I try to wipe them on my pants, the sweat keeps coming. He keeps tapping his pen on the desk. The sound of the tapping matches the beating of my heart. Ugh, I wish it would stop.

The air in the room seems to be getting thinner and I struggle to breathe. "Becca, you've broken the rules and have to suffer the consequences," he says in a cool tone.

Before I even have the chance to plead my case, I'm being dragged out of the office by my hair and down the hallway. I'm kicking and thrashing, but the men dragging me pay no attention, and Mr. Smith follows with a sick grin across his face.

We arrive at a room completely covered in mirrors, letting me see every horror within the room. There's a table in the center, covered in needles and scalpels. Two doctors, with their faces covered, wait beside it. The men dragging me pick me up and strap me down. And I keep fighting and thrashing, but it's like they've got Ania's super strength.

Mr. Smith leans in close to my ear. His breath smells like something rotted inside of him. "Your mom didn't die from an overdose. She broke the rules as well, and when we finally found her, we took care of her. Just like now...we're going to take care of you."

He stands back up and starts to laugh hysterically. I keep trying to squirm and free my arms from the straps, but I'm cemented to the table. The doctors are inching in closer, poised with needles in their hands. I need to move!

Finally, I'm able to wrench a scream from my lips and hands are on my shoulders, vigorously shaking me. The doctors plunge their syringes into my arm. I squeeze my eyes tight, welcoming the darkness and pray for some sort of deliverance.

"Becca, you need to wake up now!"

Someone shouts at me in the darkness and I can't see who it is. I try to break free, but I'm all tangled. I feel a hand caress my face and my body instantly relaxes. I would know that touch anywhere. Gregory.

My eyes crack open and he's sitting on the edge of my bed, stroking my hair. "You're having a bad dream, that's all."

My gaze darts around the room, trying to decide if this is a dream or reality. "No, I swear it was real. Mr. Smith was telling me that I was going to face the consequence for kissing you."

I begin to breathe harder, and the panic in my voice is rising as well. Gregory continues to stroke my hair and has now freed my hand to hold it firmly in his. "I promise that you were just dreaming. Mr. Smith never needs to know about that kiss."

My eyes begin to adjust to the darkness in the room and I can clearly see him staring down at me. At this moment he looks so strong, protective, and oh so comforting. A question has been lingering in my mind. "I need to ask you something."

He traces his finger through my hairline. "You can, but I can't guarantee that I'll be able to answer it."

What a response. I can already feel his defenses going up. "You said that you wanted to kiss me first. What does that even mean?"

He turns his gaze away from me. Maybe this was the wrong time to ask this question; after all, he didn't have to come in here and calm me down. I wish that he would have kissed me sooner. I wish he would kiss me now, but he's holding so much back from me.

"You're an amazing person, but I'm your mentor and I'm supposed to watch over you. But it felt right. And so I made a rash decision and kissed you."

"Well...I would be okay with you making that 'rash decision' again." If we're being honest here.

Gregory smiles, pushes my hair out my face, and kisses my forehead. "Why don't you try to get some sleep and I'll see you in the morning."

WHEN MORNING COMES, Ania and I decide to get an early start to avoid the awkwardness that might come at breakfast. I don't know if she heard me freaking out last night. Granted, Tony has no idea what happened with Gregory out in the hall, but *I* know what happened. Ania still has no idea about Gregory coming to my room last night to soothe me from my troubled dreams.

We take off on our usual path to the clearing in the woods. I keep debating whether or not to tell her about my dream. But last night was especially terrifying. "Hey Ania, do you ever have nightmares?"

She raises an eyebrow in question. "Doesn't everyone?"

That was not the answer I was looking for. "I guess what I mean is, do you still have terrifying nightmares?"

She stops dead in her tracks. "Are you having nightmares, Becca?"

I've got to unload this on her. "Ever since my mom died, I keep having these horrid nightmares. Gregory came into my room last night to calm me down from one."

Her eyes widen. "Well, thank goodness for Gregory."

I bite my tongue in impatience. "It wasn't like that. I'm just grateful that someone woke me up."

I tell her some of my nightmares and she listens to every word. I tell her about the dream I had on the way to the cabin and how some strange, cloaked man told me to question Gregory. I still have no clue what he was referring to.

Ania continues to stand there, completely silent. As soon as I'm done relaying my accounts to her, she sits down on the ground. I pace back and forth as the tension in the air starts to stir inside of me. "What do you think it means?" I ask.

When I look at her face, I see sadness. But that doesn't make any sense. "Your mom told me once of nightmares she frequently had. She said that she never told anyone about them besides your father. She feared they were more than just your average nightmare. I echo her caution to you. Don't tell anyone else about these dreams, not even Mr. Smith. Do you understand me?"

I shake my head in disbelief. "Is that all you're going to tell me?"

She puts her head in her hands.

"Ania, you can't tell me something like that and expect me not to want to know more. I'm tired of all the secrets. I know that I need to be trusting, but come on, you guys need to trust us as well."

She finally raises her head and stares straight into my eyes. Her voice drops to the sound of a whisper and I can hear the reluctance in her voice. "Your father would have to calm her down a couple nights a week, but they weren't just your normal nightmares. It was as if someone or something was trying to communicate with her. I didn't know if I believed her at the time, but the nightmares were so vivid she had a hard time forgetting them, which seemed to be intentional.

"These dreams were almost prophetic in nature. Do you remember how Mr. Smith told you that you seemed different from your mom? She was never able to move herself like you can. She was fast, but not like you. She couldn't transport herself."

Ania stops and drops her gaze from me. "She only had those nightmares when she was pregnant with you."

My eyes widen and I begin breathing deeper, faster. What does this mean? I don't remember ever having nightmares like this until after my mom died. How could she have had them when she was pregnant with me, but I didn't have them growing up? "This doesn't make any sense."

"I know it doesn't. It didn't make sense to your mom either. That's one of the main reasons why she didn't tell anyone. She didn't know what it meant."

I hesitated for a minute. "Do you think I should talk with Gregory?"

"I don't think I can answer that for you. All I can do is offer my opinion, and I think you need to wait to tell him."

Something else is bothering me. Why can't I tell Mr. Smith? Not that I really want to, but the man has a way of getting me to say things I normally wouldn't. Would he drag me back and have me examined like a lab rat? Would it change everything if he knew? Are any more strange things going to happen to me? I hope not, because I'm reaching my breaking point.

TWENTY-EIGHT

Three weeks have passed. Three weeks of training. Of awkward meetings between Tony and me. Of heated glances with Gregory. And three weeks of making sure I'm never alone with either. Thank heavens for Ania. She's like a chastity belt and Wonder Woman all rolled into one.

The sound of crunching gravel approaching the cabin is our only warning. Three weeks and it's been quiet. Apparently that ends now.

As a car pulls into the driveway, Tony and I look at each other with raised brows. All awkwardness is instantly gone, replaced with worry. We step out onto the front porch. The car comes to a stop and when the door opens, out climbs Mr. Smith.

Tony puts a hand on my clenched fist and I immediately relax it.

Mr. Smith walks toward us and looks straight into my eyes, completely ignoring Tony next to me. Tony and I stand almost at attention, like we're being greeted by an army general. Mr. Smith has the most intimidating presence. Tony still hasn't been clued in to what I can do, but I have a feeling that with this visit, that'll soon change. "How's your training going?" he asks.

My palms begin to sweat. My anxiety is off the chart. I want to flee right this moment, but I know I can't. "I think it's going really well. No doubt Ania and Gregory can fill you in on my improvements."

Mr. Smith walks toward the door and is immediately greeted by Gregory. After he enters our small cabin, Gregory signals for both of us to come inside as well.

Mr. Smith's already standing at the fire place, in all his prestigious glory. We gather around him like children ready to be schooled. "Before I meet with all of you as a whole, I need to meet with Gregory, alone, preferably in the basement."

We all share nervous glances. Guess it's soundproof down there. We all sit quietly, waiting for them to reappear. After fifteen minutes, Gregory comes up the stairs from the basement in quite a huff. "Becca, Mr. Smith wants to meet with you alone in the basement," he says in a clipped tone.

The nightmare I had with Mr. Smith materializes in my mind. What's waiting for me down in that basement? Has Gregory told him that I'm still somewhat unpredictable with my powers? Does he know about what happened here between Gregory and me? I guess I'll find out soon, but fear is filling every crevice of me.

Mr. Smith sits in a chair facing an empty one. He motions for me to have a seat, patiently waiting to interrogate me. For a minute, we just stare at each other. I'm not making a sound until he does. "I want to tell you a story."

Okay. Story time. I can roll with that.

"Several years ago, there was a relationship between a young woman and a young man. This girl was amazing. Her mere presence would light up a room. Everyone heeded her words and obeyed. The young man was loyal, strong, and attentive."

I can feel the blood draining from my face and my body sinking deeper into the chair. "These two fell in love and got married, and it had disastrous effects. At first, it seemed like together they were unstoppable, the perfect team. They completed tasks quickly and efficiently, but then all that changed. When the young man died, the girl became unhinged. Her powers and Project Lightning reminded her of her husband, and because of that, she shunned us all. She lost that spark, her light diminished, and she could no longer complete any tasks. Do you know of whom I speak?"

I stare at Mr. Smith blankly, but my heart sinks because I know exactly who he's speaking of. "My parents."

He leans in close. "Yes. Your parents are the reason we no longer allow fraternization within Project Lightning. Not only did we lose your father tragically; we lost your mother on the same day. What's worse, though, is that many watched your mother and began to doubt themselves. To see someone so high come crashing down so far, it affected everyone around her."

I can feel the tears welling up in my eyes, but I don't want to give him the satisfaction of seeing me cry. I've got to stay strong and honor my father's legacy.

"I tell you this, Becca, because I know about your little flirtation with Tony, and I couldn't care less. That's not what I am concerned about. I'm concerned about you and Gregory."

I stare at him. What's the difference? Does he think that Gregory and I could be like my parents?

"I debated long and hard about having this conversation with you, but since Gregory has not put a stop to your relationship like I told him to, I must. There are too many lives at stake. Going forward, you must only have a professional relationship."

"What about Tony?"

"That's nothing. I'm not at all worried about it. Obviously, you need to stop whatever it is you're doing, but I put more importance on what's occurring between you and Gregory. This has gone on long enough. Do you understand?"

Understand? How can I understand? He is basically telling me that even if I love Gregory, even if we are destined to be together and marry, it can never be. Forsake a chance at love and happiness, but go ahead on secretive missions that could kill me. Also, let's not forget the fact that they need us to get married and have children so that our gifts can be passed down. I can't wait for *that* loveless marriage.

I flex my fingers, desperate to relieve *some* tension. "Yes."

"Good. Now, I've already talked this over with Gregory. As far as Tony goes, I think you can handle that yourself. There is one more thing we need to discuss."

"And what's that?" I ask, completely annoyed.

"I know you've been having trouble transporting, especially when your feelings are all over the place. You have a small window of time left to train. I don't know how I can emphasize this enough, but you need to perfect your power. In fact, let's see if you can do it now."

What a hefty load to put on my shoulders. He knows that when I'm extremely upset or nervous that I just flicker and can't completely transport myself. I close my eyes, trying to concentrate, but I'm furious. Snippets of our conversation float through my mind, making me incapable of performing.

"That's enough," he commands, making my eyes snap open.

He shoots me a withering stare. "Do you think you can handle this, Becca? Can you handle your power and dealing with your relationships with Gregory and Tony? Before you answer, I want you to know what my ability is. No one can physically lie to me. Try as they might, it is physically impossible for anyone to lie. The truth always prevails."

It all makes sense. I've never lied to him. Never even thought to try and deceive him.

"I hope that I can handle this, and that's the most honest answer I've got."

He gets up from his seat. "Let's go upstairs; we have a lot to discuss as a group."

As I emerge from the stairs, I catch Gregory's eye. I must be doing an awful job of hiding my pain, because he quickly looks away. Tony looks at Gregory and then at me. It's clear he's got a question on his mind by his furrowed brow and tense, pursed lips. Thankfully, Ania has saved me a seat next to her on the couch. I slide into the seat and try to slump down to make myself seem invisible. She grabs my hand and gives it a squeeze of encouragement. She must have an idea of what happened downstairs.

Mr. Smith stands at the fireplace again, looking as if he is about to convene a war council. "You must all suspect why I'm here. The time has come to proceed with our plans. Our associates have given us the green light."

Tony perks up. "Are you finally going to tell us what we'll be doing, or are we getting another 'wait and see' directive?"

Gregory looks annoyed at the type of insubordination that Tony presents, but I can't help siding with him. The two of us have been left in the dark about the entire situation. It's extremely hard to train when you don't know what you're training for. Are there going to be other Project Lightning people involved? Are we going to be fighting anyone? So many unanswered questions, such a frustrating trend.

Mr. Smith places a tablet in the center of the floor, presses a button, and steps back. A holographic image appears in front of our eyes. I've never seen anything like it. I can't even believe it exists. The image itself appears to be blueprints of a large building—wait, not just a building, but a compound.

"This is where you'll be going. Asia."

I lean forward in my seat, paying close attention to Mr. Smith's words. "These blueprints are of a small army base. The base itself seems to be comprised of a few buildings, open yards, soldiers' quarters, and one building that goes deep underground." He points them all out on the floating 3D map.

"As you'll see from the blueprints, there are only a few ways to access the lower levels." He marks them with red Xs. "Within the lower levels is a vault with an important black box. This is the objective of your mission. Retrieve that box and get in and out undetected.

"The contents of that box could put all our lives in danger, and our families' as well. It's crucial that it's recovered, and it will be Becca's task to get it. Becca, I think the time has come for you to fill Tony in on what you can do."

I've been waiting for this moment for some time now, and I know Tony has been waiting for it too. He won't stop fidgeting and his eyes are fixed on mine. "Well, I basically have the ability to, for lack of a better word, transport myself. I see in my mind where I want to go and I take myself there."

He straightens up in his chair. "So this is why I had to train in the basement, so I couldn't see you."

"Yes, but now you're to train together," Mr. Smith answers for me. "Tony, you're to be Becca and Ania's eyes and keep them safe during this mission."

Tony gives me a wink and turns back toward Mr. Smith. "I'll gladly ensure their safety."

Mr. Smith seems to be pleased with that response, but Gregory still seems unsettled. Mr. Smith continues on with explaining the mission. We will only have a short amount of time to train together. "And there's another reason that we need to get this mission done, and soon. A couple of agents' children have been kidnapped." Time slows for a moment. I could have been one of those kids.

Mr. Smith rubs his eyes, and I finally take a moment to notice how tired he looks. I've been so focused on myself. "We're working on this situation, but I need to prevent anymore from happening. This mission should help with that." And he *really* needs me.

But what Tony doesn't know, and Mr. Smith does, is that I'm still having problems with transporting myself, especially when my emotions are getting the best of me. I've gotten much better, but I need to perfect it and perfect it quickly, or this mission will fail. I feel like the magnitude of the mission weighs on my shoulders alone.

Mr. Smith leans in close to Gregory, but makes sure we all can hear. "I expect results and for this mission to be fulfilled without any casualties. Don't forget what we talked about downstairs. I'll be in contact as the date gets closer for you all to leave. I will not accept failure."

TWENTY-NINE

As I sit looking out my window, I see Tony sitting on the steps of the porch, basking in the rays of the sun. He's waiting for me. Time's up on hiding. And Mr. Smith's warning plays in the background, telling me to end whatever there is between us. But how do I even play this? I don't want to lose him as a friend.

Ugh, too much right now. If Ania hadn't been there helping me these last few weeks...I don't even want to think about it.

I head out of my room to meet him, but at the bottom of the stairs is Gregory. The sight of him makes the butterflies in my stomach do flips. "Ania's going to work out with Tony this morning. I think you and I should talk."

He motions toward the couch. And I sit, but my gaze stays on the window. Outside I watch Ania and Tony heading down the trail into the woods.

An awkward quietness fills the room. The conversations we had with Mr. Smith hover between us. "Becca, I know what he told you in the basement."

Gregory puts his hand on top of mine. I start shifting in my seat and I can feel the tears welling up in my eyes. I don't want him to see me weak like this. "I don't like the rules, but they're there for a reason, and we need to respect them," he says matter-of-factly.

I wish I could just run deep into the woods and hide. I wish I could sit and talk with Ania. I wish I could be with them right now.

I blink my eyes and then I'm gone. Standing in front of me are Ania and a very stunned Tony. "Becca, what on earth are you doing? Are you trying to give us a heart attack?"

Tears start to flow down my cheeks and Tony's face morphs from stunned to angry. "What did he do?"

Ania waves a hand in front of his face. "Whoa, we have no idea what's going on. Don't jump to conclusions."

I'm so embarrassed. I hadn't planned on showing up in front of them. "I am so sorry, so so sorry. I need to get back." I take a deep breath, concentrate, and imagine the couch with Gregory. I wipe my eyes and I'm back sitting next to him.

He's still sitting on the couch, looking out the window when I return. "Are you all right?"

Freaking amazing, but I can't let sarcastic comment pass my lips. "Yeah, I just needed a minute. I didn't plan on disappearing."

He grabs my hand with both of his. "Focus on me right now and not disappearing. As much as I want to be with you, I can't be. Look at what just happened; your emotions got the best of you and you disappeared. It could be very dangerous during a mission."

I know what he's saying is true, but I can't—no, I *won't* disregard how I feel. My heart is breaking at the thought of having to bury my feelings. If I could just kiss him one last time, maybe that would be enough to last me a lifetime. And I don't care if that's corny or immature.

He places his hand on my chin and lifts it up so I look into his eyes. Tears stream down my face and splash into his lap. I track one on his cheek as it glistens and slowly drops down. I use my thumb and wipe it away. He grabs my hand and kisses it.

Soon, our lips meet and the sensation is so sweet and satisfying. But the feeling is fleeting, because soon it's filled with sorrow and a goodbye. As we pull away, I can't look into his eyes. I let go of him and stagger to the stairs so I can escape to my room.

I dive into my covers. I fist them, desperately trying to release the anger and sadness welling up inside of me. I grab my pillow and start punching it, but then I stop. *Enough.*

I race down the stairs and rush out the front door.

My feet pound on the hard earth, the cold air lashes at my bare arms as I race through the woods.

Why did I even agree to be a part of this? Am I to live the rest of my life in misery? How can Gregory live with himself, and why did he have to kiss me? That first kiss and the one that followed have ruined everything. I shake my head and push myself faster, needing to out run these thoughts weighing down my mind.

I have no idea how long I've been running through the woods, but the darkening sky tells me it's been long enough. I head back to the cabin.

Ania's sitting on the front steps waiting. I slow my speed and stop next to her.

"So, you work it out? Or are your hopes and dreams ruined?"

I collapse on the step next to her. Her sarcasm is not always appreciated. "I'm just tired," is what I tell her. I can't keep rehashing the same stuff over and over with her. I don't want to be that person that is constantly whining. I need to deal with this on my own.

"You know that Tony was pretty worked up after your appearing —and disappearing act. You figured out yet what you're going to do about that?"

Tony. I had forgotten all about him. He must be so confused right now. "Ania, I need fun right now, and Tony is fun. Plus, Mr. Smith told me he isn't worried about Tony and me, so that means I'm not going to worry about it either. And don't look at me like that; I've had enough lecturing."

"All right, just be careful, because I think it might be more than flirting for him."

I doubt it, but I'm not going to focus on that now. I'm tired of feeling guilty and shameful for hiding my feelings. And hanging out with him is always fun.

"Well, he asked me to tell you that he's waiting for you in the clearing. Why don't you try and transport there? The more practice the better."

I close my eyes and breathe in deeply, slowly, focusing on the clearing and imagining it in my head. I see the trees in my mind and smell the dirt in the air. When I open my eyes, Tony's there standing before me. The stars above us remind me of that night on the roof, and before he can even utter a word, I pull him close and hug him. He seems to resist, but only for a moment. I know this isn't fair to him, but I crave the affection and I know he's more than willing to give it. "Well, hello to you," he says after pulling away.

"Sorry, I don't know what came over me." *And sorry that I'm such an awful person and kinda using you right now.*

"No, I don't mind. Actually, I'm happy Ania relayed the message to you. I wanted to talk with you away from the house. Are you okay? You seemed pretty upset earlier."

"I'm fine now. Gregory knew about my nasty conversation with Mr. Smith in the basement and we were...discussing it. That's why I got upset."

He studies my face. I don't know if he's trying to see if I'm lying, but I doubt my explanation will be enough. "I'm sorry about that. Do you want to talk about it?"

"Honestly, not really. I could just use some fun or a distraction right now."

He smiles. Whether he believes me or not, he doesn't push. He spins me around. Behind us is a blanket laid out on the grass with a bucket of popcorn and two colas. "Movie?" I ask, totally confused.

"Not quite. I thought we could peruse the sky, see what we can find."

Tony lies down on the blanket and pats the ground next to him. I snuggle into the crook of his arm and rest my head on his chest. I can't believe how comforting the feeling of another warm body is.

"You have feelings for Gregory, don't you?"

He knows. I don't know how he couldn't, since it's been so obvious. I can't lie to him. I look out into the darkness of the forest. "I do."

He swallows hard. "And what about me?"

I choose my words carefully. "I'm lucky to have you."

I can feel his chest rise and fall as he breathes in deeply. "Well, you're here with me now, and that's all I can ask for."

We stare into the night sky, our fingers interlocked. He points out different satellites, constellations, and the craters in the moon. And even though I can't see what he does, his descriptions are awesome. Our conversation shifts to the task that lies ahead of us.

"Do you ever think about how we could have been those kidnapped kids?" I ask.

He lets out a puff of air. "Yeah, but if I focus on that I'll just keep playing the what-if game. And I've been trying to work on training."

"I hope you've been working really hard. How's your lip reading been going?" I ask.

He smiles as he sits up and looks toward the cabin. "Let's see if we can test it out."

He sits there for a minute, concentrating on the woods and moving his head around. "All right, here we go. I can kind of see the cabin. Gregory is on the porch and Ania is walking out the front door. He's annoyed. He's asking her where we are. She told him, and boy does he look livid.

"Ania's telling him to leave it be, and that it's his own fault. What does she mean it's his own fault?"

"I'm not sure." I know that it sounds like I'm lying, but I really don't know if she's referencing me and Tony, or Gregory kissing me in the first place.

I try to change the subject, because I feel incredibly uncomfortable. I have no desire to keep going down this path. "Hey, do you know what any of the other ninety-nine's powers are? Mr. Smith told me his, but I still don't even know what Gregory's is."

He lies back down next to me and I put my head back on his

chest, but his body is still tense. As he begins to talk, he relaxes. "I don't really know all of them. One girl, during our time at the training facility, could translate any language, even lost ancient ones. There was this guy who was able to move objects with his mind, but not himself. Oh, and remember that girl Sariah? She can replicate anyone's voice. It's a little freaky."

That is freaky. There are so many more that we don't even know about. "It's crazy to think that there used to be thousands of us."

"Wait, what can Mr. Smith do?"

I'm surprised that Tony doesn't know, but I don't see any harm in telling him. "Apparently, no one can physically lie to him. Like a freaking human lie detector."

"Interesting. That makes sense, though. Right before he left after our planning meeting, he asked me if I had feelings for you. I was thinking no, but out popped yes."

"So, you have feelings for me, huh?" I tease him.

He makes this odd coughing sound. "No, I just lie under the stars with every gorgeous girl that I meet. Actually, that doesn't sound like a bad idea."

I blush. "So what do you want to do now?"

A smirk appears across his face. "Can you transport only yourself?"

I've never thought about transporting anyone else. "I don't know. I've never tried doing it with anyone before."

"How about we give it a try? I'll hold on to you and you picture somewhere in the cabin, like the living room or your bedroom."

We stand up and Tony wraps his arms around my waist. I begin taking deep breaths in and out. I decide to picture my bedroom, because I don't know if Ania and Gregory will be in the living room. Tony presses his body against mine and whispers into my ear. "Just relax and take your time. If all else fails, we can stay here in the grass."

My breathing starts to slow and I focus on the image of Tony and me in my room. The impression becomes clearer as I keep picturing us.

When I open my eyes, he's still there in my arms, and we're in my room. I hug him tightly. I'm so excited that we did it. I want to go tell Ania, but as soon as I let go of Tony, he slumps to the floor with a loud thud. "Tony!"

Ania and Gregory race up the stairs at the sound. They look over Tony and check him for injuries. He's just lying there on my floor, his skin as white as my sheets. I don't know what went wrong, but soon Gregory's doing CPR on him. After a few agonizing moments he begins to stir, and Ania grabs hold of him and lifts him onto my bed. "Tony, are you okay?"

He tries to lift his arm, but it slumps back down. "Where's Becca?"

Gregory clenches his jaw, but motions for me to come over to the bed.

"I'm right here."

He breathes in a deep, ragged breath and winces. "When you started breathing slowly, it was like my life was being drained from me. I could feel all my energy being depleted. When we were finally in your room, my body just shut down."

Gregory turns and grabs my arm, dragging me to the hallway. "What were you trying to do?"

I try to rip my arm out of his grasp, but he hangs on tightly. "He asked if I could only transport myself, and I told him I didn't know. We decided to try and see if I could bring both of us."

"Why didn't you transport to a main room where Ania or I could have been? Better yet, why didn't you wait to do it around one of us?"

"We wanted to be alone."

And that was the wrong thing to say. His nostrils flare and he begins to breathe faster. "To your bedroom? You sat on that couch earlier crying and kissing me, and then raced to the next guy?"

I finally rip my arm away from his hold, disgusted at his presumptions. Apparently he's going to think the worst of me. "You get no say in what decisions I make. That was made perfectly clear to me this morning. As far as what happened with Tony, I didn't even know there was a chance of this happening. I don't have those same effects after I transport myself."

He's fuming now. "Do you think it's easy for me to be in this house with you, let alone know that you're off with him?"

I turn away from him. I can't bear to look at him anymore. "I really don't know, Gregory. Maybe you should think about what Ania said to you earlier; it's your own fault."

He grabs me by the shoulders and forces me to look at him again. "How do you know about that conversation?"

"Tony saw."

Gregory's eyes begin to shift nervously. "What else did he see?"

I look at him curiously, trying to figure out what he's hiding. "He didn't tell me anything else."

Ania peeks her head out the door. Her sad eyes shift between the two of us. "I'm going to take Tony to his room."

"Doesn't he need to go the hospital?" I ask.

Gregory rubs his hands over his face. "No, he'll be okay. We'll just watch him tonight. It's too risky to take him anywhere."

"Becca, he's wondering if you'd come with us," Ania calls out to me.

"Yes, of course." I open the door wider so she can fit through with Tony. I smile at her, because I sometimes forget how strong she is, and seeing her carry a big guy like Tony makes me want to laugh. Gregory heads to his own room and we walk down the hall toward Tony's.

Once he's all situated in bed, Ania excuses herself and we're left alone again. The feeling of guilt washes over me like a tidal wave. "I'm so sorry, I had no idea—"

Tony cuts me off. "Becca, I asked you to try it. This isn't your fault. At least we know now and it didn't happen in a serious situation."

He pats the open space on the bed next to him. "Will you stay with me for a while? I'm still a little shook up."

"How can I say no? I might have killed you back there. I guess I owe you."

I climb on the bed and lie right next to him. He brushes my hair out of my face and I lean in and kiss him on the forehead. "Go to sleep. Hopefully you'll feel better in the morning."

THIRTY

As the sun's rays stream through the window, I almost forget whose room I'm in. Tony lies next to me, still entranced in his dreams. Last night was a dreamless night for me, and thank goodness for that. Ever so gently, I slide out of the bed and back out of the room, only to bump into Ania.

"Spent the whole night, I see." She stands there with her arms crossed over her chest. "Nothing happened, I swear."

She smirks. "Oh, I know. I just wanted to give you a hard time."

My body slumps, the weight of the past few days taking its toll on me. She tries to force a smile, but it falls short. "Why don't we have some breakfast and you unload on me? It might do you some good."

I nod in agreement. Maybe she's right, and getting all of this off my chest will help. Not to mention that in a few short days we'll be on an important mission and I need to be focusing on that.

On any other day, the breakfast Ania made would probably taste amazing, but my mind is spinning so much that I can't focus on anything. Gregory appears in the doorway to the kitchen. "Becca, you're working with me this morning. Be ready to go in twenty."

Ania begins to protest, but he waves her off and turns out of the room, heading for the front door.

She looks back at me confused, but I'm fuming. "Really, he has some nerve." I say.

He infuriates me to no end. One moment he kisses me, the next he's barking orders at me. I know he has my best intentions at heart, but can't he cut me some slack? All I know is that if we're doing any hand-to-hand combat, I'm going to kick his trash. Forget waiting twenty minutes; I'm ready to have it out with him right now. I stand up so fast my chair goes crashing across the kitchen floor.

Gregory stands there waiting for me at the foot of the porch steps. He starts running down the usual path and I follow suit. Instead of heading for the clearing, he turns right, into a part of the woods where I haven't been yet. We keep going deeper and deeper into the trees, but I'm not backing down, because I can outrun him any day. We come upon another clearing and he comes to a stop. His eyes are like daggers. I size him up, trying to remember all that Ania has taught me. He breaks the silence. "Maybe you should be a little more discreet about where you sleep at night."

Are you kidding me? "Nothing happened."

I've had enough, so I take a swing at him and he blocks my punch. And then it begins.

I continue swinging, jabbing and kicking, but he just blocks me and doesn't bother to fight back. I try faking a left hook and come up with my right fist, but he just swats me away. My muscles are screaming in pain and begging for a break, but I need to land at least one blow. The frustration keeps building and I start moving faster. Every kick or punch I try he continues to block. Is he trying to wear me down? It's working, because I'm almost out of strength.

I bend over, trying to regain my breath. I feel him step closer to me, maybe to comfort me, but I have no clue. But he's given me a golden opportunity and I'm going to make the most of it.

I turn away from him and clear my mind, still bent over, but with my fist clenched. As he reaches for my shoulder, I turn as fast as I can and hit him square in the eye. He stumbles backwards to the ground, looking completely stunned. I fall to my knees, because I'm still grasping for my own breath.

We both lie on the ground, not speaking. All I hear is our panting, and an occasional moan escapes my lips. I'm still raging inside.

"You want to hit me again?" he asks.

The question startles me. "Actually, yes, I would love to hit you again. I'd love to give you two matching black eyes." But that's all a lie. I feel sick that I sucker punched him.

He starts laughing and I manage to roll on my side. I don't know what he finds so funny, but I'm certainly not laughing. He makes me want to scream.

He crawls over to me and grabs the front of my shirt. I lie paralyzed with fear. I close my eyes, waiting for a blow to come, but it doesn't. Because suddenly I feel the firm pressure of his lips. I open my eyes and meet his as he pulls away. All thoughts flee from my brain. "I know that I told you we can't be together, but I can't do it." He stares in my eyes, not saying anything else and I really want to shake him.

"Where are you going with this?" I ask, because I don't know how much more my heart can take. And I'm impatient.

"I'm falling in love with you, Becca, and I suck at pretending that I'm not. I don't know what we're going to do. We can't let anyone know about us, because I don't even want to think of the consequences."

He's falling in love with me? Whoa.

A memory comes to the forefront of my mind, my nightmare about Mr. Smith punishing me for kissing Gregory. But it's not just the nightmare—didn't he say something about wiping my mind? "What do we do, then?" I ask.

"You need to act like nothing has changed. If you suddenly reject Tony, it'll throw up all sorts of red flags. You need to be angry and indifferent toward me."

"Wait, so you're okay with me flirting with Tony?"

He strokes the side of my face. "No, not in the least bit. I never want anyone else in this life flirting with you but me. Just back off it slowly, so slowly that he has no idea. Do you think you can do that?"

I look into his gorgeous green eyes. I don't think I'll really ever be able to say no to him.

"I know I can, but you can't keep changing your mind. If you pull this stunt again, I'm done."

He stands up, brushes off the dirt from his clothes, and helps me to my feet. His eye is beginning to swell. I reach up and caress his face. "I'm sorry about the shiner."

He wraps his hand around mine. "I deserved it."

I won't argue with that, because he's been driving me crazy.

We head back toward the cabin and as we reach the porch, Ania is waiting for us. She stands up and immediately takes note of Gregory's black eye and my red, swollen hands. "What's wrong with you two?"

"It's okay Ania, we were just sparring. We're both all right, nothing broken. I think it was a good way for Becca to release some tension."

She shakes her head, throws her arms up in the air, and then turns around. "Tony's asking for you upstairs," she says and walks into the house.

When I reach Tony's room, I automatically enter, figuring he'll still be in bed, but he's not. He hands me Gregory's phone. "Becca, Mr. Smith would like to talk to you."

My voice freezes with fear in my throat. I grab the phone and step out into the hallway, walking away from Tony's room. "Hello."

There's a moment of silence, but I can hear him breathing. "I know, Becca."

What can he know? Millions of thoughts and ideas are swirling in my mind. I know I have to be very careful of my choice of words with him. I decide to ask the most obvious question. "What?"

Laughter comes across the phone. What the hell? "I decided to call and ask Tony how training was going. He told me about you trying to transport him. Let's not do that again, okay?"

Even though Mr. Smith's answer isn't what I was expecting, I still can't release the tension in my body. I let out a fake laugh. "Yeah, we definitely won't be trying that again."

"And how is everything else going that we spoke about?"

My eyes widen and I realize that I need to be so, so careful, or everything will come crashing down. I decide to be completely blunt and honest when it comes to Tony. "Nothing has changed yet in regards to Tony, but I wouldn't be too concerned. Everything is going well. I actually sparred with Gregory today."

He breathes a deep sigh of relief into the phone. "How did that go? Did you wipe the floor with him?"

I laugh, but it's more a relieved sound than anything else. "No, but I did give him a nice shiner."

He laughs harder into the phone and my body relaxes, but only for a minute. Because I don't like this banter with him; it feels forced. "I'm glad to hear everything is going well. Keep it up. I'll be talking with you again soon."

He hangs up before I have a chance to say anything else.

I knock this time on Tony's door and he tells me to come in. "How are you feeling?"

"Much better than last night."

The guilt weighs so heavy on me. "I'm sorry," I tell him again, but he waves his hand like it's no big deal.

Tony must have finally gotten a good look at me, because his lips tense and he starts breathing harder. "I'm okay, Tony. I just did some sparring with Gregory. I actually went at him pretty hard. He didn't even hit back, just blocked."

This seems to diffuse him for a moment, but not long enough, because he decides to go down to the kitchen. No matter how much I protest, he's determined.

When we reach the kitchen, Gregory and Ania are sitting at the table. Gregory's nursing his black eye with a bag of peas. Tony laughs at the sight of him. "See you got your butt handed to you by a girl."

Ania clears her throat. Tony backpedals. "No offense Ania, you're not your average woman. Your strength and abilities are your powers."

It's time to step in. "Enough, I'm tired of all of this. Now, we have a mission to prepare for and I would really like to survive it. So let's work together so we can all make it back home safe and sound. And hopefully be a help with finding those missing kids." Everyone pauses and then I see the resolve in their eyes.

TRAINING IS GRUELING. Gregory has Ania and me out in the cold woods multiple times a day on some sort of treasure hunt. Apparently this is the best way to have Tony direct us where we need to go, because he guides us through an earpiece. Not only are we hunting through the woods, but I'm running at least ten miles a day. Ania times me, trying to push me faster each time.

The biggest training exercise, though, is getting me to transport somewhere that I've only seen a drawing of and have never been.

Gregory pulls up a map on his phone. "Okay, so we're here." He points at the blue dot on the map. "I want you to go here." He makes the map smaller and a red pin appears.

"It's an abandoned water treatment plant." He taps his phone again. "Here are some recent photos." I scan the aerial photos with him.

"Don't worry about getting inside. I just want you to get to the front gate," he says, pointing at another photo.

Of course it's abandoned; it looks like a serial killer's paradise. They could have filmed those *Saw* movies there.

"It's isolated; that's why I picked it," he says, like he's picking up on my discomfort.

"And what if I end up somewhere else?" I ask.

He slides his phone to me. "Take this. I can track you on my tablet."

I look at the photo one more time and then put it in my pocket.

"You've got the image in your mind?"

"Yeah," I tell him.

He puts his tablet on the table. "Whenever you're ready."

I close my eyes and picture the creepy gate with its bent barbed wire. I think of the X on the map, the arch of the roof from the photos, and how it kind of reminds me of the photos I've seen of Auschwitz.

The phone vibrates in my pocket. I open my eyes to a night sky and a freezing breeze. Where the hell am I? The vibrating continues in my pocket and I finally answer it. "Becca, why are you in Germany?"

Germany? I look up at the infamous gate above of me that I can just make out. Auschwitz.

"Becca?" His voice raises in volume.

"Apparently, thinking about Auschwitz right as I'm transporting is not the smartest idea."

And man does this place feels heavy, but with what happened here I'm not surprised.

He blows a heavy breath into the phone. "All right, come back."

I shake my head. "No, I'm going to try that place again."

"Are you sure?"

"Yeah, I can do this." I hope I sound a lot more confident than I feel.

"Good luck," he says, and hangs up the phone.

I shut my eyes tight and put all my focus on the images Gregory showed me, and nothing else.

I slowly open one eye. Success. I would drop to my knees if the ground here wasn't filled with trash. I pull out the phone, anticipating the ring. And it only takes ten seconds.

"I think you're ready, Becca. I have faith that you can do this. Come back to me."

THIRTY-ONE

"Well, that's strange," Tony says.

I look toward Tony from my perch near him on the porch. He's looking out across the forest before us. His head tilts to the side. Suddenly his body goes straight and stiff. I jump to my feet. "What is it? What do you see?" I ask.

He squints his eyes like he's trying to focus even further. "Dirt is getting kicked up like a car is at the end of the drive."

My heart starts pounding. "What does the car look like?" I slowly ask.

He narrows his eyes at me and then turns back to the woods. "I think it's a gold sedan. Hard to tell."

Everything stops for a minute. Tony fades; the sounds of the birds in the trees are cut off abruptly. The only thing that I can focus on is the freight train that once was my heart. "They found me," I whisper.

Tony jerks at my comment. "Who—what are you talking about, Becca?"

I walk down the porch steps, controlling each movement of my body. I don't know how they found me, but they did. I haven't seen the car since joining Project Lightning, so I thought they'd lost interest in me. They're going to keep coming, and I don't even know why. I'm done with this. Done with the constant fear.

Tony calls my name again, but I'm too far gone to really register it. Ever since my mom died, I haven't felt completely safe unless I'm with Gregory. Everyone keeps making decisions for me, but no more. I'm going to find out who these guys are.

As I take off at a mad dash down the drive, Gregory comes rushing out the front door screaming my name. He's too late.

Within seconds I've run all the way to the two men. They stop their conversation as soon as I appear. A fleeting look of surprise crosses the face of the man on the right. He quickly wipes all emotion away and then straightens to his full height of at least six and half feet. His large arms cross over his huge chest, which is clad in a white dress shirt, and his black brows rise as if daring me to speak.

The man on the left lets out a menacing chuckle. He licks his pinched lips and rakes his hand through his greasy blond hair. Gross.

"Well, beautiful, you made things a lot easier for us," the sleazy blond says. His lips curl into an evil smirk as his eyes rake over me from head to toe.

A repulsed shiver rocks my body.

"Shut it, Thompson," the other man, who's completely brooding, snaps. He turns toward me. "Now, let's save some time. Just get in the car, princess, and we'll explain everything."

Did he just call me *princess*? I freaking hate when anyone calls me that. And does he really think I'm just going to get into that car with them?

Idiots.

But there's something I need to know before I take off. "Have you guys been following me?"

"I guess this isn't going to be easy," brooding guy mutters. "Yes, we've been following you. Our boss has really wanted to meet you since your mother died. You don't have to work for Smith."

I take a step back. They know too much. How do they know all of this? "Who are you working for?" I ask in a whisper.

"We're just like you, Becca. Now come with us and you'll learn more about our people, and become stronger than you can here," Broody states.

This is like a bad Lifetime movie. Do people actually fall for this? I'm not getting in that car. They may be like me, but seriously, the blond guy, Thompson, creeps me out. Who in their right mind would go anywhere with these guys?

"I'm not getting in that car," I state firmly.

The night at the bar flashes in my mind quickly. *This* time, I can fight back.

Thompson rubs his hands together and his eyes light with a sadistic glee. He turns to his partner. "This is why you brought me, Henderson. Let me at her."

What?

Henderson slowly nods, and all the bravado I built up fades away on the breeze. I won't even try to transport, because I know it won't happen. I'm way too scared— I'll just flicker. Plus, no one can know; I can't let them see. What have I gotten myself into? I turn to run, but my body is completely immobile. Nothing even twitches; only my eyes move. My breath starts coming in heavy pants.

Henderson curls his lip in an annoyed sneer. "That would be Thompson's power. You aren't going anywhere," he snaps.

I try to scream out, but my mouth stays frozen and I can only manage muffled screams. What am I going to do? They're going to take me. Gregory and Ania will never find me. I don't even get a chance to fight back.

A car comes screeching behind me and two doors slam. I can't turn to see who it is, but I can almost feel Gregory's presence. He better have Ania with him, and I hope she kicks the crap out of these guys.

Henderson mutters a curse. Then the weirdest thing I've ever seen happens, but I've seen it before. That night at the track at school. One minute Henderson is standing there, but in the blink of an eye, there are five Hendersons. Still incredibly creepy.

Ania's laughter washes over me in a soothing balm. This will be easy for her. I hear her advance from behind, but as soon as she's beside me, Gregory's voice roars, "Ania wait—!"

His plea is cut short as suddenly my body is free and Ania is frozen in place.

Everyone stills. An eerie silence descends. The five Hendersons run for us. "Try to free Ania!" Gregory screams at me as he ducks one guy and throws a punch at another.

How am I supposed to do that? I look at Thompson. Maybe if I distract him it'll free her. I make a run for him, but he's ready for me.

I kick out at his legs, but he dodges to the left. I regain my footing and fake a punch to the right and then follow with a left jab. I score a hit to his jaw, but he comes back with a swift punch to my stomach. I double over, gasping for breath. His fist swings, connecting with my kidney. I stagger away and he kicks out with his leg, but I duck away at the last second. Staying crouched, I sweep my leg at his ankles, taking him by surprise. As he stumbles, I stand up, swinging my fist at his jaw. It connects, and pain radiates up my arm from the impact. Thompson drops to his knees and I swing once more for his temple, knocking him out cold. Before he even hits the ground, Ania rushes past me.

Gregory.

I spin around and suck in a breath when I see his battered face. A trickle of blood flows from his lips. His left eye is already swelling, along with his jaw line. He's clutching his right side. The five Hendersons surround him, but Ania comes barreling through like an enraged bull. In a flash of fists and feet, only one Henderson is left. But he's out cold on the ground.

I finally release the breath I've been holding.

Gregory takes his cell from his pocket and tosses it to Ania. "Call headquarters. We need this situation neutralized. Becca, go to the car and get the rope out of the trunk. There should be a briefcase in there as well."

Rope? Seriously? "Now, Becca!" Gregory roars.

I rush for the car and pop the trunk. I grab the rope, some duct tape, and the black briefcase. When I turn back, Gregory's slumped on the ground with his fists clenched tight. I run for him. "Are you okay?" I ask him.

One of his eyes is already swollen shut and his bottom lip is huge. He shifts toward me and then sucks in a sharp breath. His good eye focuses on mine. "I will be...eventually. Becca, what were you thinking?"

I bite my lip and hang my head. "That's the car that was at my grandparents' and then followed me to the FBI. I didn't think...I just wanted to know if it was them. I just wanted to do something for myself." My voice drops to whisper. "I just wanted to feel safe."

Gregory's face softens and he runs his fingers across my hand on the ground next to his. "They could have taken you—" his voice cracks. "They could have taken you away from me—us." I watch him take a deep breath, and then he looks me straight in the eye. "I'll always keep you safe."

My eyes shoot up to his. I only thought about myself. I didn't think about him or Ania or Tony. Gregory's always thinking about me, protecting me, and now instead of lecturing me, he's being kind. Some days I feel like I don't deserve him. "I'm sorry," I whisper.

He grips my hand and gives me a tender smile. He nods his head and motions toward the briefcase. "I need you to open that up. Inside is a syringe and bottle. Fill the syringe up to five milliliters. Each man needs a dose."

I cringe at his directions. "Why? What am I giving them?"

"It's just a medicine to keep them unconscious. Can't have them waking up and using their powers."

I nod my head and open up the briefcase. I've never even handled a needle before. Gregory guides me through giving each man an injection, and soon Ania joins us.

"What's the plan?" Gregory asks Ania.

I look around, just now noticing that Tony's not here. "Wait, where's Tony?" I ask.

"He's back at the house. Not very happy about it, but we needed him to stay away in case something went wrong," Gregory says. He shifts and his face scrunches in pain.

Ania takes the rope from the ground and begins to tie the men's arms and legs behind their backs. "Well, we need to get both of these guys and their car back up to the cabin. A clean-up crew is coming to take care of them." Ania answers.

"What do you mean 'take care of them'? They're not going to kill them, are they?" I ask, somewhat horrified at the thought. Yes, they were going to take me, but they weren't going to kill me—I hope.

Gregory places a comforting hand on my shoulder. "No, they'll arrest them and take them back to Project Lightning. They'll decide what to do with them. We don't usually kill our own people, Becca. There are only a few of us left now."

Ania takes a deep breath, bringing our attention back to her. "There's more. We need to get packed and ready to move. Mr. Smith wants us leaving for Japan tonight. With people knowing where Becca is and the importance of this mission, we need to move now. There's a chance our location was leaked."

My mouth drops open. We're actually doing it. I don't think I'm ready.

THIRTY-TWO

The plane ride to Japan is taking forever. It doesn't help that my body is still stiff from the brawl yesterday. We set out early this morning, but this leg of the journey is the worst. I would have thought we would be flying in a private government jet, but apparently not. Next to me is a rather robust American businessman who snores like a foghorn. His poor wife must relish the times he goes on business trips, because that has to be the only time she gets good sleep.

Ania's across the aisle from me, so I start poking her.

"Rebecca Hunter, I'm going to kill you if you keep me awake this entire trip."

I point to the man next to me and then pretend to be pulling a noose tight around my neck. She laughs. "I feel like I have a slumbering bear next to me. Wanna switch places with me?"

The snoring isn't the only reason I want to change seats. On the other side of her is a sleeping Gregory, and I would do anything to sleep on his shoulder. But of course, she knows me too well. "No way. You stay over there with your bear and I'll stay here playing chaperone." She lowers her voice to a whisper. "Where's Tony?"

"He's all the way in the back, near the bathrooms. Maybe I'll just go back there and see if there's an empty seat."

I get a disapproving look from her. She may be right, but I'm dying sitting here. This has to be the longest flight in history. And nothing will wake this man. No matter how much I shift in my seat or how loud I cough, he just keeps snoring. I'm a little jealous of him. I want nothing more than to pass out, but my nerves are on edge about this mission. It doesn't help that every time I close my eyes lately, I have horrific nightmares. "How much longer do we have on this flight?"

She opens her eyes and sighs. "A couple of hours at least. If you really can't sleep then go see if Tony is awake and chat with him. I'm going to sleep."

I make my way to the back of the plane and find Tony staring out the window. He's got the whole row to himself. "See anything interesting out there?"

He perks up at the sound of my voice. "Nothing special. It's pretty dark. Couldn't sleep?"

I plop right down next to him. "No, I have a buzz saw sitting next to me and he's dead to the world."

"If you want, you can lie down back here."

"Tempting offer, but then you'd have to deal with the slumbering bear."

He lifts up the arm rests and pats his knee. "Use me as your pillow. I don't snore."

I curl up on the seats and put my head in his lap. He strokes my hair and I begin to relax. Sleep comes swiftly.

I'm lying in a lush green field with the warm sun beating down on me. In the distance I hear a voice, and then I see her approaching. I'm not quite sure if what I'm seeing is real. "Mom?"

She sits down next to me in the grass. "You're more beautiful than I could ever imagine. You look so much like your father."

My breath catches. It's her. "Isn't this a dream?"

She smiles and it makes my heart sink. "It's a dream of sorts, but I'm real."

I close my eyes and open them to find her still there in the grass. "Last time I checked, you're dead. I watched them lower your body into the ground."

She grabs my hand. "Haven't you learned? Anything is possible. Stretch your imagination. Maybe I'm just a part of your subconscious. I don't have a lot of time, though, so let's get to the point."

I stare at her blankly; this is too strange.

"I'm just here to tell you to continue trusting Ania. She promised me that she would always look out for you. More importantly, your dreams are essential. Stop fighting and fleeing them. Try figuring them out. Don't run from them, run to them."

"Figure them out? They aren't dreams. They're terrifying nightmares."

She strokes my hand. "They're still your dreams, and you can control them. Unless you want to fear going to sleep every night, figure them out. You're going to be landing soon, but maybe I'll be able to visit you again." She hugs me, stands up, and walks back over the hill.

I lift my eyelids and stare into nothing. Tony's still stroking my hair, but the way that he's looking at me makes my guilt surge. He isn't looking at me with lust in his eyes, but something so much more. I'm such a horrible person.

"I'm glad you were able to get some sleep."

I give him a small smile. "Yeah, I actually had a dream about my mom. It's been years since I've dreamt about her."

I sit up. It doesn't feel right lying in his lap anymore. "I'm going to go back to my seat before we land—don't want Ania worrying."

He doesn't reply, just smiles as I get up and walk away.

Ania's still asleep, but Gregory isn't. I only catch his eye for a brief second, but I won't hold his stare. Nothing bad happened back there, but this whole situation leaves me feeling...wrong.

I can feel him still staring at me and finally work up the nerve to look at him. He gives me a loving smile. My stomach twists. I shake my head and look back down at my feet. Not only do we have to worry about staying alive, but what kind of future can we have together? *What have you gotten yourself into, Becca?*

Finally, the captain gets on the loudspeaker, telling us to prepare for our impending landing. That's what I need to do right now: prepare myself for things to come. I might not make it out alive. I might not fulfill this mission. Even if I do, Mr. Smith will be waiting for me with questions regarding Gregory and Tony. This is a no-win situation for me. *Calm down, Becca. The last thing you need is to flicker out of the seat and get everyone around you suspicious.* I breathe in and out, relaxing myself. Ania catches my arm. "I'm okay, just a little anxious, that's all."

She doesn't buy that explanation, but I can't say anything else without worrying Gregory or exposing us to anyone watching.

As the plane plunges down toward the landing strip, my heart drops into my stomach. I don't feel ready. I don't feel qualified for what we're going to do. The plane's tires strike the tarmac, bringing me back to life. We'll be spending the night in Japan and then moving to mainland Asia, but they still won't tell me exactly where we're going.

THE HOTEL we're staying in is nothing fancy, but it's nice to be back in some sort of civilization. Living in that cabin for weeks on end made me miss things like people watching. Japan is amazing. I just wish that I could have the opportunity to enjoy it. My bed is such a welcoming sight—until the knock at the door. Ania answers it while I stay sprawled out on the bed. It's Gregory. I don't need to see him because I *feel* him and smell his own natural spicy scent. "Can I have a moment alone with Becca?"

Ania makes an irritated noise and grabs the ice bucket. "Sure, I'll just go down the hall and get us some ice."

She pauses. "How are you feeling?" she asks him.

He gives her a tight smile. "I'll be fine," he says, and then I hear the door close.

I don't bother moving from the bed. I'm too tired and I'd rather just fall asleep. He gingerly takes the spot next to me on the bed, getting as close as he can. His warmth seeps into me. "I might not get another chance to talk to you alone until after this mission. Are you ready?" He watches me and I can almost guarantee he knows how I'm feeling right now.

I keep my eyes fixated on the ceiling, blinking back tears. "I just... I don't...I'm scared."

He interlocks his fingers with mine. "You've worked hard. Just remember to keep calm and you'll be able to do this."

I know he's right, but I'm still afraid about the mission and what could happen afterwards.

"Becca, all we have right now is this moment, and I don't know what tomorrow will bring. So I want you to know that I'm falling in love with you, and we can figure out the details later."

My throat tightens. I don't want to cry, but I know he's right. And I'm so afraid to say those three little words back to him. I loved my mom and she left, and my father died before I had a chance to know him. I can't predict what's going to happen. If I can't tell him, I need to try to show him. I kiss him, over and over again, until Ania clears her throat, interrupting us.

"You two need to make sure you don't compromise anything about this mission." She rubs her face in frustration. "I suggest that once you walk out that door, Gregory, you go back to just being her mentor until this is over with."

He agrees, and I walk him to the door. He kisses me out of sight of Ania and then whispers into my ear. "I do love you, and we'll figure all this out."

I smile in reply and as our hands unlink, my heart drops because it feels too much like a final goodbye.

When I turn back around, Ania stands there biting her bottom lip.

"What is it?" I ask.

She sighs. "You might want to slow down, kid."

I stay silent, waiting because I know more is coming.

"Emotions are already running high right now. It's expected, especially with these types of missions. When we finish this, take a breather, because I think the two of you are in over your heads."

I laugh, but it's more a tortured sound than anything else, because I know she's right.

We talk for hours about love, boys, and how Ania wishes she had waited until she was married to be with a man. She loves her daughter and wishes she could be with her more, but she continually stresses the importance of waiting. Whether I like it or not, this is where I really missed out on having my mom. I never talked about guys with my grandma; I think it made her too uneasy. And my grandpa would only tell me that he would kill any guy who touched me. Meeting Ania has been such a blessing for me. "You know, you're like the big sister that I always wanted, but never got to have," I tell her.

"Thanks for that. I can only hope that maybe you can do the same thing for my daughter one day."

I know the sentiment is meant to be encouraging, but the reality strikes me with such force. We're going into hostile territory, and there's the chance that one or both of us won't make it out alive. "How do you deal with the possibility of not going home?"

Her expression changes to one of complete seriousness. "I try not to think about that. What I focus on is the task at hand and getting it done. We take huge risks on every mission, but I try to remember that the greater good is what's important. I always see myself succeeding, nothing less."

"Do you even know what's so important in that black box?"

"No, and I don't try to question it. I figure it's better if I don't know. That way I have no emotional connection to it. It's safer sometimes to be ignorant."

I trust her and can see her logic, but there's such a temptation to know.

"All right," she says. "Friend time over, mentor time back on. We need to get to sleep or we won't be any good to anyone tomorrow." She flops onto her own bed.

"Good luck tomorrow," I whisper.

"Becca, we don't need luck. We've trained for this, and I trust you and Tony."

The sound of his name brings the shame back to the forefront of my mind. "Tony. I had almost forgotten about him."

"This is coming from a friend: make sure you deal with him after all of this. You're going to break that poor guy's heart."

I hate it, but she's right. The way he looks at me now is so different. No longer does he have a playful look in eyes. It's much more intense and serious. I can't go to him just to have fun anymore—that time has come and gone. "I'll deal with that once we're done and back home safe."

He deserves so much more from me, and he deserves someone better as well.

THIRTY-THREE

In the morning, we assemble in Gregory's room. Apparently he's been in communication with Mr. Smith already, and we need to get moving on to the next leg of our trip. "We have enough time to grab our stuff and have a quick breakfast, and then we are off again," Gregory says.

We depart the hotel and soon pull into the parking lot of a marina. Tony's facial expression says it all. "Where are we headed now?" he asks.

"On a boat ride, and that's all you're going to get," Ania answers, grabbing all the bags by herself.

We set out into the unknown, with only water stretching out for miles. I resolve to stay up on deck with the cold breeze whipping at my hair. It makes me feel alert and alive.

Looking over the rail of the ship, I try to imagine what lies ahead. The saltiness of the air corrodes my thoughts, so much so that I don't even realize that I'm not alone anymore. Tony stands beside me and breathes deeply as if drinking in the air. "Are you nervous?" I ask him.

"Nervous? No way. Look at me. Don't I look like the epitome of cool and calm?"

I glance over at him. He's such a bad liar. "Well, I would say yes, but you're all sweaty and it's really not that warm out here."

He rests his chin on my shoulder. "Of course I'm nervous. I never thought in a million years that I would be halfway around the world on a secret mission, especially one that could get me killed."

His words ring true in my mind. I'm nervous too, but what choice do I have? It's not like I can run away or go hide under my covers. There's so much more to face than just this mission. I feel like I'm living a lie, too. This business with Gregory is clouding my thoughts and emotions.

Tony stands tall next to me, unmoving and strong. "I'm really scared," I admit.

He pulls me close, my back to his front, his arms around my waist. We stand there staring out to the distant shoreline. Our fate lies behind those green hills and mountains. "I can't really tell you that it's going to be okay. But I promise to do my best to guide you and Ania. I want you safe more than anyone in this world."

His promise is reassuring. After all, he'll be our eyes, the man who could put us in the path of safety or disaster. He'll show us the way; I don't doubt it.

If it weren't for what lies ahead of us, I might be admiring the beauty of our surroundings more. We're out in the ocean, still miles from land, with nothing but this greenish blue water underneath, and the clouds above.

Ania joins us at the rail and Tony releases me from his arms. Natural sunlight makes her look more beautiful than ever. She leans over the railing, looking at the water below. "I remember the first mission I went on."

Both Tony's and my ears perk up. No one's ever really talked to us about what they've done in the field before. I lean closer to her so I won't miss a single word.

"I was about the same age as you guys. They sent me to Egypt to find some hidden artifacts that were important to our ancestors and our operation. They were scrolls, and some said they contained prophecies from our ancestors. There used to be a man who could see the future. He was killed during the time of Moses, but not before he recorded what he had seen." Her eyes stay fixed on the horizon.

"I don't know what they said, but they were important enough that I was given the task of retrieving them. I was part of a small group. The plane ride there was the worst part. My stomach wouldn't settle and I didn't even dare eat anything for fear of retching it all back up. I kept telling myself that this wasn't going to be another training." She shakes her head, a sad smile on her face.

"When we got to the secured location, it was up to me to subdue the guards. The air was thick with sand and heat. My palms were so sweaty, and I didn't know how effective I would be at hand-to-hand combat, but I had no choice. That was the first time I had to kill a man. It was awful. It was the worst feeling in the world, but I kept telling myself that he would kill me first if I was caught. I had to get us into the room." Her eyes are still looking out at the water, but it's like she's not even here with us anymore. Like she's back there. Her hands shake.

"This isn't always a pretty business we're in, but it is not always so horrible. I've saved hundreds of lives and protected those I work with. I once got to save a young girl who had been kidnapped and taken halfway around the world. With everything in life, there are wins and losses. I want this mission to be a success. I want you two to know that by doing this, we are protecting the innocent. If we can enter and leave without ever being seen, I would be so happy."

I haven't even let myself really think what will happen when we encounter other people. Sure, I've been training with her to fight, but could I take someone else's life? I shudder at the thought.

Ania turns and leaves us at the railing, heading back down below the deck. For the first time I see fear in Tony's eyes. What did he have to fear? He would be miles away from any real danger. Was that fear for me? He grasps my shoulder tightly. "Whatever happens, you remember how fast you are and all that Ania taught you."

I nod in agreement.

"I second that notion," Gregory says from behind.

I turn and see him standing there. It's the first time since we said goodbye last night that he has spoken to me directly. "Could you give us a moment, Tony?"

He releases my shoulder and pushes past Gregory, smacking him in the shoulder as he walks past.

"He's just nervous, that's all."

Gregory scowls. "You don't need to defend him, Becca."

We stand at the railing together, basking in the warmth of the sun. I would give anything for it to be just the two of us out in the ocean alone. "Ania told us about her first mission."

"Really?" I was expecting more of a response. He doesn't seem that surprised, but he tries to act it all the same.

"What was your first mission like?"

He rubs the back of his head and squints up at the sun. "Now is not the time for me to tell you that story."

He keeps a treasure trove of secrets from me. What are we doing with each other? I feel like he knows the world about me, but I only get bits and pieces from him. And yet my heart just wants him. He lets his fingers stroke mine. "Promise me that you'll be careful and do your best to come out unharmed."

"I will. I know I can be stubborn at times, but I don't have a death wish."

He pulls me in close and hugs me tightly. I know he doesn't dare kiss me—too many prying eyes. The warmth of his body gives me such comfort and the smell of his skin makes me weak in the knees. What if something goes wrong?

When he pulls away, an unnamed feeling washes over me, like an impending doom. "Better get down below deck and join Tony. It won't be long till we reach shore."

ONCE WE REACH LAND AGAIN, we're hurried into an SUV with blackened windows, and a driver I don't recognize. I don't get a chance to look at our surroundings, but there's an unmistakable smell of sea water, dirt, and dead fish.

As we buckle our seat belts, Ania pulls out two black pieces of cloth. It doesn't take long for Tony and me to be blindfolded. "Is it really necessary to keep where we're going a secret?" I ask.

Before anyone answers, our eyes are covered and we enter into darkness. "It's for your own protection. We haven't schooled you on ways of withstanding torture. You won't be able to give too many details in case of capture," Gregory says matter-of-factly.

The sound of his voice momentarily puts me at ease, until I realize he said the word *torture*. Hell. My nerves are on edge and I wish he could hold my hand.

The ride is smooth at first, not a lot of turns or stopping. A deep exhaustion washes over me. I try to fight it, but it lulls me nonetheless.

It takes me a minute to realize that I'm dreaming.

Before me stands Gregory, with his emerald green eyes staring at me. Wait, he's not staring at me; it's like he's staring through me. I turn and see a vast forest before my eyes. Thousands upon thousands of trees stretch out for miles. I don't even know the names of the plants I'm looking at. I can't tell what he's looking at.

I turn back to him and he's just standing there, unmoving, unflinching. In an instant, Mr. Smith is standing beside him. Something is clutched in his hand, but I can't make it out and I'm frozen where I stand. When he looks toward me, I realize that he can see me, unlike Gregory. His lips turn into a cruel smile. "I told you to end things, but you wouldn't listen. Now I have to take care of this...problem...for good."

I don't understand what he's telling me until he raises his hand. Light glints off the blade. He reaches toward Gregory's throat. Quick as lightning, he slashes at his jugular. In one fleeting moment, he's taken the man I love. Gregory slumps to the ground, his lifeless eyes looking through mine.

I want to scream, but I can't. I want to run and save him, have him in my arms, but my body won't move. Mr. Smith looks into my eyes. "All part of the plan."

He turns and walks away into darkness. I draw in a deep breath and release a roar. "What plan!? WHAT PLAN!?"

When I open my eyes, I'm still in darkness. It takes me a minute to realize where I am. These dreams are going to give me a psychotic breakdown. I know I need to figure them out, but the stress is weighing on me. Why did my mom want me to in the first place? I can't deal with this now.

After what I assume is an hour, we're no longer on a paved road. It's evident by the constant thrashing of the SUV. I swear the driver is trying to hit every hole and rock he can find. It's bad enough being tossed around, but not being able to see is driving me crazy and making me a little queasy. Not to mention that my palms are sweaty and my knees won't stop shaking. I feel like I'm waiting for the beginning of a championship basketball game to start. The anticipation is killing me. We just need to get there and get this over with.

Another hour passes and we finally come to a stop. Ania takes my blindfold off, and at first I close my eyes at the bright sun, but then I see the view. White peaked mountains, lush trees with their leaves turning brilliant shades of red and yellow, and the unbroken blue sky for miles. I take a deep breath. The air is so clean and crisp. Definitely not the dead-fish stench from earlier today. This has to be where Tony will be guiding us from; the advantage of the height is clearly evident.

Gregory steps out of the SUV and tells the agent in the driver's seat to wait a minute. "All right, Tony, this is where you will be stationed. Here is your two-way radio. The girls will have earpieces."

Tony looks around. "Are you leaving me alone here?"

"Yeah. This is far enough away that I'm not worried," Gregory says, and nods his head.

Gregory gives Tony more instructions while I take in the view. I wish I had my camera, because this is amazing. Such a random thought considering what we're about to do.

With one last meaningful look from Tony, we turn to leave. We hop back into the vehicle and Gregory turns to face Ania and me. "I'll be at our pre-disclosed rendezvous point. Do you have your map of the building?"

She pulls out a little device that looks like a cell phone and presses a button. The hologram of the compound appears and we go through it again, exactly where we are to retrieve the package, where to exit the building, and how to get back to Gregory. No matter how many times we go over the plan, I'm always afraid that I'm going to miss something.

"Good. Now, the town is pretty close to the compound, but hopefully that'll help provide cover," Gregory tells us.

Last night Mr. Smith called, giving us the go-ahead on the mission. "Tomorrow seems to be a local holiday with lots of tourists, a perfect opportunity to hide in plain sight," Mr. Smith said.

We haven't been driving for long when we stop again. Gregory looks into my eyes and I see fear in his. "This is where we say goodbye for now. I'll see you two soon. Be smart, be safe, and above all, don't get caught."

THIRTY-FOUR

Ania and I head off on foot through the woods. The view's not as amazing as where Tony is, but the surroundings are still pretty remarkable. Thankfully, most of the trees haven't dropped their leaves yet. The sounds are unfamiliar and strange. The air is cool but bearable. Not too cold yet. Ania signals me to stop and we drop low. We check over our gear and make sure that our earpieces are working. "Do you read us, Tony?"

A slight crackling penetrates my ear. "Loud and clear, Ania. I'll let you know if I see anyone coming your way. It looks like it gets pretty steep, so watch your footing."

We move at a pretty fast pace, dodging tree limbs and roots. The whole time I keep thinking how surreal all this feels. It's almost like we're back in the woods near the cabin. All we have to do is find the clearing, just like any other day.

I know I can outrun Ania, but I keep pace behind her as she takes the lead. It doesn't take us long to reach the outer fence of the compound. Tony chimes in our ears. "There looks to be a guard about a hundred yards to the west. The fence doesn't look electrified. I would still check it, though. There's a hole in the links about fifty yards to your east. It looks big enough for you two to finish with wire cutters pretty quickly."

The fence does look a little ragged, and we soon find the hole that Tony's talking about. Ania puts her ear close to the fence, waiting to hear if the fence is electrified. It seems to take forever and I keep looking, waiting for a solider to come strolling our way. She nods at me and then starts cutting more fence. She squeezes through it first and I follow suit.

We duck behind a building and she brings out the hologram. It's about a hundred yards to the central building. She signals Tony with her hands concerning guards.

"There are three watchtowers. All three are occupied, but they seem to be distracted with the festivities going on in the town square."

Tony's voice crackles in our ears again. "Don't try to mix and mingle with the people— you'll stick out like sore thumbs, but utilize all the commotion to move swiftly in the shadows."

We carefully move closer and closer, the crowds of people not too far away from the border of the compound. We keep low and out of sight. I notice the laughter, the smiles, and the sounds of people having fun. My heart sinks a little bit. I've been missing out on so much these past few months. It wasn't long ago that I would have been like one of them, completely clueless to the dangers in this world. Everything has turned on its axis.

Yes, I've found Gregory, but the repercussions we could encounter scare me nightly. I think what scares me most of all is not being able to find joy with him without having to constantly look over my shoulder. Now, however, is not the time for self-pity. I've got to concentrate on the task at hand.

With all the commotion and noise, it's easy to slip in and out of the shadows while the crowd and soldiers are unaware. We move stealthily into the center building as planned. Ania crouches down and I do as well. All I want to do is close my eyes, but I need to keep watch while she digs in our only bag, which I'm carrying for when I grab the package. She pulls out our map and signals that we need to maneuver to an adjoining stairwell.

The building is silent, but we step lightly so our feet make no noise. I'm used to running at fast speeds, but having to move quietly is a whole different game.

The door to the stairs is unlocked. I can't believe the lack of security in this place. Something makes my hair stand on end, but when I stop, nothing but silence surrounds us. We begin descending several levels, moving quickly. She stops at a door, crouches down, and opens it enough to see if anyone is coming. She signals me to follow. Suddenly she stops, puts her arm up, and pushes me back into the stairwell. Her face is a neutral mask, not even breaking a sweat. It's taking everything I have to stop my knees from trembling.

She pulls out what looks like a stun gun from a holster on her ankle and then puts a finger up to her lips to silence me. She slowly opens the door again and inches the top half of her body through. Before I even have time to react, she has already subdued the man by stunning him. As he falls, she slams the butt of the stun gun against his temple. His body goes completely limp. He's out cold. "Holy... Ania," I whisper.

She smiles at me and then points to her watch. We need to be quicker if we're to get out of here unseen. She drags the man into the stairwell. We've been in the building too long. Who knows how long we have until someone finds this guy in the stairwell or not at his post?

We proceed down the hall, only slowing down for corners. She's come rather equipped for this mission, using mirrors on corners, another stun gun poised for use. She stops at a plain-looking gray door. "This is it," she says as she pulls out the map for me to look at.

It would be ideal if I could transport from another location, but Ania and Gregory are afraid something could go wrong. I sided with them on this, because I could easily end up in enemy hands.

I've seen this room a thousand times in my imagination and on a map, but it's different to be standing right in front of it. Ania got us this far, but I'm the one who needs to go the rest of the way.

I stare at the image on the map and close my eyes. I picture the room: no windows, only one door, a table in the center and rows of computers. I breathe in and out, keeping the image in my mind and focusing on seeing myself in the room as well. When I open my eyes, I see the black box sitting on a table. I grab it quickly.

The sound of typing hits my ears. I'm not alone. Someone is sitting at a computer, but dark hair and dark clothes are all I'm able to see. Something strikes me as odd, though. The smell is familiar, like musty cologne. I'm out of the room before I can even register who I saw, but there's a familiarity about whoever is in that room. Chills run down my spine and I feel uneasy, but Ania is directing me to hurry down the hall. "Is everything always in a black box?" I ask.

She looks at me, annoyed, tapping her watch, and I slip the shoe-box-size container into my backpack and catch up with her.

We come upon a different set of stairs and head up a few levels. We haven't yet reached ground level when she starts to slow down, but I blindly trust her to lead us to safety.

We come to another door, but Ania stops, pulls out wire cutters, and then disarms an alarm attached to the door. I'm surprised this door was armed when none of the others were. The sun blinds me for a minute after she opens the door, but I notice we're at the bottom of a long ramp. We crouch down. Ania tries calling for Tony, but all we hear in our ears is silence. I start getting anxious. "This is taking way too long," I whisper.

"Just give him a moment, I know he won't let us down." Her voice is hushed as well.

Finally there's a crackling in our earpieces. "The soldiers are still busy with the civilians, and you have a clear shot to the fence," Tony says.

Ania moves up the ramp slowly and I follow suit, but soon she's quickly backing up and pushing me back down the ramp. "Tony? Come in Tony are you there?" she asks.

Her eyes never look back toward me, even as she continues to move us. "What's going on?" I ask.

Static fills our earpieces.

As it continues, her entire body freezes and she slowly turns her gaze back to me, a look of horror crossing her features. Her face is drained of all its color by the time we get back to the bottom of the ramp. She rips off her earpiece. "He—he lied. There are at least a hundred armed soldiers between us and the gate."

I stumble backwards and fall flat on my butt, then rip out my ear piece too. I hold my head in my hands. What's going on? Why would he do this to us? She slumps to the ground as if she's at a loss too. I have no idea what we're going to do.

"Can we go back through the building?" I ask Ania, my voice taking on a slightly hysterical tone.

She considers the door for a moment. "It'd take too long. Any moment now they're going to sound an alarm. I'd rather not get trapped in that building."

How are we going to get out of here alive?

THIRTY-FIVE

Betrayal. The feeling coats me, suffocates me, as we stay crouched down on the cement ramp. The sky above is painted with white puffs amongst a blue sea. It's beautiful. At least I got to see something beautiful before I died. At least I got to love someone, if only for a moment.

I know I'm not alone in my feelings, because Ania's face shows signs of pure shock and fear, but mostly anger. How could Tony do this to us? I trusted him, became vulnerable with him. He was my friend and this is the way I'm thanked. I let him in.

A memory flashes before my eyes. He let that man at the bar take me outside, never did a thing to save me. Was he trying to get rid of me then? How am I any threat to him? If I could only go back and not confess all those deep feelings with him, then maybe this wouldn't cut so deeply. If he could only see us right now, I would have a few choice words for him to read off my lips. But being crouched down here, I highly doubt it. However, now is not the time to play a girl scorned, because looking at Ania, I have no idea what we're going to do.

I can see that she's trying to calculate a new plan. At the moment, we're undetected, but as soon as they discover that the black box is missing, they'll sound the alarm. This stupid black box. Life and death reside with this abysmal thing. Every special ops team, at least in the movies, has to steal something in a black box. I grab Ania's wrist and it snaps her back to reality. "So what's the plan?"

She looks at my hand in confusion. She has no more answers than I do. "I'm not sure yet, but I need to think about this before we make a move. It'll get too cold when the sun goes down, and we aren't exactly prepared for temperatures close to freezing. I didn't think Tony would deceive us like this. I can't believe Gregory didn't pick this up."

Gregory? What did she mean by 'pick this up'? "How would Gregory know?"

She stares into my eyes. There's pain reflected in those beautiful eyes of hers, but I can't tell why. She takes a deep breath and then releases it slowly. "Becca, there's a lot you don't know, and I don't have much time to tell you. So I'm going to be blunt and honest. Gregory can read minds."

What. The. Hell. Everything seems to still. Is this all I'm going to find at Project Lightning? Treachery from the guys? My heart drops to my stomach. All this time, all the thoughts I've had about him, Tony, this entire operation, he's known what I'm thinking. He's known my fears and worries. All the times I fantasized that he would just lean in and kiss me—how humiliating! He told me he loved me and for what? To play some sick joke? Do I even know him? How could I have been so wrong?

I snap to attention at what Ania referenced before my thoughts turned selfishly toward my own humiliation. Something isn't adding up. Gregory should have known if one of us was planning on double crossing. "Wait, could Gregory be in league with Tony? Could someone be using Tony?"

She sits there biting her lip, tapping her finger against her knee. "I doubt it, but I really don't know. You need to be very careful in Gregory's presence now. Becca, before we go any further, I need to tell you a few more things. I know this is a lot, but if something happens, you need to know."

Be careful in his presence? I don't even know if I want to go anywhere near him. How close does he have to be to read my mind? My thoughts will never be safe.

Ania begins to talk about my mother. Apparently she never trusted Mr. Smith and Project Lightning. "It's true that after your dad died, she was never the same. I can understand why; she loved him more than anything in this world. His death completely wrecked her, and in her eyes, the only way to cope was through drugs. It was the most selfish path she could have ever taken.

"About two years ago, your mom sought me out. Once she had left the operation, I never thought I'd hear from her again. Actually, Mr. Smith ordered me not to speak with her at all. How could I say no, though? She was there when my mother died and the best mentor I could have ever asked for. She was the sister I had always wanted.

"We had a system of communication out in the field. It wasn't standard protocol, but something we devised. She left me three silent voicemails, and the fourth was a wrong number, which was a code leading me where to meet up. Your mom loved her navigational coordinates."

Anger begins to boil up inside of me. I never even got a birthday card from my mother, but she had a secret code with Ania. Nothing for years—no phone calls or visits, nothing. I clench my fists at the burst of rage.

"When I met up with her, she seemed anxious. Her eyes never fixed on one point, always surveying the area. Your mom knew that she wasn't going to be alive for much longer. She asked me to make sure I looked after you and told me that when you're ready, you need to question her death. She didn't die from an overdose. She'd been clean for a while and was working in a diner at nights. She was clean the day I met with her."

It's as if bombs keep going off around me. I grab the coin my pocket. She kept that coin on her. It had to mean something to her.

The world is spinning, and I'm waiting for the ground to open up and swallow me whole. Tony's deceived us, there's a chance that Gregory has as well, and now Ania tells me that my mom was probably murdered. There's not much else to lose at this moment, and I need to tell Ania about my dream. "She came to me in my dream on the plane ride to Japan."

This makes Ania sit straight up.

"She told me to continue trusting you and to try and figure out my dreams. Ania, how is this even possible? She's dead. There's no reasonable explanation for her being in my dream."

She's still, as if trying to figure something out in her brain. "Some believe that the soul never dies. Our dreams can be the gateway between this world and whatever comes after this life. If you've learned anything these past several months, it's that there are things we don't understand. We know you're different, and I bet there's something in those ancient prophetic scrolls that points toward you."

Who would have ever thought that I would be able to 'magically' appear some place I thought about? It's too much right now, not to mention the hordes of soldiers waiting at the crest of this hill. I close my eyes and the feeling of being overwhelmed washes over me. Should I pray? Would prayer help me right now? It couldn't hurt.

Ania places a hand on my shoulder. "You're doing it again."

"Doing what?"

"Flickering."

We stay crouched on the ground and I continue to watch Ania trying to figure out something to do. I know she's running game plans in her mind. Where do we go from here? "Why don't I just transport the both of us?"

I had done it with Tony that one time.

"Tony almost died when you guys did that. What if we get caught or, heaven forbid, Gregory actually deceived us? If I'm weak, who knows what the consequences could be, especially if we need to run? Your emotions are all over the place and I can't let them take both of us. It's too risky."

"We should still try." My words are little more than a hiss.

The sun's sliding behind the mountains, and the sky still shows a brilliant hue of red and orange. I don't know how long we've been out here, but it feels like hours, and I can feel that the temperature has been steadily dropping. The sound of footsteps echoes somewhere above us raises an alarm in my mind. What if they find us hiding here? Finally, Ania's body sags a little and she reaches into her pockets, pulling out two grenades. My jaw drops.

"This is what we're going to do. We're going to crest the top of the hill. As soon as we do, you're to run to the south and make for the rendezvous point. Do you understand?"

Is she insane? What if I can't get there fast enough? What's the plan with the grenades? I raise an eyebrow at her. "What are you going to be doing?"

She squares her shoulders and a firm resolution settles into her eyes. "I'll be the distraction. I can fight them off without a problem; you can't. We did *not* come this far to fail. I'm your mentor as well, and this responsibility falls to me. You're to meet up with Gregory and fulfill this mission."

"But what if he..." I don't want to voice it. I don't want to say the words and make them true.

"We don't know anything. But if there's anything wrong, you get the hell out of there. You run."

Her voice is so determined and stern. I don't dare defy her right now. Given all that I feel, she's right. No matter how much I try to argue with her, she's right. We check over our weapons and the precious cargo in my backpack. Ania pulls out a letter and hands it to me. "Before every mission I embark on, I write a letter to my daughter. I want you to give this to her if something happens to me. She never needs to know how I died, only that I went down with a fight. I also want you to make the same promise that I made to your mother. Take care of my daughter."

Death is a part of life, but without my parents, Ania is the only one who has helped me through Project Lightning. Now that I don't think I can trust Tony or Gregory, who do I have to turn to? I told her myself that she was the big sister I always wanted. I take the letter and put it into a small pocket inside my shirt. "I promise, Ania."

I may say those words, but what I really want to do is shove the letter back into her face and tell her to give her daughter the letter herself. I don't want to be the one to tell someone that their mother is dead. Giving me this letter is a death knell, and I don't want to be a part of that. But I've promised her I'll watch out for her daughter, and I refuse to fail her.

We begin slowly moving up the cement ramp and I try my best to stay within the shadows. An alarm begins to sound. Boots pound on the pavement up ahead. Either they just realized that the black box is missing or they found the man in the stairwell.

As we crest the top of the ramp, she signals me to start hugging the building and heading south. She moves from her crouched position and stands up straight with both grenades in her outstretched hands. What...?

In front of her stands an army lined up in their ranks and ready for orders. Some start to take notice and yell in a foreign language. She pulls the pins out of both grenades with her teeth and coolly walks forward. I stop and stare at her. What on earth is she planning on doing? How is she so calm? Maybe this is just a distraction. Hopefully. Just a distraction.

Making my way along the side of the building, I can see the gate about a hundred yards in the distance, but I stop to see what Ania's doing. She's still walking at a steady pace toward the soldiers and they finally take notice of what she's clutching in both hands. Anger has left their screams and is being replaced by confusion and fear. Ania starts screaming something in Polish, and she's running at full speed into the center of the regiment, swinging her arms like they're battering rams. Men go flying in all directions and more try to fill in the gap, but she kicks them, sending them into the other men. Her hands are still clutching the grenades, but her whole body is a weapon. The sound of gun shots blazes over the screams of the soldiers.

I bite down on my lip hard to choke back a sob. I know this is my cue to get the heck out of here. I can't watch anymore.

I start running as fast as I can for the gate. If I could just picture the rendezvous point, I'd be out of here, but there's too much going on. I can't seem to trigger my powers; my emotions and adrenaline are out of control right now. The gate is only a few yards ahead of me and currently unmanned, since every soldier is either trying to find cover or defuse Ania, and that's when I feel it.

The explosion sends me flying into the fence and I land with a thud. There's ringing in my ears. The coppery tang of blood fills my mouth. Those were not normal grenades. There's no way they would have sent me flying like that. Ania must have made them more powerful. I roll off the fence and lie on the ground, trying to regain my equilibrium as the sorrow begins to wash over me.

Ania. She just sacrificed herself for me. Tears begin to roll down my cheeks, but the feeling of my backpack reminds me that I need to keep moving. I can't break down now. I have a mission to fulfill as well as a promise to her.

I push myself off the fence. My body screams in pain. Crap, I think I broke a rib. All the sounds around me seem muffled and I have no idea if anyone is heading after me, but I take off.

I run through the streets that were filled with tourists and festivities only a short time earlier. Chaos is my cover now. People are running through the streets as if more bombs are going to start falling out of the sky. The rendezvous point is only a few more streets away.

I round a corner and make for the waiting SUV. Gregory is hanging out the door beckoning for me to run faster. I can't make out what he's saying. He's pointing behind me and I see them hot on my heels. There are about five Humvees chasing after me, with soldiers leaning out the windows. The SUV starts moving and I scream at Gregory to wait for me. "Please!!" I beg.

He's still hanging out of the door. "Come on, Becca, move it!"

I try so hard to imagine myself inside the SUV sitting right next to Gregory, but fear and urgency keep washing over me. I flicker and for an instant I think I'm sitting behind the driver's seat, but I'm back running on the pavement. My body is screaming in pain with every step I take. The SUV speeds up, and I'm only inches from the tailgate. Gregory is pleading with me to get into the car. "I can't do it. Slow down and let me in!"

At that moment, the driver slams on the gas and I can see Gregory yelling at the driver as they fade into the distance. My heart sinks. If he hadn't betrayed us, he could have hopped in the back and opened the tailgate to let me in.

I'm still not alone, still being chased. All the anger I feel, the rage at being left behind in a foreign country. Ania's death will not be in vain. I made her a promise.

I skid to a stop and turn at my chasers and scream into their faces. The Humvees stop dead in their tracks.

I will not go so easily. I will not be looked at like some helpless little girl by Gregory, Tony, or Mr. Smith. I. Am. Rebecca. Hunter. And I am extraordinary.

The world fades.

And as it focuses back in, I'm in the clearing in the woods near our cabin.

I fall to my knees and look up at the night sky looming overhead. I have no idea what time it is. The woods are quiet.

I did it. I was able to funnel all that rage and make the jump, but what to do now? I pull at my hair in frustration. Where do I go? Tony's betrayed us, Ania sacrificed herself for me and this mission, and Gregory's left me behind.

I take off my backpack and check the contents. The box is still safely inside and seems unharmed. I need shelter.

I head off toward the cabin. I know that Gregory and Tony won't be there, but maybe someone else will be. Quickly, I'm at the front steps. The cabin is completely dark and quiet. So many memories here. Were any of them true? Can you fake the connection that

Gregory and I have? Or was everything a lie? How many times am I going to have to ask myself these questions?

A sob threatens to break free, but I smother it. I can't break now. Strength. I need strength.

I find an unlocked window and hop inside the cabin. I don't dare make a phone call because I know that will signal to headquarters that I'm here. Do I want them to know I'm here? If Tony betrayed us, I should call Mr. Smith and let him know, but if he's in on it, that could be disastrous for me.

I pace about the living room, not really sure what to do. Maybe if I knew what was in the black box, could help me make a better decision?

I take my bag off and place it on the floor. The box doesn't seem too heavy, but that might not mean anything. I undo the unlocked latches on the case and slowly lift the lid. It's like they wanted this to be stolen. A sick feeling fills my stomach and I scoot backwards. I shouldn't have opened this. What did I just do?

A slip of paper sits in the box. So insignificant.

A sound escapes my throat, a tormented laugh. A bunch of letters and numbers that mean nothing to me. *Ania died for this?*

I march to the kitchen and pick up the house phone. I dial Mr. Smith's direct line, which I was made to memorize. On the third ring it's answered. "We've been betrayed," I whisper into the phone, and then I hang up.

End of Book One

ACKNOWLEDGMENTS

There are so many people I need to thank right now.

First and foremost, I'd like to thank my husband Nick, for loving me, supporting me, dealing my stress, and keeping the kids away as I tried to finish this.

Next, to my children. Thank you Mena, for being so excited that mom was writing book. And thank you Xander for being willing to just sit with my while I made these words come to life.

I need to thank my WeeWa girls: Sara, Kathy, Emily, Carrie, and Dena. Thank you for your advice, for telling me when things suck, and when they're great. I couldn't have asked for better friends who share the love of writing with me.

Kathy, thank you for proofreading for me, and answering my million questions.

Dee, thanks for being one of the first to read this.

To the wonderful writers of ANWA. This group holds a wealth of wisdom, and I get to take part of it.

To my editor Jana Miller. You helped me beyond measure with this book. Bet you can't wait for the next one, huh?

My amazing cover designer, Molly Phipps, with We Got You

Covered Book Design. You created such a beautiful cover, and I can't wait to see what comes next.

I'd also like to thank some musicians that helped me find the right words: The Strumbellas, The Lumineers, Vance Joy, Birdie, and so many others. The music you create has greatly inspired my writing. Without your talent, I don't think I could fully realize mine.

To my parents. You raised one seriously independent daughter. And I doubt I would have taken this on if you hadn't. You filled our home with books and learning. And mom, I know you're just as excited for this book as I am.

Finally, to the readers. Thank you for taking a chance on this book and me.

ABOUT THE AUTHOR

Pam Eaton lives in the deserts of Arizona, but she'll always consider herself a New Englander at heart. She graduated from Arizona State University with degrees involving education and history. While she loves history, it'll always take a backseat to the fictional world she stumbled into as a young girl.

She lives with her husband, two kids (with one on the way), and two crazy, but lovable labs. It's a chaotic life, but she wouldn't have it any other way. Especially since they let her read an insane amount of books, and watch way too many Food Network shows.

You can find out more at Pam's website

www.pameaton.com